A Barrow Boy's Cadenza

PETE ADAMS

A Barrow Boy's Cadenza

In E Flat Major

Book Three
Kind Hearts and Martinets

U RBANE
Publications

First published in Great Britain in 2015
by Urbane Publications Ltd
Suite 3, Brown Europe House, 33/34 Gleamingwood Drive, Chatham, Kent
ME5 8RZ

A CIP catalogue record for this book is available
from the British Library.

ISBN 978-1-909273-96-2
Ebook 978-1-909273-97-9

Design and Typeset by The Invisible Man
Cover design by The Invisible Man

Printed in Great Britain by
CPI Group (UK) Ltd,
Croydon, CR0 4YY

urbanepublications.com

The publisher supports the Forest Stewardship Council® (FSC®), the
leadinginternational forest-certification organisation. This book is made from
acid-free paper from an FSC®-certified provider. FSC is the only forest-
certification scheme supported by the leading environmental organisations,
including Greenpeace.

To Havant Rugby Club,

I have neglected for too long, too many tremendous friends made over a long time and I suppose I will have to continue neglecting you – that's the problem with being an enigma

– MC Mariner

By the same author

CAUSE & EFFECT - Kind Hearts and Martinets Book 1

IRONY IN THE SOUL - Kind Hearts and Martinets Book 2

are available as Kindle editions on Amazon.

Acknowledgements

Thank you to Nicola Lovett and Sandra Jones who have introduced me to the 21st Century, in a gentle way, and then in a cajoling way. They will say that I have never got the hang of anything, but I know they like a laugh. And always to Jan Fowler of Aposites – patience personified, designer of my blog site, reader of my manuscripts and a wonderfully warm hearted woman, though a tough critic. Please note Jan, a lot of your comments have been addressed. And of course I am grateful for the support of my family, there at all times with a nudge and a friendly push; this was on the platform of Waterloo Station, but they like a laugh as well.

The story is principally set in my adopted City of Portsmouth but I have adapted some of the locations, settings and buildings to suit my imagination and the narrative. I love my adopted home town of Portsmouth and Southsea and I apologise to any citizen if they feel that I may have taken one or two diabolical liberties.

Pete Adams

'Where justice is denied, where poverty is enforced, where ignorance prevails, and where any one class is made to feel that society is an organised conspiracy to oppress, rob and degrade them, neither persons nor property will be safe.'

- *Frederick Douglas*

Pete Adams

Preface

Barrow-boy - Originally the term used to describe a London street hawker, commonly selling fruit and vegetables from a barrow, often used to describe a social climber from the East End of London, noted for his above average ability but lack of refinement.

Cadenza - An elaborate, ornamental melodic flourish, interpolated into a piece of classical music by the soloist.

E Flat Major - often associated with the bold, sometimes heroic; grave and serious. The major introduces the humour, the upbeat contrast to the mellow.

Pete Adams

Prologue

London, Whitehall, or just off it, near Pall Mall, one of the classical white stucco terrace buildings, appearing from the outside as it has done since Georgian times, but stripped out and modern inside.

It was just after midnight. The House rarely sat late these days, and so the MP was able to attend with the PM's Cabinet Secretary, the Head of Armed Forces, and the man known as Pomerol; as in the ruby red wine he always brought to these meetings, supplied by his City of London wine merchant. This is what they were now sipping out of crystal goblets, sitting around the large conference table, a single central and powerful light punching white light onto the diamond polished surface, the distant walls lost in the peripheral darkness. It was a rare meeting of these men who were driven politically and ideologically. The room was silent; everything that needed to be said had been said and their course was set. They savoured their wine and waited. They would wait all night if necessary.

The light reflected back up from the table surface into the faces of the men. A romantic might think they looked like the severed heads of Olympian gods, floating in the heavens; they were far from gods but it wasn't far removed from how they viewed themselves. Their faces were fixed and did not even respond to the delicate tapping on the distant door. It opened and the room was flooded with light for the briefest of moments then plunged back into the previous halo and gloom. There was a whirring and gentle snap as the electronic door lock engaged once more.

The harsh rap of metal heel taps on the polished hardwood floor and a chair pulled back with only the hint of a scrape. Len took his place at the table, part filled his crystal goblet, swirled the ruby liquid, sniffed, sipped and gave the obligatory Mmmm of approval. He put his glass down and placed his hands flat on the table in front of him; he was ready.

* * *

The dog was dead when they took it out of the harbour; a savage beast who had in turn been savaged. He chucked it back. Strewth, what's that, the seventh this month? He was just a crane operator, so why should he care? The Ministry of Defence Police Inspector however, did.

* * *

Colonel Horrocks, nicknamed The General, insisted they accept his resignation. 'The Chief Constable position is not for me; the job is not what I thought it would be. I suggest that we get the previous Chief back,' he told the committee. But it was not accepted.

'Colonel Horrocks, you are the man we want in this job and I suggest that you think long and hard before you say no to us; am I making myself clear?' The ramrod straight Colonel of the Marines was making himself quite clear to Horrocks.

This is not what retirement was meant to be like, Horrocks thought to himself as he clanked out of the Royal Naval Officers Club and onto the street. The salty sea mist did little to settle his churning stomach; what should he do? His options were clear, the consequences of saying no very certain. This was not a game. He could think of only two people who could help him, but would they?

* * *

Jack settled the banker into the rather palatial safe house, a jewel in this part of leafy Southsea.

'I'm not sure I can do this Inspector. You have my statement and my affidavit, can that not be enough?'

'Enuff to bang the bastards away but not to save the economy stupid,' Jack said, thinking he was cutting a rather presidential pose, and wishing he had a mirror to look in. He did however feel some trepidation; this would be dangerous and took balls, and he thought merchant bankers had none. It just goes to show, he thought.

'The 'ouse is nice though...' he said to reassure the uncomfortably plump, sweaty banker, ''bit 'Ansel and Gretel for me, all that flinty stuff, but nice garden for you to stay out of,' he chuckled. The banker looked confused but Jack Austin knew about the gun running and didn't want this banker popping his clogs just yet.

There was a message on Jack's phone, which he studiously ignored. It read:

> *Well done BatBat and Dobbin*
> *I'm in Jack*
> *List of those involved on its way*
> *Those bankers need to be on the naughty step.*
> *Shall we go gunning for them?*
> *Mor.*

Pete Adams

Chapter 1

'I'm dying.'

'Again?' She sighed; it would not be the first time he had died on her. A little over two months ago he had been shot rescuing children held by a paedophile ring on a Solent fort. He had died and been brought back and now here she was, listening to his delirium.

'I see a fairy at the bottom of our garden, sunlit water, dappled pixels of sunlight, its magical and it speaks to me...' he said, in an ephemeral, cotton candy voice, '...don't go to work; take Amanda off to a world of tranquillity, beauty and seafood...escape as two lovers. You've done your bit.'

She looked over to his prone form in the bed. She saw beads of sweat on the puckered skin that sank into the void of his right eye socket. They refracted the early morning summer sun that penetrated to the back of the bedroom; strong, blinding, punching through the crack in the curtains. The vertical white scar that ran from his forehead to about an inch or so onto his right cheek was raised a brilliant white, an iridescent reminder of a most horrific injury. Mumbling incoherent frontier gibberish, his good eye closed, he was unaware she looked at him. Sometimes, it was as if she had never before seen the disfigurement. She returned to her work.

'Retirement is like dying...listen, like only the dying can,' he called out like a poncy Larry Olivier, and Mandy stopped her flurry of housework, this fragmented sentence catching her attention. They'd spoken about retirement and whether they could hack it. She had this romantic notion of just taking the ferry – what he called the fairy - out of Portsmouth and going on the missing list in France. Jack became aware of the sudden inactivity and opened his good eye; his vision was blurred. He saw not a ferry but a more traditional fairy in a knee length silk nightdress gently lowering herself onto the bed and sitting beside him; he gave an involuntary gulp. She stroked his brow, looking into his still unfocused one good eye. He responded with a throaty, rumbling groan to her soothing and gentle touch, worried he might be uttering a death-rattle. He sensed her breath in his ear, shivered, and despite his failing health was excited by the proximity of her radiant beauty.

'Shut the feck up Jack, you are not dying, you have a hangover; getting pissed with Alexander Petrov and Milk'O. Now get up and give me a hand.'

Oh the cruelty of the fairy world. He was awake now and any thoughts of a day off in bed were gone, uncomfortably reminding him of his own childhood. If he was ill his Mum would say "Go into school and ask the teacher if you can rest yer 'ead on the desk". Other kids had days off.

Groaning and expelling his sour breath into the dusty atmosphere, he replied to her clenched nose, 'Ooooh Amanda, you can be so insensitive. What're you doing anyway?'

He propped himself and twisted his aching body, so his good eye could face her without having to turn his painful head. His neck hurt; could it be meningitis? How could he ask Mandy to put a glass on his skin and check?

Familiar with his hypochondriac panics and reading his thoughts, she replied, 'I'm picking up my clothes from where you threw them last night, and your tutu, which is covered in mud and grass stains, and if it's meningitis get your own bloody glass. I'm getting the flat ready for Liz and Carly who are coming to stay for a week while they look for somewhere to live.'

'God, really? I thought that was next week,' he said, his vision clearing; was this the clarity you are supposed to sense before death?

She stood, grasping a bundle of clothes to her chest, predominantly stiff pink netting, and looked back at him, 'I appreciate you have your head full of the important things like Millwall feckin' football club, Bernie having a cheese sandwich when you asked him what he wanted to drink, and of course the overthrow of the Government, but I thought there may have been a little room in your noggin for a modicum of domestic information.'

He thought that was it and began to relax, but it wasn't. She stayed there and appeared to be looking for an answer. What could it be she wanted to hear; what was the question?

'What are you doing with my tutu?' Nice save he thought.

'Putting it in the wash,' she said, standing up and sitting immediately back down again as he tugged her hand. She fell across him and as he planted a kiss she noticed his eye was better focused and the Stratford upon Avon moment appeared to be over.

'Oh that's nice love' she said, and he kissed her brow. 'Come on let's get up and have some coffee, they'll be here soon.' Mandy gave a token struggle but was enjoying the warmth of this irritating man and then she raised her head just in time to see a cheeky thought make the tortured journey across his ravaged face.

'Have I got any clothes here?' he asked.

She gave a hint of a chuckle at his imminent embarrassment. 'Crikey,' she said, and thought for a bit more, 'there's your old shirt I wore that time, when I had nothing at your house.' She was thinking of clothes but Jack was remembering and recalling how beautiful she looked in his shirt, reflecting also how in the sixties the screen sirens were often seen in just a man's shirt and it affected him as much now as it did in his non-spotty youth. In fact, this woman had ignited a desire in him he thought may have been totally extinguished, and not just because he would be sixty in a few days. He had lost his lust for life and the lust for anything else after Kate, his wife, had been killed in a car crash a little more than three years ago.

'Just need some round the houses (trousers) then?' he said in his spiky, cockney accent. People didn't really know what Jack's accent truly was as he bounced from estuarine, cockney, Jane Austen English and anything else that entered his mind at any prescribed time, especially cod Irish.

3

Mandy went to the wardrobe, grabbed the shirt and tossed it to him, 'Let me think on the trousers, as revolting a thought as that is, but let's get up and have breakfast, and please, not too much Stratford upon Avon eh?'

'What?' Jack said, as he raised himself from the pillow with only a modicum of groaning. He found his boxer shorts on his face and as he lifted them off he saw Mandy smiling at him. He acknowledged the accuracy of her throw and Mandy picked up the shirt and held it open for him. One arm in, he spun into her arms and embraced her.

'Amanda Bruce I love you.' She was about to reciprocate when the phone went. 'Leave it love; it's bound to be the Nick.'

'Jack you are a DCI and I am a Detective Superintendent, and half of Portsmouth was blown up last night. You were there. We also stopped a battle between Crusading Knight Templars and Saracens; you were there as well and both times dressed as Angelina Balle-fucking-rina. So I think our colleagues may want us in today?' To mollify the strength of her rebuke she applied her syrupy southern belle smile which he saw as a special treat for him.

She leaned over to pick up the phone, not taking her eye off him, and again it appeared as if she looked to him for an answer. He sensed as he always did a feeling of mild panic; what to say? That was twice this morning, which was not good for his apolloxy which he was convinced he had, along with oldtimers (Alzheimer's) and florets and now menintitearse. One day he'd have to learn what these ailments were really called.

'You were going to say something?' she asked.

The cavalry came over the hill and something occurred to him, 'What about Connie, dressed in her yoga stuff?' and Mandy roared a laugh into the telephone receiver.

On the other end of the phone, Detective Inspector Josephine Wild, known as Jo Jums or Mumsey (which had become Ma'amsie since being promoted to Detective Inspector), reacted appropriately.

'Mandy you do realise you have just deafened me.'

Mandy walked with the portable phone, her eyes following Jack who had taken advantage of the distraction to beat a strategic retreat to the loo for a quick pit-stop, and then to the kitchen. She watched him getting his mocha pot ready.

'Sorry Jo, but Jack was remarking on Connie's part last night, saying she was dressed in her yoga kit.' She stopped talking to Jo Jums and turned, reacting to Jack's cry having dropped his pot. The coffee strainer and metal bottom pot had fallen onto his bare feet; she watched the mocha pot explode and the shattered black handle skitter, along with a cloud of coffee grounds, across her formerly clean floor. Shaking her head, she still managed a chortle at his reaction to the pain and described the picture to Jack Austin's long-standing and long-suffering colleague.

'What?' he said, as he scrambled around the floor, mentioning occasionally that he may have a broken foot, as he used the toe of that broken foot to push some of the coffee grounds to god knows where, hoping they would miraculously disappear.

'It's a ninja Jack; she was dressed as a ninja.' He'd not heard, as was so often the case when he didn't understand something. He did have poor hearing but Mandy often thought some of this was selective.

'The 'andles broke and who's ginger, are we having Golden Syrup?' he said from the floor.

Mandy returned to the phone, not understanding a word of what he said, 'He's okay Jo, thanks for the call, we'll be in for the not the *nine o'clock briefing,* about ten; we want to call into the hospital to see Father Mike, they kept him in the Assessment Ward last night.' She carried on listening on the phone whilst looking at her man scrabbling on the floor, trying to pick up the coffee grounds with his hands and looking to see if the handle would magically reaffix itself.

'Jo, tell the Commander to sit in on our briefing, save time. I will handle the press conference later, set it for five, I have a feeling lover boy will need an early night, me too if I'm honest - see you later.'

Chapter 2

Still hopelessly floundering on the floor, looking to see if he could push the debris somewhere, anywhere, rather than get a dustpan and brush, Mandy sashayed to Jack. A welcome distraction and he dipped his head under her nightdress. She knew her man and had positioned herself deliberately - Detective Chief Inspector Jack (Jane) Austin, a self-confessed, fully paid up member of the dirty old man brigade.

While he played ging-gang-gooley, camping happily under her nightdress, she remembered that he would be sixty in a few days and she would be fifty four not long after, and they hadn't discussed how to mark the occasions. The investigation had been preoccupying, but he was in denial about his age - well about most things if she was honest - and this was how he managed to keep going, denial being his core faith. C of E, Church of Egypt, De-Nile.

She lifted her nightdress, 'Close your mouth we are not a codfish,' she said, accompanied with her best coquettish smile, and dropped the nightdress onto his open mouth. It was a thing with Jack, he quoted films, adverts, and TV programmes. A lot of *Pride and Prejudice* of course, he was known as Jane Austin after all, misquoting for the most part and more often than not very inappropriately applied and out of context, but she liked it. He liked the film *Mary Poppins*, except for the penguins, "Nobody liked the penguins" he would say, and then looked anguished because he liked *A jolly 'oliday with Mary*. How many men worried about *Mary Poppins*? Were there any at all?

People thought Mandy to be as equally mad to fall in love with Jack, but their relationship gave her life a certain frisson that had been missing for a long time. That is, when she is feeling benign and loving towards the feckin' eeejit. Other times it was a source of agitation, particularly at work where he dug ever deeper holes for himself but often miraculously escaped.

'What were we talking about?' a muffled voice called from beneath the nightie.

'Ninjas Jack, not gingers. You could get the dustpan and brush,' Mandy said, and headed to the kettle, the trim of her nightdress receiving an emergency sniff as it dragged across his face.

'I'll make my own tea then shall I,' she laughed, always pleased when managing to catch him with one of his own idioms. It was a game and she thoroughly enjoyed it; enjoyed her relationship with Jack and shared his rejuvenation. She switched the kettle on and flicked her eyes to the floor, Jack on all fours, spare tyre over his boxer shorts, shirt riding up his back exposing giant love handles like a spare set of buttocks; not your classic fantasy image. She often categorised him as a *Jack Nicholson* type, a boyish charm in an aging and not lean body, and promised herself a trip to Specsavers, just after she got her brains tested.

'What's a feckin' ninja when it's at home?' he said, still on his knees, still resisting the dustpan and brush, trusting that the floor would clean itself.

There are some frustrating times with this man, but he made her laugh and sometimes deliberately so.

'It's a Chinese or maybe Japanese, martial arts expert, silent and deadly. You never seen a ninja film Jack?' Mandy saw where he was about to go and put up her hand, 'I forgot, you only like Rom Coms and before you say it, it's not a fart.' She chuckled, starting to feel nice despite the carnage and mayhem of the night before, and despite the fact that her kitchen floor was covered in bits of mocha pot and coffee grounds. Liz and Carly would likely be treading on debris for weeks, as Mandy would live with Jack in his house while her pregnant daughter Liz, and her partner Carly, stayed in the flat while they looked for a new home.

'You don't have any water at the bottom of your garden anyway,' she said to the floundering walrus.

'What?' He was getting up now, and making a song and dance about that as well; she thought he's looking for me to pitch in and help him clean up his mess. She got the dustpan and brush. Was this my role in life now, cleaning up after this bloke? Kate, Jack's late wife, used to say, "He's like a big ugly ship ploughing through the waters and we all live in his bow wave".

Mandy, a single mum with two children, had been friends with Jack and Kate and their two kids for more than eight years, and Mandy thought Jack might never get over the loss. Still, here they were, slowly growing together; on her part at least, for Jack never did any growing up. Nevertheless she thought they had a good foundation. Certainly they loved each other, though she was not so foolish to believe this was anything other than an energetic flush after a prolonged period of deep mourning for Jack. It was exciting for her too, but she'd been in love with this eeejit for a while, waiting to see if his one eye would ever open again and in her direction.

'I said you do not have any water at the bottom of your garden for any ferry, or fairy for that matter, to be dancing upon.'

'I was using dramatic irony,' he said with a smug-ugly grin on a face only a mother, or Mandy, could love.

He was doing her tea whilst she returned the floor to a semblance of a shine. She liked this about him, he did her tea, he cooked, did a bit of cleaning except she was always first to see the dirt before it ever came onto his radar; he never saw dust at all and claimed he was hyperallergenic, meaning allergic, but in a manic way. However, he did so many things that came from his heart and it made her feel cared for, loved.

'Dramatic irony? You twat, what's that got to do with the price of fish?'

'Be nice to have fish this evening eh?' Jack responded.

She shook her head. His ability to change direction never failed to amaze her, as did his love of fish and seafood.

'Jack; dramatic irony?'

He brought her tea over and kissed her neck; the toast was in, she could smell it burning.

'I like mine lightly toasted!' she shouted into his ear as he was also notoriously deaf.

'Shite...' and Jack reached the toaster, not in the nick of time. He inserted more bread as the replacement mocha pot began bubbling, increasing Jack's sense of panic. Mandy relaxed and sipped her tea, alert to Jack's ooooh's, fecks and shites, as he dispensed his robust coffee with just a bundle of tea-towels to grip the pot. He succeeded with only two or three tea-towels becoming doused in black tar that masqueraded as coffee; he hid them behind the bread bin.

'Not having muesli Jack?' she teased him. Kate had introduced Jack to muesli and after some time of whistling, which he did all the time anyway, and sitting like a bird with its legs hanging out of a nest, he began to like his bird seed. In fact his muesli had become an art form, making it himself with his own gathered ingredients and a formula that people ran miles from if he threatened to tell them about it; which happened often.

'I'm having toast today sweetheart, I need to soak the oats and then put the coconut in...'

She flagged him with her eyebrows, 'Stop, or we can talk about dramatic irony.'

He knew when to stop, in fact Jack knew women; leastways this is what he told himself, though the whole of womankind knew different. Mandy sat, sublimely relaxed with her tea and now lightly toasted toast, looking at her eeejit of a bloke sat opposite her, agitated, burnt toast breaking as he buttered it and squashed it into his mouth. She had swapped her burnt stuff, which he'd nonchalantly tried to pass to her, with his immaculately toasted bread. Still, he was happy with his demitasse of bitter-black coffee; that was really all he needed.

'You could have made more toast,' she said. He ignored her,

he was committed to the black bread and black tar and she saw the patent relaxing of his ugly face as he took his first sips. Jack erroneously considered his face handsome, with character. Mandy thought it was more like a cross between *Geoffrey Rush*, the actor, and a slapped arse; she giggled.

'What you laughing at babes?'

'Nothing, just thinking,' she replied, taking pleasure in a warm glow as he looked at her with a loving though dodgy eye. She did not consider herself a beauty, but Jack did, he considered her a real woman, said it all the time and she liked it. He would say she was his Sophia Loren of Portsea Island, which was the Naval and Commercial port of Portsmouth; nice, but not Capri.

'Okay lover?'

'Fine Jack, I'm thinking about the nice things you say about me.'

He stopped crunching, slurping and mmmming, and moved his chair to hers and sat so their legs squashed together; he tried to do this wherever they were. The intensity of his coffee and charcoal breath grew as his hand stroked her cheek, 'I love your face Amanda. You have hazel eyes that flare to green when you are energised.' This could mean when she was angry or sexually aroused. It was of course one of his favourite *Pride and Prejudice* rejoinders, all completely out of context, but it made her feel good so who gave a toss.

'You have perfect Olive Oil skin (he liked *Popeye*), and I love your thick, black, arching eyebrows,' and she shuddered as his index finger traced the eyebrows and brushed her closing eyelids, 'and your raving hair, how it shines, blue and green in the sunlight as it swings and touches your shoulders,' he was touching her shoulders now and she Mmm'd. 'I love to kiss your full and lush lips, but most of all Amanda, I love your nose,' and he kissed it, blowing the essence of toast and coffee up her nostrils. This was always his final sentiment. She had a large roman nose that had been the bane of her life, but he loved it.

Jack's hand dropped from her shoulder, caressing her breasts en-route to encircle her waist. Mandy rose from the chair and sat facing him on his lap. They kissed and he held her tight, her breath was lost; Father Mike will have to forgo their hospital visit she thought, as he fumbled lifting her up, tripped, felt his back for an injury, but eventually guided her to the bedroom. Fortunately she knew the way.

Chapter 3

Mandy had come to relish her post-coital reverie after making love with Jack; he slept, and she savoured the subsequent quiet. The buzzer intruded and she continued to drift, but she did respond to "Coooeeeh" from the hallway.

'Are you decent?' Liz called as she poked her head into the bedroom; Jack and Mandy scrambled the quilt around them. Liz giggled and Jack could see the likeness of her mother and knew that if he had met a younger Mandy, he would have been equally as attracted.

'Thank you Jack, that's a lovely thing to say,' daughter and mother said in unison.

'Did I say that out loud...?' Mandy and Liz nodded and smiled, still in unison.

Jack spoke his thoughts. Mandy thought it was endearing but often wondered where she would put Jack when Alzheimer's really had got a hold; still the Tourettes was under control.

'We will meet you in the kitchen directly,' Mandy replied. Mandy excused herself to take a shower whilst Jack entertained Liz and Carly in his boxer shorts and shirt. This was not just making sure the girls had refreshments; it meant light entertainment, jokes, singing and whistling. Mandy could hear the girls groaning as she slipped into the bathroom, smiling as he called out, 'Welcome to my world girls.'

Mandy reappeared refreshed and dressed. It always amazed him how quickly she could get ready, though it helped that he liked her with very little make up, her hair wet and drying naturally. It was hair that swung as she moved her head, like in the shampoo adverts, and had a wonderful lustre and depth; he really loved it.

'Thank you Jack, I know you do and I like it too.'

He rolled his eye as he made his own way to the bathroom, with Mandy calling out for him to leave the extractor fan on supersonic; guffaws from the kitchen and the groan this time from Jack in the loo. He reappeared twenty minutes later with an inscrutable look; it was his enema look, also not inappropriate in context.

'That was quick Jack, and why the enema look?' Mandy knew Jack well; even the dozy Mr Malacopperism enigma look.

'One, you have not got the new Cosmopolitan and there is only so many times a man can read about the female orgasm, so clearly I would be quicker, and two, I can't go to work...' he paused for dramatic effect, '...as I've no round the houses (trousers) and my tutu is in the washing machine.'

He sat at the kitchen table and applied an appropriately smug grin, crossing his spindly legs. 'Day off I think...' and he tapped the table top, an erratic beat with his fingers which he made rhythmic. 'What's this tune girls?'

They replied in sighing unison, 'Doctor Who, it's always Doctor Who.'

He laughed, 'Well done girls, douze points,' and looked to see if they were impressed with his French.

Liz spoke, 'Mum told us about your school arts festival, Milk'O, Alexander Petrov and Fee DePrune; that was such a lovely thing. We'll watch it on catch-up telly.'

They'd not noticed the French, he will have to try that one another time and filed it away and forgot it. 'Did she also tell you we had to bounce some terrorists and some cretin kids who were playing out their computer games of Crusaders and Saracens, and I had to do all this in my Tutu?' he folded his arms, determined to justify a day off; how could they miss the signs?

Mandy pricked his balloon, 'I did Jack, as well as I didn't break your coffee pot and we do have to go into work. I've phoned Jo Jums and had the briefing put back to eleven; she didn't seem surprised, said she had enough to be getting on with. She'd also checked and Father Mike was out of the hospital and back at the Rectory,' and she smiled.

He shuffled his chair closer to the table almost conspiratorially, his smug grin reinforced; it was what Mandy called his shitebox grin, and she wondered what was going through his mind. The finger tapping was not Dr Who but nerves, she thought, he's not confident of his argument, 'Jack; the grin?'

He wobbled his head to assure everyone he was confident, 'I've no trousers, hmmm, hmmm,' he reasserted, sure that he had mentioned this before and he stood and gestured with his hands along his skinny and extremely long, varicose-vein infested legs; the three women made retching noises. Mandy stood and told him to sit down and give their stomachs a rest while he pointed out that of course Liz and Curly would not like his legs, as they were from the Isle of Lesbos, which was received by the girls with additional convulsive laughter.

Mandy disappeared, returning with a huge pair of khaki shorts, 'Me Morecombe and Wise shorts, you found them,' and Jack stood and kissed Mandy gratefully, excitedly, genuinely believing she had indeed just found them, not even beginning to think that she had found them so readily because she had in fact hidden them. He disappeared to complete his dressing while Mandy briefed the girls on his ridiculous shorts that had huge leg holes that flapped around as he walked, and when he sat, presented all and sundry with more than a glimpse of his bits and pieces.

Carly and Liz were in hysterics as he came back and paraded like a supermodel, the irony being that they were laughing at how stupid he looked and he actually imagined he could have been a super model, and not one of those skinny frights either.

'Let's get to work then!'

And they continued giggling as they took in the full ensemble, baggy shirt, the eeejit shorts, legs looking like they were hanging out of a nest in a vine of black grapes, socks with dogs and penguins and size twelve tan brogues.

Mandy turned to Liz and Carly, 'Make yourself at home; I'm sorry I haven't made the bed nor tidied up, can I leave that for you?'

'Of course Mandy,' Carly replied taking control.

Mandy had noticed before that Carly was the dominant one in the partnership, probably why her daughter was the pregnant one, then admonished herself for the stinking thinking and looked to make sure she had not said this aloud. She hadn't, but Jack had read her thoughts, he was good at that and she liked that about him as well. She kissed and hugged her daughter, two Continental pecks for Carly. She noticed Jack still did one, stubbornly clinging to the English reserve he never ever had in the first place.

He smoothed Liz's belly, 'Is this a bump I see before me?'

Liz giggled and ran her hands over the slight tell-tale sign of a pregnant woman. Mandy shed all of her actual English reserve and hugged her daughter, then rubbed the belly. Jack had shown her the way again and he did it all without thinking; then again, did he ever think?

Chapter 4

'Jack, you've not mentioned I'm wearing my swirly gravy dress.' They were in the semi-basement car park of Mandy's apartment block.

'Sorry babes, I love you in that dress, d'you 'ave the complete ensemble?'

She smiled, 'I do Jack.' She was wearing a pale cream dress with tiny blue and white flowers. She had worn this on their first weekend away, which would have been a lot better if they had not been accompanied by Len (also known as Norafarty) the criminal they had been tracking; Del Boy, Jack's MI5 contact; and Jimbo, an MI5 body protection man.

'You thinking about when we went away with Len, Del and Jimbo?' He was holding the car door for her, something he always did. It irritated her at first then she realised she liked it. She tilted her face to his. She was tall herself - five ten to his six four - so she tipped her toes slightly to kiss him and giggled into his mouth.

He stepped back. 'Okay, what have I done?'

'Nothing lovely, I was thinking that you thought I was joking when I said these were cornflowers,' she tittered, smoothing her hands over her dress, 'you thought cornflower was for making gravy.'

He hemmed in anticipation, 'I was right about the swirl though wasn't I?'

As she stepped away and spun the dress floated in a swirl and he could see her tight white briefs underneath.

'See them?'

'I did, and I thought nothing could get better than stockings and suspenders.'

She walked back to him and this time she did kiss him, long and deep, 'Jane Austin you ARE a dirty old man,', then whispered in his ear, 'but you are my dirty old man and I love it.' She stepped into the car and enjoyed him looking at her legs as she did so, and she giggled some more; she could not remember giggling so much since she had left school. This man had been so good for her.

'What now? You certainly have the giggles this morning.'

'I like you looking at my legs, but then thought to myself, if only I could say the same to you!' And she mocked covering her head, as if he was going to bash her. Instead he leaned in and kissed her and told her he loved her, even if her vision was impaired.

'Yep, should have gone to Specsavers, no doubt about that one lover boy,' she replied.

He closed the car door on the giggling Superintendent and went to his passenger seat, studiously buckled his seat belt and so did she; this was a ritual that did not elicit mirth. Kate had never worn her seat belt and this is what killed her. Jack blamed himself but his son Michael had told Mandy Jack was forever telling Kate to buckle up and getting grief back for his labours. He still thought about it whenever they got into a car and Mandy, sensitively, allowed him his moment of silent reflection. His melancholic moments were thankfully getting better, though he was still an emotional man, her wuss actually, and his son and daughter's *girl's blouse*. She smiled again.

'What?'

'Michael, calling you a girl's blouse.'

'Yeah, well he's off to college with Winders in a couple of weeks.' Jack called his son's girlfriend Winders, an affectionate and poignant epithet. Jack's dad had been a window cleaner in Stepney, East London, and had been known as "Winders" and Jack as "Winder's boy". Michael knew that for his dad to nickname Colleen thus was a big thing. Mandy often wondered if this was where Jack's propensity to give out nicknames came from; he always said that everyone in Stepney knew him as *Winder's Boy* and it made him feel welcomed, a part of the community, and that's how it was at the police station; Mandy was known as Mandy Pumps, Mandy Lifeboats or lately Dobbin. However, in their intimate life he called her by her full name, Amanda; that was just for them and she loved it. She even liked her own name now, whereas she had grown up hating it; a bit like her nose.

They reached Kingston Police Station and Mandy pulled into the secure car park. He held the door and helped her out in his dirty old man style. She popped the boot, collected her bag and handed him his iPhone saying, 'Message from Len last night.'

'I'll 'ave a look in a minute,' and she gave him her look. 'What?'

'You and technology.'

Jack Austin was not known for his grasp of the twentieth century let alone the decade or so of the twenty first. They walked across the car park and into the Nick, a brief hug and a kiss for the CCTV that they knew would be relayed into the Community Policing office, the CP room.

They trotted past Hissing Sid the desk sergeant, 'Your family, they are well?' the expected *Pride and Prejudice* greeting from Jane Austin.

Sid responded, 'Tolerably well thank you.'

They wandered up the stairs together. This morning he had a sedate manner about him. Unusual you might say, but Mandy had her gravy dress on and was sashaying provocatively, exaggerating the sway of her hips for him; he took his ogling duties seriously.

'When are you two going to grow-uap?' It was Jo Jums on the top landing; she had seen the car park CCTV and gone to meet them. Jo Jums, Detective Inspector Josephine Wild, was an all-pervading presence, a formidable officer and even more formidable mother of four. She was ably assisted by her husband Tanner, a name given by Jack of course. He was a gentle man, a hands-on dad; and he needed to be as Jo's role was becoming increasingly serious. Tanner didn't mind, but their relationship had only just survived a rocky patch, Tanner fearful he might lose his job, which would have left them floundering. He now had a secure consultancy position with an obscure Government Department, courtesy of Jack and his MI5 spook colleagues - not that Tanner was aware. Importantly, this enabled him to work from home. MI5 wanted Jo Jums to take on the running of Community Policing which Jack had established and was generally perceived as a benign, almost wooden-top, police department, but was in reality an MI5 front operating in the strategically important Commercial and Military City of Portsmouth.

Jo Jums had worked with Jack for many years, unaware until very recently of his MI5 involvement, and as a consequence was inured to his childish antics. She had thought that his blossoming relationship with the hitherto strong female Superintendent, would relieve her of the oft irksome task of looking after her boss, but it seemed that the Superintendent had allowed herself to become almost as juvenile as the DCI. It now fell to her to look after the both of them. She had observed them from her perch on the landing, and watched them now, hugging, shouldering the wall and giggling.

'Is this the two accomplished professionals that I left last night at a crime scene, albeit one of them was in a pink Tutu?' she said, tapping her foot.

They had no answer other than, 'Naughty step?' and replied in unison.

Jo nodded, 'But first, if we can talk in your office please Superintendent?' She stressed the Superintendent title more in hope than in any realistic expectation of mature behaviour.

They stopped giggling at the sight of the Commander coming down the stairs. Jamie Manners, nicknamed Good or Bad, depending on what mood prevailed. It was Good Manners this morning.

'Hello you two, heard the delayed nine to ten briefing was to be eleven.'

Mandy demonstrably bit her bottom lip as they entered her relatively spacious office, a workmanlike, masculine space that Jack often thought unusual for a very feminine woman. Jackie Phillips, the child psyche friend and colleague, had said it was likely a subconscious response to a male-dominated work environment, which also explained the two comfy chairs that she had in front of her desk. They were low with reclining backs and Jack called them her psychologically challenging chairs, because this is how he felt if ever he sat in them. He always opted for the spare upright, orange, PVC chair and sat by the far wall, which had the added benefit of allowing him to look out the window. He participated in meetings only if he felt like it; a bit like now.

'Earth to Jack,' Jo said.

He did not respond and Jo Jums thought he had gone to sleep, which had happened too many times to mention.

Mandy saw Jo wanted Jack's attention, 'Jane!' she shouted mischievously.

He jumped 'What?' Mandy flicked her head to Jo Jums. 'What?' he was irritated, 'I was thinking.' Mandy knew this was impossible but Jo seemed preoccupied so she let it go, and gestured for Jo to say whatever it was on her mind.

Jo kicked off, 'First of all please sit upright, I don't want to look at your revolting bits and pieces!' She turned to Mandy. 'What are you doing letting him wear those shorts? I thought you'd thrown them away.'

Mandy pulled a face that said harrumph, looked truly stumped and slowly turned her head to Jack who was tucking his flapping trouser legs in, whilst responding to Jo Jums, 'Mandy found them this morning, I only had my Tutu and she'd put that in the wash.'

'Well, there's no answer to that,' the Commander said standing, and thus no longer psychologically challenged, 'I just wanted to say a brilliant result last night, the arrests and the festival. I've had nothing but good calls all morning and that makes a change I can tell you.' He clapped Jo Jums on the back, acknowledged Mandy and Jack and moved to the door. 'Good to see Bombalini and Bookshop again. Nice one Jack, good additions to the team since we lost Half-Bee. I can cover Bookshop's cost but we will need to look carefully at Bombalini. Leave that to me.'

The Commander left with Jack mumbling "He intended to".

It went quiet and Jack thought this was unlikely to be because the women in his life were concerned not to disturb him. He ventured a glance. Mandy was at rest, it was Jo Jums doing the real looking.

'This is what I wanted to talk about before briefing,' she said, looking like a seaside picture postcard Mumsey, puffed out rosy cheeks, folded arms with bingo wings, missing only the rolling pin. 'I am used to not being consulted on many things, but recruitment to my team, and having to welcome Bookshop and Bombalini like I was expecting them, is another.'

She sat back on the reclining bit of the chair and looked at Jack; she seemed not in the least psychologically challenged and Jack thought about that. He switched his eye to Mandy; no help coming from that quarter and he considered running, but bearing in mind how good Jo was at the tripping-up game, he likely wouldn't make it. He looked at the tree outside Mandy's office window, avoiding an answer, when the phone rang and saved him.

'Amanda Bruce,' Mandy answered and listened, then mouthed it was Hissing Sid. 'Sid, why should I give a flying feck if a dead dog has been found in the harbour?'

Jack thought that Mandy's swearing had really been coming on lately, and he put this down to his good influence. Mandy of course had been trying to kerb her enthusiastic use of Jack's colourful language; it seemed just okay from him, but not from a mature woman of respectable rank.

She held the phone away and they could hear Sid talking to himself. 'Did I just say that?' she asked, and Jack and Jo Jums nodded smiling and they could hear Sid saying, "Yes you did, and tolerably well".

'Sid, slither up with a memo and we will add it to the briefing.' This seemed to satisfy Sid, and Jack as well because she had referred to Sid in the simpering, snake like form that he personified.

Jack leapt up, scaring the bejesus out of Jo and Mandy, 'Right briefing,' he said and headed for the door in a masterly fashion, passing Jo without being tripped. He heard Jo say "Fucking hell". He thought, why fuck in hell when you can wank in heaven, noticed a sharp intake of breath, harrumphed, looked back to see two nodding women confirming he had spoken his thoughts, and beat a retreat, closing the door quietly behind him. Never slam a door, you lose what you have gained inside the room, or lost in this case; another bit of Austin psycho-babble that was really catching on; well he thought so anyway. He also thought he could be in trouble, but cheered up in the short distance from Mandy's office to the CP room.

"Eh Bombalini, whatsamatterwivyou" Mandy and Jo Jums looked at each other as they heard Jack's shout from the CP room. They each shrugged and got up, 'Let's join the feckin eeejits Jo. Well, one anyway.' Mandy said.

'Three at least Mands, I know Bookshop and Bombalini from Jack's distant past.'

'Oh God help us,' and Mandy sketched a Father Mike blessing, giggled again, and followed Ma'amsie into the CP room for the *Not the nine o'clock* briefing.

Chapter 5

'More in hope than expectation, Mandy called for calm as she entered the CP room. Jack looked back at her as he was encouraging Bombalini from his deckchair, while Bookshop was pushing a feather duster up Jack's flappy trouser leg. Remarkably the office settled and apart from the fact that Bookshop had nabbed Jack's work space and wheelie chair, they were almost there.

'Bookshop, let Jane have his workspace and chair back please.' Jo Jums asserted her matriarchal presence.

Jack looked to Bookshop, 'Said you'd get in trouble.'

'Jane, a modicum of grown up behaviour for a short while at least please.' Mandy turned, wiping a care worn brow. 'Jo Jums if you could brief us on where we are after last night please.'

Jo waited for Bookshop to get a spare chair from the Sissies section (Sissies is what Jack called the serious crime squad). Jo stood and Bookshop hurried up, 'Updates from last night,' she said and counted off her stubby fingers. 'One, the News is reporting a phantom ugly bloke in a pink Tutu, blowing up a van at the top end of the Eastern Road and then rampaging in the, oh so nice, suburb of East Cosham. We have a lead on that one, but I understand the Superintendent has Jane's Tutu in the washing machine, so thankfully there will be no trace evidence.' She allowed for the expected laughter, 'It is also known that he had newspapers and his phone thrust down his tights, so the gay community and the blind women's club have stopped looking for him.' There was more general chortling at Jack's expense that he took in good part.

Jo Jums frowned and got quiet, 'Two, Connie you should be on a fizzer for jumping in on the affray last night, but well done anyway, and Jane wanted to know where you got your Yoga outfit?' More laughing at Jack's expense. Connie was the short and slight Chinese Computer officer, real name Way Lin, nicknamed Confucius by Jack and now called Connie by her partner in computers and life, Frankie. Frankie was a strong woman in all respects and there was no doubt that she was a real computer whiz, and known only to a few, a spook colleague of Jack, and now Mandy and Jo Jums.

Jo and her fingers moved on, 'To cut to the chase; a good night last night, well done everyone. Half-Bee and Brenda have been arrested for leaking information, Brenda folded immediately, seems she was only reacting to her anger at Sitting Bull being forced to retire as Chief. She admitted to abetting in the kidnap of the General, sedating him under his desk, pretty much as we surmised. Half-Bee was more pro-active in his resistance to the cut backs and government policy and he held his hands up eventually to helping Moriarty, whom we all now know is Len; one Lionel Thacker, aka Lionel Thackeray, and often called Norafarty. So pick the bones out of that.'

They all did and with laughter, and Jack thought Jo was good and getting better. In his way he loved this woman who had stuck with him through thick and thin, proving herself worthy of his recommendation for promotion and taking over this specialist unit he had developed for his MI5 bosses.

'Four...' Jack was convinced it was three, can nobody count these days? '...Len is still out there and that will be our focus.'

Jo sat. Last night had been hairy and it was really only good fortune and ironically, Jack's foresight, that prevented a major disaster. The spooks, monitoring a caravan of explosives, had not seen the exchange into a transit van. Jack, using his dubious and villainous street contacts was aware, and eventually the terrorists were diverted from their original target, a demonstration in the Guildhall Square, to a spot where Father Mike and Jack lay in wait. Father Mike drove the van off the road, the van subsequently exploding.

Those were the facts of the matter but the story being relayed by the authorities had to have some of the narrative doctored to save the not so innocent, not least the assistance from Jack's colourful friend Kipper and members of his local crime family.

Jo Jums allowed the frivolity to subside. She had learned from Jack you had to have wind-down time after a big operation. This she was doing, but knew also that Len, or Moriarty or whatever he was called at the time, would not rest, and if he was being steered by people as yet unknown above him, they would want to keep the pressure on the police. She put her hand up and the noise died, 'Frankie you have Jane's phone?'

Frankie was wheeling down Silicone Alley, which is what Jack called the array of six computer screens run by Frankie and Connie. Frankie read out the message that she had also put onto a split screen on the crime wall.

> *Well done BatBat and Dobbin*
> *I'm in Jack*
> *List of those involved on its way*
> *Those bankers need to be on the naughty step.*
> *Shall we go gunning for them?*
> *Mor.*

Jo continued, 'For those of you that do not know, Jane has made contact with Len,' and she wiped her brow in an exaggerated manner, 'and if you can believe this, Jane has turned him,' she said, waving her crossed fingers demonstrably in the air. 'So, he will become our own source of information. I happen to think this is dangerous but the powers-that-be have sanctioned it, and so...we get on with it. We have already received details from Len of the key players in the Crusader and Saracen gangs and these will be rounded up by uniform. We will question initially but we do not have the resources to go out ourselves, which brings me onto Bookshop and Bombalini.' Everyone spun in their chairs to look at the two new team members. 'Jane, since you recruited these two, why don't you do the introductions for those poor eeejits who do not know them.'

Jack looked like he had been shocked from a deep slumber. He stood, stretched, and his hefty six foot four was a powerful image in itself, but it was the non-existent eye that got those who did not know him, the sunken wrinkled skin that Mandy called his Klingon effect. The prevailing story that Mandy believed up until recently, was that Jack's berserking nature had caused him to be glassed in a pub fight; she knew now that this was not the case. Just over twelve years ago he had rescued the daughter of Fatso and Maisie, a local fishing family, from a serial rapist. The ensuing fight caused them both to fall from the dock onto Fatso's trawler, where the rapist clawed Jack's eye with a boat hook. Jack, well known for his mindless berserking, continued the fight, which ended up with them both in the harbour, the assailant drowning. Jack was badly disfigured and blinded in his right eye.

Unknown to many, Jack was awarded the Queen's Gallantry Medal for that act. Nor did many people know of the CBE he collected when he purportedly retired from MI5 as a senior analyst. Jack Austin was a large and often loud presence for a quiet and relatively modest man.

He faced Bookshop, 'Nigel Gallagher – take a bow my old son,' and Gallagher duly obliged. 'Take note girls, the founder member of the Wandering Hands Society, WH Smiths, we call him Bookshop. He's to be watched at all times and not just by you girls, I've often caught him looking at my arse, but then it is a pretty nice backside eh Mandy Pumps?'

'For an elephant, yes it is Jumbo,' more laughter; he loved Mandy's humour.

'Bookshop is in from the sticks at my request; a country boy but a good copper.' Mandy saw Bookshop as a man of about fifty, who had more of a tame presence, especially standing next to Jack. Tall like Jack, a lot slimmer and more powerfully built, but then Jack was turning to seed. Mandy smiled to herself. She knew Bookshop to be a little dour, but only until you got to know him. He had an acerbic wit that took some getting used to; a complete contrast to Jack, whose humour was juvenile and obvious. He was good looking in a conventional sense but to Mandy, he lacked character. It was a shallow face, a slight snub nose, eyes close to the surface, blue but pale, thin lips and a shadow beard that looked cultivated; well, he was a country boy.

Bombastically Jack called up Bombalini. The Italian stood, bowed, gave a cursory wave and sat straight back down, 'Fernando Pescassaroli, a bit of a mouthful so we call him Bombalini. Europol originally and still feeds back to them. Seconded to us as Norafarty is on Europol's radar. He will be our link at Inspector level and when we go out for a pizza.'

A little titter and Jack was noticeably disappointed that Jo Jums got better laughs, and then felt okay because he had taught her; he made a mental note to remind people of that. Bombalini laughed heartily, he had that light hearted bonhomie about him. Mandy had met him once before on a police op in Guildford, more than ten years ago, and she was not sure if he recognised her. He was very Italian, dark and swarthy, deep olive skinned and bottomless brown eyes, intense, almost black; and a beautiful smile that set off his contrasting pearl white teeth. Shortish, medium build, probably mid-forties, this man had a real presence, you would not ignore him and if you were a woman you would likely go out of your way to be noticed by him. He was smiling at Mandy; he had recognised her and her stomach gave a flip.

Jo was back on her feet, 'Okay, we have a lot to tidy away from last night.' She waved her notes, 'Sissies lead the interviews of the Saracens, Jed Bailey with Wally and Kettle. Bookshop you lead on the Templars with Nobby and Alice please. I hear they are all talking, so probe to see what corroborative stuff we can get with Len's list, and let's not forget the information we got from the paedophile ring and the sources there. It is still our belief that this is all linked to civil disruption in some way, so look for connections. Uniform are reporting notices of proposed demos as the public wake up and react to the government policies. So who are the prime movers?

Let's look for links and get it snuffed out.'

It looked like she was finished and the Sissies began to wheel away, 'Not finished...' There was mumbling from Jed, who had got a particularly good start on his chair. Jo picked up and waved the memo from Hissing Sid, 'A report from MOD (Ministry of Defence) police...a dead dog in the harbour; seventh this month and we are only halfway through.' She scanned the memo, 'They've asked for you Jack and you Mandy, the MOD police stupidly thinking that the name Community Policing meant what it says on the tin I suppose; the naïve Military buggers.'

'Ma'amsie, no can do, I have a report to send upstairs and prepare for a press briefing.'

'Spotty has already been on,' Frankie called out. Spotty was Jack's name for the young press relations officer. Not spotty at all, called Jeff something or other, but nobody knew. Jack called all young men spotty, he said it gave older men a chance.

Jo Jums continued organising, not even breaking stride, 'Alice Springs, a chance for you to get out and about with a dirty old man; are you okay with that?' Another example of Jack's management philosophy adopted by Jo Jums, always polite; authority was not there to be thrown around, but to be used creatively.

'I'm okay Ma'amsie' Alice replied, 'I've got my car back and it's nicely tuned up.' Jack blanched, he considered Alice a nutcase driver, but she had calmed after falling pregnant and was about to get married to Nobby. Alice saw Jack's panic and decided not to relieve him of it just yet. Jo Jums wound up the briefing.

Mandy asked Alice to go into the Gunwharf shops while they were out and get her dipstick some trousers and to be sure to throw the shorts into the harbour.

'Good, I can get a new mocha pot, Mandy broke mine this morning,' Jack said.

Mandy decided not to contest this either, her experience was if she did, it could go on forever, so she let it roll. Just for now.

Chapter 6

Alice collected her raincoat, tapped Nobby on his shoulder as she passed, and they exchanged a smile. She went to meet Jack in Mandy's office. Alice Herring was a relatively new Detective Constable and a stunningly beautiful young woman, twenty two and blossoming in different but equally radiant ways in her new pregnancy, soon to marry Nobby the Commander's son. Alice was the niece of the notorious villain Alfie Herring, a background incongruous with the police force. Jack, also incongruously, was fast friends with Alfie Herring, whom he called Kipper, erroneously classifying the vast crime family as *Friendly rogues*.

Alice knocked on Mandy's door and went straight in with her hand over her eyes. The last time she had barged in, Jack and Mandy were well on their way to sexual union; since then Jack had located the snib lock, 'We're just talking Alice,' Mandy chortled and Jack grinned like a juvenile delinquent.

'I'm ready Jane, the car is in the front car park,' Alice said as she turned and wafted away. Alice always wafted, had there been any trees Jack would say she would waft like a wood nymph. Nobody pressed for an explanation as the logical extension was nymphomaniac and frankly, although naturally savvy with a rather fruity upbringing (Alice would never take even the hint of offence at Jack) she was a nice girl, and the other women felt protective of her. Jack did as well and Mandy sensed something between them, but couldn't put her finger on it, yet.

Mandy swung in her office chair and looked at him; he recognised the look and so stood awaiting his final instructions. 'Be good, and don't kiss her,' she swung more energetically and leaned to look out of her window, 'looks like rain, don't get wet.' She swung back from the window; saw his look, 'What?'

Jack replied as he reached the door, 'Nothing, just I could see your bra down the front of the gravy dress,' and he made a run for it.

She shouted her reply, 'And I could see up your feckin' trouser legs and I'm about to be sick, Bozo.'

Normal relations established, Jack whistled and sung his way down the stairs and heard, "Shut the fuck up" from the Commander at the top of the stairs. He felt good, he liked normality and they'd not had a lot of that lately; time to relax and enjoy life. 'Sid, cod and chips twice and have you got a number for me?' Jack said as he stepped into the reception foyer.

Sid offered up the obligatory, "I heard you the first time" and handed him a card with the police station credentials and an MOD pass number that would allow them onto the Naval Base, and access to the secure area where his presence had been requested. 'You'll need your warrant card Jack.'

Jack began vacantly rummaging around and unsurprisingly couldn't find it. Sid sniggered as Mandy tapped his shoulder and made him jump.

'Your card.'

'What would I do without you?' And with that he was out the door, shorts flapping.

* * *

Back in her office, Mandy swung in her chair, her legs extended, and then chastised herself for enjoying life especially after all of the shite there had been and still was happening. She dialled up Father Mike, a Catholic Priest who was also Jack's long time friend and his MI5 liaison. Since Mandy was now, to all intents and purposes, living with Jack, and had insisted on knowing everything about him, she had been co-opted into his nest of benign and inept monkey spies. So Mike had become her contact as well.

'Mike, yes top of the feckin' morning to you too.' Although it was Father Mike O'Brien, he was no more Irish than Jack, but you wouldn't know it as the two of them spouted cod Irish all of the time. 'How are you Mike, Jack couldn't give a toss of course but I was worried about you last night.'

Father Mike had been involved the previous evening in the blowing up of the terrorists and the subsequent fight between the Crusaders and Saracens. It had left him concussed and he had been held back in hospital overnight for assessment. 'I know you were love and I thank you for it, so what can I do for you this fine morning?' Mike asked.

Mandy had previously disliked and been very wary of this priest, unaware of his role in Jack's life, but now she trusted him. 'Fine?' she answered, spinning in her chair to look out the window, 'looks like rain to me and my turnip has gone to the Naval Base in his Morecombe and Wise shorts without his kiddie's anorak.'

'He'll need that as well if he's with Alice,' a reference to when Alice sat on Jack's lap in a pub and kissed him. Jack had to hide his embarrassment with his red anorak.

'How did you know he was with Alice?' Mandy asked warily, knowing that this man had sources all over the place, 'you are creepy at times Mike.'

'I'll take that as a compliment,' Mike laughed, 'but Jack just phoned, asked me to light a candle as Alice was driving him to the dockyard.' Mandy laughed now. 'I know, but it was Jack's way of finding out how I was without appearing to be all sensitive and caring. Okay Mandy, it's nice to hear from you but you phoned for something, you forget I know you too.'

'You do? I bet you don't,' she said and then got onto her mission, 'Jack's sixty this weekend Mike, and I want to go away with him to France, without Del Boy, Jimbo and hopefully without Len. Can you arrange that?'

Mike gurgled a laugh, recalling the fiasco of Jack and Mandy's attempted dirty weekend away. 'I will speak to Del, I'm sure it'll be okay. You know today is Friday don't you, and if you are going for the weekend maybe you should have booked up; thought I'd mention it as it is the holiday season.'

'Oh feck, I must have lost track of time. Shite Mike, I wanted this to be special for Jack, seafood and everything.'

'Relax-a-cat Mandy darlin', and I don't need to know about the "everything" but he will certainly like the seafood. So tell me where you want to go and let me sort it for you, okay.'

She was aware of Mike's *Mr Fix-it* epithet, he did this for Jack and now she supposed he would do it for her. 'Will you Mike, thanks...' she hesitated, '...you will just book Jack and me in a cabin and a hotel...without Del Boy won't you?'

Mike, clearly amused, took the details and hung up. Mandy then realised he hadn't said that he wouldn't book Del, but surely he couldn't be that crass, and if they kept it quiet Len wouldn't find out either. She wanted this time with Jack; they needed to talk about their future together, in love and in the MI5. In particular, they needed to discuss what Del had mooted with the main MI5 man Dr Jim Samuels, which was that Jack and she should set up the extension to Community Policing, whatever that would entail. MI5 were content for Jo Jums to run CP, and Mandy was not sure how she felt about any of that at all.

Chapter 7

While Mandy was fixing up their little getaway, Alice was held up at the Naval Base security gates frisking Jack, rummaging through the infinitely deep pockets in his vast Morecombe and Wise shorts for his warrant card and the security pass. Jack was relatively oblivious to Alice's rummaging; he was distracted, concerned about keeping a look out in case Mandy was watching. He knew she couldn't possibly be there, but she had a knack of appearing at the most inconvenient of times.

'She's not looking Jane, you turnip, come here,' Alice spun him and he cooperated casually. She looked him in his eye, 'Can't you remember what you did with them?' They were watched by amused security guards; the sight of this gorgeous woman going through her Granddad's pockets pleased them, and they said so, which was when Jack made a mental note to tell Uniform to nick them all for speeding when they left work.

'You can stop laughing Detective Constable Springs,' Jack said in his best serious voice, which had Alice convulse in hysterics as Jack reacted to her ticklish frisking. Her hands descended, bumped over his varicose veins and eventually came up with the card and pass, which had been tucked into his socks.

The guards seemed satisfied and let them through, directing Jack to where he was to meet the MOD Police Inspector. When they returned to the gate about ten minutes later, Alice asked if they would pretty please let them turn around and come back in, and could they this time give the directions to her.

The dock area where they were due to meet the Inspector was a huge expanse of vacant concrete apron, where, of course, they were not allowed to park. Alice swore under her breath at the nature of the military beast, dropped Jack off and drove to the distant allocated parking spaces. She was watching him as she ambled back to the quayside. Jack was peering over the edge, looking for a dead dog she presumed, swivelling his head, leaning outward, hands on the small of his back. And then he fell in. Hardly able to run for laughing, she reached the side and looked down but couldn't see him. She heard a shout; it was the MOD Police Inspector, running toward her whilst speaking into a radio, and summoning help from two crane operators who were clearly enjoying the spectacle. The Inspector said something that wiped the smile off all their faces, 'There's an undertow at the wharfs edge and it's dangerous.'

Alice looked further out into the harbour and saw Jack floating on his back; the harbour police had reported they were nearby and she could see the launch approaching. Alice could do nothing except watch. She phoned the Nick and spoke to Jo Jums; Mandy was in a meeting with the Commander. Jo's immediate response was to roll-up laughing before grasping Alice's serious tone. She instructed Alice to stay put and ring in when she knew something. Jo hung up and remarkably sprightly, loped the stairs two at a time and barged through the door of the Commander's office with a hint of a knock. The Commander began to remonstrate but Jo breathlessly splurged, 'He's fallen in.'

Mandy said nothing but the Commander did, 'What?'

'Jack, he's fallen into the harbour,' Jo said, at which point Mandy and the Commander guffawed but Jo wasn't joining in.

'What is it Jo?' Mandy asked straightening her grin, aware something was amiss and sensing bubbles in her tummy.

'There's a dangerous undertow and he's been dragged out, Alice is there and the harbour police are on the way...but...'

Mandy jumped up, 'Oh fucking hell, that feckin' man, fuck it, fuck it and shit on it. Jo get me a blue bottle cab,' and she took off down the stairs to her office.

Jo phoned, 'Sid, we need an urgent bluebottle cab with blues and twos to the dockyard; Jack's in trouble.'

Sid was good, always was, he was just fun to take the Mickey out of. He had a patrol car at reception by the time Mandy got there and she jumped in and they drove off with the blues and two's. The driver was Bobby, Jack's Millwall mate, and he took a call. Sid had come up trumps again and arranged for the dockyard police to meet them at the gate and to take her straight to Alice; "No military shite stuff", as he put it. It was only a short drive down from the Nick and they were soon at the dockyard gate where Mandy transferred to the MOD patrol car that sped off, soon to be spinning onto the concrete apron where Alice could be seen looking out to the harbour. The patrol car pulled up, Mandy got out and ran to a very distressed Alice, 'Any news? ...what the hell happened?'

'No news.' She pointed out to sea, sniffing and rubbing her red raw eyes, 'See the police patrol boat, that's where he is, they're getting him now.'

'What happened Alice?' Mandy repeated.

She shrugged, 'I don't know, I dropped him here and went to park the car,' and she flung her hand out to point to where her car was, miles away. 'I was walking back, he seemed to be looking over into the water and he just went in. Mandy I'm so sorry, I laughed at first. I ran here but I couldn't see him. Oh Mandy I am so sorry,' Alice sobbed.

Mandy thought Alice was maybe overreacting and it should be her crying, 'What are you sorry about?' she asked, and Mandy thought about the baby and maybe it was Alice's hormones.

'I should have looked after him, I'm so sorry.' Alice was about to say more when they heard an escalating throaty, clacking racket, and looked up as an air ambulance helicopter passed overhead, hovered and landed. They were being ushered out of the way by the Dockyard uniform police, who had appeared unnoticed.

They watched the police launch approach and dock at a set of concrete steps built into the harbour wall. A patrolman had a body slung over his shoulder, Mandy mewed but Alice was there.

'He has a blanket on him, so he must be okay.'

Mandy took comfort in this logic and ran with Alice and got to the boat just as Jack was taken aboard the helicopter, already firing up to leave. Mandy looked around lost, noticed Alice speaking to the harbour police and when she returned she seemed even more agitated and distressed, 'They've taken him to QA Mandy...' she paused.

'What? What are you not telling me; Alice?'

Alice was blubbing and looking like she would wail, 'He's been shot Mandy, he's been shot in the back.'

Alice started running to her car and Mandy followed. As Alice zoomed off, Mandy became strangely aware that she was thinking calmly. She phoned Jo Jums, told her what was happening and asked her to rally the troops.

Jo had the Commander beside her and she told him. There was stunned silence in the CP room. Jo took command, 'Jamie get in touch with the dockyard police, tell them to keep their feckin' size twelve hob nails away from the crime scene; we want this one.' He started to say that it wasn't their jurisdiction but saw the look on her face.

'I will do what I can Jo.'

'And so will I Jamie, now go please,' he did and Jo looked across to Frankie, who nodded back and Jo knew she had let Father Mike know already; he would make sure they had the scene. 'Jed, take Bookshop, you have jurisdiction, well you will have by the time you get there; secure the scene and the Uniforms work for you; thankyou; Pronto Tonto please.'

Chapter 8

The operating theatre waiting area was very familiar to Mandy. A few months ago, Jack had been in an explosion and shortly after was shot, had died and been brought back, twice. Jack had joked it was DDT, drop dead twice, and here she was again with a very tearful Alice and facing a man in blue surgical scrubs. She prepared for bad news. 'Mrs Austin?' She tried to speak but couldn't. She would like to be Mrs Austin.

She heard Alice answering, 'This is his partner, Amanda Bruce.'

It was good enough for the surgeon, 'He has taken a high velocity bullet in the back. It passed through cleanly, close to the shoulder and has hit nothing vital; he will be fine, so you can relax.'

Alice sobbed, this time in relief.

Mandy raised her head and finally she cried, 'Thank you.' The doc remained facing Mandy and Alice, their red rimmed eyes looked back at him quizzically.

'He was here a few months back wasn't he?' and Mandy and Alice nodded silently. Mandy became aware that Alice and she were doing things in unison; the two women looked at each other. The surgeon continued, 'That was a serious one. I suppose I am curious to know what he was doing back at work so soon.'

Mandy felt unusually guilty and didn't know how to answer, but just then Jackie arrived and she whisked the Doctor to one side, introducing herself as they went. Dr Jackie Phillips was a child psychiatrist primarily, but was also briefed by the spooks to monitor and look after Jack for Post-Traumatic Stress Disorder. She knew

Jack as a patient and also as a friend of his late wife, and now a firm friend of Mandy's. She spoke for some time with the surgeon; in the meantime the family began arriving.

The surgeon returned and addressed the gathering crowd; 'I take it you are all family?' They nodded. 'He will be okay and should be out in a minute. I am grateful to Dr Phillips who has briefed me. We'll keep him in Intensive Care overnight, to keep an eye on his progress.' The surgeon was done and walked off but stopped, 'Oh, who is Spanner?' Alice put her hand up. 'He was asking if you got his mocha pot and said...' the Doc pondered, arms spread like Julie Andrews on top of a mountain, '...to keep Mandy away from his...' and he chuckled as he shook his head, '...his Morecombe and Wise shorts? Do you know what that means?' He looked at Jackie. 'May be one for you Doc,' and he pointed to his head, indicating a possible loose screw. He turned and left but looked back when he heard the raucous laughter, shook his head again and disappeared; shock affected people in different ways.

Mandy remained standing, she had Jackie, Maisie, Liz, Carly and now Dolly around her. Alice stood aside, ashen, looked to Father Mike who had floated in like the Holy Ghost and they stood with Michael, Jack's son. 'I think this is the, How to live with Jack Austin support society,' Alice said, flicking her head to the gaggle of women. 'He's okay so I'll go; can you give a lift to whoever needs it please?' said to nobody but Mike gestured okay, and Alice left. Father Mike looked at the gaggle of giggling women and thought they will all likely be in the Bridge Tavern tonight, and thought he might just join them.

* * *

Jack was wheeled out of the recovery room, awake but dozy; he could hear them all. The nurse said, 'He's okay, just a bit dozy,' and almost in unison, "No change there then", a response which Jack decided to ignore. He wanted Mandy and could hear her asking the nurse to swap sides by the trolley. Jack lay still while Mandy and the nurse had a discussion about how this was the side the nurse liked to be and Mandy, deceptively and dangerously polite, pointed out that she was on his blind side.

He decided this called for his best 'not very well voice', which he had practiced a lot lately, and noticeably straining, weak and sickly sounding, he called out, 'Amanda, are you there? Please, I need you.'

The nurse, guilt stricken, swapped sides with Mandy as Jack winked with his good eye. Mandy knew then he would be okay and funnily enough, she would be too, especially after a few drinks at the Bridge Tavern tonight. Mike stood with her while they set him up in ICU.

'How are you Mandy?' Mandy looked at the Priest, pensive, everything was changing in her world and she was about to tell him so, but Mike continued, 'Something about your fella Mandy, he goes out on a dead dog case and winds up shot. He was set up Mandy. I've spoken to Del Boy; he has people on it and has touched base with Jo Jums.'

'Mike, do you think it was Len?' she asked.

'Not sure,' he said, 'I would like Jack's take but my guess is it's not Len; probably someone who feels Len is too close to Jack.'

'Mike I shall be here for a while, can you organise Jack a new phone. I am guessing Jack's is likely at the bottom of the harbour.'

Mike smiled, 'See you at the Bridge tonight?'

'No, I'm staying,' and as Mike turned to leave, 'Mike can I ask you something?'

'Sure,' Mike replied and returning to the bedside, he rested a hand on Mandy's shoulder; she felt comforted.

'Jack and I want to get married...and...I want that to be soon... and well...'

'Am I qualified to marry you?' he interrupted, 'Yes I am, and I would be honoured; are you Catholic?' She nodded, 'Well that's a turn up...what is it?' he noticed her questioning look.

'Jack, he's Church of Egypt,' and she laughed at his regular joke about denial (De Nile).

Mike chuckled with her, 'Mandy darling he's a Catholic; converted for Kate, didn't go to church much, said he sent Martin (his dog) in his stead, but he did convert.' Mike smiled warmly, flexed the hand that remained on Mandy's shoulder, 'I'll fix this for you, the Cathedral okay? Jack will want a Registry Office you know?' She nodded and Father Mike carried on, 'But if you say it's what you want, then he will give it to you, you know that as well, I can see.'

He turned to leave, 'Okay, I'd better talk to Del; he'll have to go to France on his own this weekend.' Mandy looked at Mike in horror and the priest backed up in mock fear, 'Kidding,' and he put his hands up defensively.

Mike left and Mandy recalled how she felt the last time Jack was shot, and the other whole host of incidents that had happened to him over the short time they had been intimate. She was aware something had changed and she tried to fathom that feeling. She was secure with Jack, was that it? She knew he loved her and they were extraordinarily compatible. Maybe it was because they seemed settled and she did not see every incident as a catalyst for a trauma that might lead to a break up? She shook her head and did as Jack would do, parked it firmly in the denial bay for a time, let it sort itself out; Jack's psycho babble.

'It will sweetart you'll see, it will all work out and I will marry you in the Cathedral if that's what you want. Bit of a turn up eh, my girl a Roman Candle.'

'How long have you been listening?'

Jack was coming round, 'Long enough. I'm sorry if I scared you; I love you.'

'You did scare me, but it felt like a natural scare; can you understand that?

He looked at her for some time, she waited, thought maybe she should prod his shoulder, 'No tomfoolery eh?' he finally said.

She nodded, stood and leaned over him, 'I love you John Austin,' and they kissed.

'And I love you Amanda Bruce. Feckin' shoulder hurts though. Where were we going by the way?'

She giggled, pulled the chair closer to the bed and settled down with her eeejit of a man and talked about what she had planned for his birthday, fairy to France, Honfleur - seafood heaven; all for him.

Chapter 9

While Jack and Mandy were billing and cooing, Jo Jums was galvanising her team. She had already arranged for the Sissies (Serious Crime Unit) to reinforce her team and was coordinating the feedback from the scene, processing it, and feeding that information to MI5 via Frankie. When Alice returned from the hospital she reported to Jo and the Commander on Jack's condition, firmly suggesting that Mandy not be contacted and more than suggested that Jo should do the press conference. Jo looked at Alice, the girl was assertive and clearly upset; something else was there, Jo was not sure what it was but her antennae was rarely wrong.

It was agreed that Jo would do the press briefing with the Commander and this was causing her a degree of anguish. She had briefed before but just local news, never televised - and this was going out nationally. She had taken several calls of reassurance and even one from Bernie at the local Evening News, fishing for a lead regarding the explosion and a reported gang fight in East Cosham. They would break the news of Jack at this briefing. It would likely be long, detailed and electric. Jo was nervous; the Commander was standing beside her.

'Ready Jo?'

She nodded, rose from her seat and scanned the CP room; the team were already sat around the TV. She was ready and felt some fire in her belly.

Spotty, the youthful Press Liaison Officer, met them at the door to the press briefing room. Other than telephone conversations, Spotty had never spoken to Jo before today; this was a first for him also. He put his hand on hers, patted gently and said in a gangly youth, patronising, gobshite manner, 'You'll be fine Inspector.'

She looked taken aback, recovered, and threw out a repost, 'Feck off Spotty,' and walked in first, followed up by the Commander. Spotty was aghast; this was completely against his rules, he was supposed to go in first. Jo reached Mandy's seat, turned and mouthed, 'Close your mouth you are not a codfish,' then flicked her head, 'spit spot' and he came to heel; most did, even dogs apparently. There was a buzz amongst the journalists; noses twitched.

Spotty regained control, or so he thought, and kicked off.

'We will break this briefing into five sections.' He sat back as the reporters responded with a buzz of excitement; they expected two, maybe three items. Spotty used the dramatic pause technique of the Jane Austin School of amateur eejit dramatics, and when he had the quiet he sought, he continued. 'The Commander will brief on the demonstration in the Guildhall yesterday, then the explosion on the northern section of the Eastern Road. We will then take some questions.'

He turned to face Jo Jums, 'Detective Inspector Wild will brief on the operation she led in East Cosham last night, and we will wrap this up and move on and take questions about the Arts Festival at King Dick's school...' There was laughter and he allowed it, he was getting better. 'Sorry, I meant to say King Richards School.' He waited for the gentle laughter to fade, 'Then DI. Wild will brief you on breaking news of a shooting in the Naval Base this morning.'

The expected regaling of questions energetically ensued at that revelation. Spotty put his hand up and waited for quiet, 'We have a lot to get through and you will get all of the information you need...' he paused, looked at the Commander and then Jo Jums and continued in Mandy fashion, '...well, all that we are prepared to let you have anyway.'

There was an appreciative chuckle from the journalists, an attempt or two at questions which were all related to where the Superintendent was, but the Commander had started and the press corps quieted.

'You are all aware of yesterday's demonstration in the Guildhall Square,' he said, 'you will also be aware that the police were not consulted, and we only found out about it via intelligence sources. And the newspapers of course...' and he looked to the ceiling. 'We do not wish to frustrate freedom of speech. However, in the interests of public safety and indeed the marshalling of our dwindling and stretched resources, it would be helpful if future demonstrations could be coordinated via the police.' The Commander paused and this was seen as an invitation to question but only half-heartedly. It had, in the Press's opinion, been a benign demo, but their misinterpretation of events was to be radically affected.

'As you have all reported, the demonstration went off without any real problems but I can inform you now that the police were also aware, via Home Office intelligence sources, that the demonstration had been prompted in order to be targeted with a bomb.'

There was pandemonium. The Commander sat back from his directional leaning on the table and waited while Spotty did his job, which he did quickly and efficiently. With peace restored Spotty nodded to the Commander.

'As I was saying,' the Commander said, 'we had late intelligence that the Demo was to be targeted. We were able to trace a van with explosives and DCI Austin, with a small team, tracked that transit van and managed to divert it from the Guildhall. When they thought they had a clear space, they tried to stop it. The van detonated almost immediately. Forensics are at the scene on the northern section of the Eastern Road and we are not sure if we will be able to determine if it was an accidental or deliberate detonation, but we can confirm that two occupants, known to the Intelligence Services, died in the explosion.' There was a flurry of bellowed questions and the Commander batted the cacophony away. 'I can also say that the intelligence was late because the MI5 agents, who were tracking the individuals, had to react to eleventh-hour movement by these men.'

He stopped, looked at Spotty, who in turn asked with just a hint of a wry smile, if there were any questions. There were, and the Commander dealt with them all and wrapped up saying, 'These are difficult times and the police should be seen as allies not the enemy. The police do not intend to enforce draconian regulations, but any future demonstrations will have to be viewed as suspect unless coordinated with police officers.'

There seemed to be a general acceptance of the Commander's announcement and this was soon replaced with an energised anticipation of the next bit of news, and Spotty kicked this off with the introduction of Jo Jums. He announced what they had agreed.

'Detective Inspector Wild is now running Community Policing. Detective Superintendent Bruce and DCI Jack Austin are still attached to the unit but will be taking on more strategic duties, to include the development of the intelligence systems that led to the discovery of the terrorists and the source of the recent religious murders. The Inspector can report on this now.'

Spotty handed over to Jo, and with fluttering butterflies, she waited for quiet; it was not long in coming.

'First of all, I believe you are all aware that in our unit if you do not have a nickname then you do not belong. So, to save you the trouble of looking, I am known as Jo Jums or Ma'amsie.' She allowed time for the expected laughter to fade, 'Good, now we have that out of the way, I can say that related to the various incidents that have been reported, and in particular the religious murders in the past few weeks, DCI Austin and Superintendent Bruce's investigations led to a computer game called, *Echoes of God – the Crusader Creed.*'

This was big news, and as if there had been an electric current passed through the seats, every journalist was on their feet clambering for a personal response. Jo was not going to answer questions and so she allowed the noise to ease and the press to sit back down, albeit on the edge of their seats. After she had quiet, she continued, 'The game in itself is relatively innocent,' and she allowed herself a little personal aside, 'if you can say gaming that encourages executions is healthy relaxing fun for youngsters that is.' There was a murmuring of assent and Jo reckoned there were a number of worried parents in amongst the press corps. 'The computer game encouraged online play and as you stepped up levels, so you became sucked into a dark trap that eventually led to acting out the fantasies the games had created. It was the culmination and acting out of these fantasies that we experienced in Portsmouth these past weeks with the religious murders. It is also our belief that this was motivated by the same people who had steered and enabled the paedophile ring, which was broken up recently and has been covered in past briefings.'

She allowed once again for the excitement to subside and Spotty came back in, 'A press pack will be distributed afterwards and this will have the detail you are looking for.' He handed back to Jo.

Jo continued, after a brief acknowledgement to Spotty and his growing expertise. 'I can report that the investigation is still ongoing and on several fronts, and this is being led by Detective Superintendent Bruce and DCI Austin. In the meantime it will be me briefing from this podium. Any questions?' Of course there were many and Jo fended some away and dealt with those she felt comfortable with. This included the detail of the attack by swordsmen, known as Saracens, on a Christian brotherhood meeting, defended by the so called Knights Templar; all characters from the computer game. Gradually the journalists were sated and they could see Spotty anxious to get the next topic going.

Spotty did, 'The Arts Festival was more than adequately covered by the television last night, as well as being in many of the dailies this morning. This was a festival instigated by DCI Austin and was meant by the Inspector to be discreet; for the children only. It was announced to the press with the eventual consent of the school, because it became known that the people organising the bomb and the Crusade attacks had also targeted DCI Austin at either the Guildhall or the ground conflict area in East Cosham. We wanted it known that the Inspector would be otherwise engaged. I will now hand back to Inspector Wild.'

Jo waited, there were no ill-disciplined interruptions, the look on her face threatening the naughty step. 'We were aware of the risk to DCI Austin but in the event, Jack Austin left the Arts Festival early and was involved in the satisfactory conclusion of both of these incidents...' she paused and the press could see that she was dealing with some emotions. 'However...,' she paused again, choking a little. The Commander looked over, concerned, but Jo Jums recovered. '...This morning, we had a call to go to the Naval Dockyard and DCI Austin responded to that call,' she stopped again, '...we are still gathering details but when DCI Austin got to the site, he was shot. He fell into the harbour and was subsequently rescued by Harbour Police.'

There was a crescendo of shouts, the scraping of chairs, and one or two falling over as the press leapt to their feet again. Spotty shouted 'Stop!' It made everyone jump and Jo noticed he was also upset. She touched his hand, nodded it was okay and grasped the reins.

'It appears to have been a long range, high velocity sniper shot and fortunately the wind was gusting. The DCI has a shoulder wound and will be okay. Least ways, when I spoke on the phone an hour or two ago to the hospital, he was joking with the Superintendent and so his life is very likely to be at risk again.'

This caused an eruption of laughter from the Press Corps, a combination of relief at the news, and knowledge that Jo Jums was as funny as the Superintendent. They had come to like the CP press briefings; Jo Jums stood and left, the Commander and Spotty following.

* * *

Len was still in his dressing gown, not long up from bed after his late night in Pall Mall. He watched the briefing on BBC News and was not pleased. From his flat he made some calls and then readied himself for a trip to Portsmouth.

Chapter 10

Mandy was still at Jack's bedside. He'd had a little tussle with a nurse, but in the end they allowed Meesh onto the bed and she snuggled into his good shoulder.

Meesh was actually Michelle. Nobody knew her second name or whether she was six or eight years old and the girl's upbringing was so traumatic that she had either blanked all this information out, or never knew in the first place. Jack had rescued Meesh from a filthy house run by a paedophile ring, the same house where she had also witnessed the murder of her mother. She had formed an immediate bond with Jack and Mandy, and vice versa. Jackie Philips, the child psychiatrist who was looking after the girl's well-being, had brought Meesh to the hospital, along with her foster mother Gail.

Gail was a big presence in all senses, and together with her comparatively diminutive husband Mickey Splif, they were doing a marvellous job of giving the girl something she had never had before, a family, unconditional love, and a safe home. Jack rarely talked about the incident because it made him cry; this was not just Jack being a wuss (although he clearly was), it was seen as another symptom of his Post Traumatic Stress Disorder (PTSD). Jackie Philips, as well as caring for Meesh, was monitoring Jack and had identified that he had probably been suffering something of this disorder since his eye incident, so long ago. Jackie had suggested that a strong reaction had been brought on by the recent traumas he had suffered; caught up in an explosion, shot (now twice), run-over and being knocked off his bike can take its toll on a person. She had alerted the hospital psychiatrist of this and charged him to watch for a reaction.

Jackie had always joked with Mandy, out of earshot from Jack that is, that he was her personal crisis magnet. In all her professional career Jackie had never experienced anyone having so much happen to them in such a short period. Jack, if asked, just said he was clumsy and a tad unlucky. This was also seen as a symptom of his PTSD and a consequence of being Church of Egypt. The hospital psyche reported that Jack had told him to "fuck-off" and he was concerned. Jack later explained to Jackie that "She was his gal" and, all in all, Jackie and Mandy saw this as amazing progress.

It was late and Gail wanted to take Meesh home to bed, and it was a further testament to the mothering qualities of Gail that Meesh resisted like any other child. Jack, the sentimental wuss, cried. After six or seven waves from various distances down the ICU ward, Meesh and Gail finally left. Jackie prepared to leave as well and asked if Mandy was going for the drink at the Bridge Tavern to celebrate Jack being shot. Anyone listening in would be shocked, but this very assured and elegant psychiatrist knew exactly how to deal with her patient, and he respected her for it. Jack grinned, 'Go on love I'll be okay. I'll have another visitor anytime soon anyway.'

'Who?'

He gave her the think like a copper look.

'Oh, you think he will come?'

He nodded, 'I'm certain of it, so tell Jimbo to let him through will you please.'

She looked around her, 'Jimbo? He's here?'

'Don't know for sure, but I would be surprised if he wasn't.'

Jimbo was MI5, generally assigned to bodyguard duties. He had even shadowed Mandy and Jack on their recent dirty weekend away in Exeter, where they had been tracking "Len" Lionel Thackeray.

Len (despite his mental instability and privileged background), was thought to be a deeply motivated socialist who saw it as his mission in life to get the country back to good core values and support systems. Views echoed by Jack, which was a dilemma for the Home Office and especially for MI5. Len and Jack 'got on'.

Len had been on MI5's radar for some time and they had done nothing to treat Jack's PTSD in order to keep Jack out there operating. It was to suck in Len and any of his confederates; Len had attached himself emotionally to Jack, maybe even loved him. Mandy now knew there was no choice; Jack had to stay in the game. But when this was over he would get the treatment he needed and deserved. In the meantime she looked out for him, along with Jackie Philips, Father Mike and apparently Jimbo. Jack had ostensibly agreed to this but sometimes you never knew whether he was in denial; he often said of his PTSD, "Just need a good kip and I'll be as right as rain; misery was optional". He was her delusional bozo; nice, but definitely delusional and obviously a bozo.

'I'll meet Len with you Jack, and then I might meet you down the Bridge later Jackie.'

Jackie left, knowing it would be highly unlikely she would see Mandy at the Bridge Tavern.

Alone now, she sat with Jack in the comfortable silence that he so loved and she often felt uncomfortable with. His good eye focused, 'Go find Jimbo and tell him we're expecting Len, he'll want to tell Del.' He noticed her looking at him strangely. 'What's up babes?'

'Just, I'm feeling okay and I can't reconcile that feeling. I should be angry or worried or both, but I'm not,' she said. He continued looking at her and she knew more babble was coming, even said, 'More babble?'

He nodded, 'More babble,' and smiled. 'Look at Michael and Alana.' She was confused at him mentioning his son and daughter. 'Don't be confused darlin', all I'm saying is that they worry but they know I'm doing what I'm good at, not the action man stuff granted, but I am good at what I do, and the most important thing is this...' He paused for dramatic effect and she gave him the *I'll tear yer skin off yer* look that he secretly loved, '...if you and I don't do this, then who will? And will they be good enough, and what will happen if they fail? Then again what will happen if we fail? We have the experience, a feel for what needs to be done or can be done, or even what boundaries can or need to be pushed. It's the age old question of balance, of how far you can afford to go, the means to the end, the means justifying the end, the moral paradox; what are you prepared to do to achieve something that you believe in, when something that you might have to do is against your beliefs? Shite that hurt my head; must be all the swimming I've done today.'

She laughed, told him he had only done floating, and then thought how lucky it was he had surfaced on his back. A tingle of fear but it was gone in a moment.

'Hallo you two, having a nice weekend?' Mandy smiled, secretly relieved Jimbo was here to keep an eye on Jack. 'I've got Len outside. Del said to check if you want to see him or to nick him?'

Jack responded, 'Give me two minutes then let him in. And Jimbo, I'm glad you're here this time.'

Jimbo shaped to leave, turned and spoke to them in his calm and assured tone, 'I'm glad you're glad, because I'm not. You're more dangerous to guard than the Queen!' But he seemed amused, and left to sort Len and then settle back into his shadows.

Jack put his hand on Mandy's; she looked into his eye.

'Be nice, okay.'

'Claws retracted sweetheart.'

She smiled and made a couple of fists; it was the best she could do as Len sauntered in, booted and suited, hands in pockets, totally relaxed. He was six foot, slim, good build, probably worked out, and they knew he was in his early thirties. Clearly financially well off, Len conveyed it in his manner and his dress. Top-end public school, with all the confidence that the system instilled, regardless of the other emotional damage that they also knew was inflicted upon him when he was a boy at Winchester. His hair was black, medium length, trimmed regularly and controlled with nancy boy gel as Jack would say; a tad smarmy but assured, and clearly bonkers.

'Hello Len, been expecting you.'

Len's reply set them both back, slipping through estuarine to posh that in any other circumstances would be funny.

'You're a bleedin' tart Jack Austin...' and then in his classy, public school tone, '...why I chose you, I will never know; I've been extremely worried.'

Mandy thought, that's what I would normally say. Feck, Jackie and Jack were right; the turnip is in love with him. She didn't know what to say, so relied on Jack knowing; not normally advisable, but what's a girl to do?

'Not sure I follow the banter old chap,' Jack said in his RAF Biggles voice, and Mandy waited for him to loop his fingers as flying goggles; he didn't, probably because his shoulder hurt.

Len carried on, unabashed, 'I mean Jack that I was concerned that you had been targeted. I sent you messages to watch your back, one from Joe Moss, and a text this morning saying stay put, to go nowhere until you heard from me.' He then slapped his forehead in exasperation and Mandy thought, bloody old woman and what happened to the text, but Len was still on his rant and Jack was encouraging him.

'I have to watch your back all the time. What happened to the back room Walla stuff? Christ Jack, I need to be able to relax and not to have to worry about you; how do you expect me to work if I have to worry about you all of the time - eh?'

He stopped only because a nurse had arrived and put a firm hand on his shoulder and told him to calm down or she would ask him to leave. He did calm and he pulled up a chair and pushed it between Mandy and Jack. She had to shuffle aside so he could fit in. She thought if he holds his hand I'll clump him. He didn't, but he did rest his elbows on the bed and place his chin into cupped, well-manicured hands; gentile and slightly effeminate.

'So how are you then Jack?'

'I'm okay; sorry to worry you Len. You should know I'm not that good at technology. I've also lost my phone in the harbour, I thought going to do a bit of Community Policing would be safe; so what can I tell yer?' and Jack touched Len's hand.

Mandy steamed, felt like saying something, but Len was talking to her now.

'Are you getting him a new phone and will it have the same settings?'

Mandy was shocked at Len's terse and assertive manner and stumbled over her reply, 'Err, yes... it's being organised now.'

'Well go and check when it will be up and ready, so I know – go on,' and he waved his hand in a wet rag manner, but the gist was there.

Jack smiled, 'If you wouldn't mind love,' and she got up and left, riled, mumbling to herself as she walked to the corridor. As soon as she was out of earshot she phoned the only person she could think of, Father Mike, and he was able to reassure and calm her.

'Sounds like Jack's winding him up to get some information.'

'I know Mike and I have been so good today, even thought I was getting into my stride.'

'And so you are, but unlike Jack, try the baby steps. Remember he has been at this a very long time, trust him Mandy. To tell you the truth, I'm a little relieved that Len is trying to cover his back.'

Mandy smiled to herself, 'Mike, thanks for not saying his arse, and you are just as bad as Jack, you know that?' and they shared a chuckle.

'I do Mandy, and to tell you the truth I am a little bit proud of that; can you tell?'

'I can, you are both tosspots...hang on...' it was Len butting in, 'What?' She said, in a manner conveying her agitated mood.

'Oooh Mandy, calm down dear.'

'What is it you posh, patronising, feckin' gobshite?'

His hands were up as if he was pushing her away, then went to his cheeks to check his squirrel nuts, 'I'm just saying goodbye and making sure Jack's phone will be working, and when?'

She calmed and spoke to Mike and closed the call, 'It's ready now.' He just said "good" and sauntered off and Jimbo appeared. She shook her head, and Jimbo let Len go and returned to his shadow.

She went back to Jack, 'When Maisie said things happen around you she wasn't kidding was she?'

He smiled warmly, touched her hand and she felt a current of electricity; it was nice. 'You were worried for a bit there babes. I did tell you that I thought he loved me didn't I, but then I am attract...'

She stopped him going there, clearly he was not good looking, but strangely she found him attractive; God help her and God help Len she thought, he clearly needed to get to the opticians as well.

'Yes well, what else did he say?'

He smiled a warm and loving smile. 'You are very good you know, even when you are upset, you have that interpretive brain that I like so much.'

She smiled back at him, but it was more of a tight grin, 'That sounded nice but what did it mean?'

'It means that you can think well, even when you are emotionally riled, and that is good for what we are about to do.'

She looked worried now, her shoulders slumped, 'Oh no Jack, what are we about to do?'

The smile never left him; it just got broader. 'Get married you banana.'

She laughed and hugged him, he winced in pain and the nurse came running and with a stern face she chastised Mandy, counselled that visiting hours were over and asked her to leave. 'Listen love,' Jack asked, 'get the phone wherever it is, his parting gift, apart from a kiss on the cheek...' she looked in horror, '...just kidding,' and she restrained herself from punching his shoulder. 'He said he will sort the people responsible for the shooting, so we need to watch this space; it will help us understand what we're up against.' He squeezed her hand, 'When I come out, we'll stay indoors; no field trips, okay?'

She nodded, kissed him and left, resisting the rude ushering of the nurse. She got out into the corridor and burst into tears, her body racked with sobs. She felt strong arms around her and comforting words, it was Jimbo.

'I've arranged a lift for you,' and a man appeared from nowhere. 'You're staying at Jack's I take it?' she nodded. 'Okay, this is Wilf, he will look after you and will stay with you at Jack's tonight; we don't think there's any risk, but Del wants to take no chances okay?'

Chapter 11

Jo Jums organised the team well, gathering information from the various scenes that was supplemented by matter of fact data provided by Len. Some tasks she assigned to neighbouring forces, but she was acutely aware of keeping her own unit tight and secure; they'd recently been subject to a mole that had caused great difficulties, and this Len Op was a long way from being over.

It was a Saturday, and conscious of Jack's way of doing things, she wanted her team to have some time off with their families. Jed and Bookshop had done all they could at the dockyard. It had been a professional job; the sniper had been positioned in a redundant tower due to be demolished in a week or two and had collected the spent cartridge case. The bullet had gone right through Jack, and the only thing they could do was to track back through visitors to the secure area. Fortunately the Military Police were going to deal with all of that, and she allowed this with only token resistance; she knew it would gain them nothing even if they found the sniper. This smacked of high level collusion and that information presumably would come via Len. At least that's what she hoped.

Jo had visited Mandy at Jack's house earlier. As Jo shaped to leave she whispered "He's drop dead gorgeous", looking towards Wilf (who was waiting to take Mandy to visit Jack) with raised eyebrows and nudging Mandy. Mandy laughed and told her to feck off, but secretly agreed; Wilf was a hunk. But then so was any man beside Jack, physically anyway.

There was no rush to get to the hospital. She had phoned first thing in the morning and he'd had a comfortable night and was now moved to a recovery room of his own, and would be let out after he had been fitted with a shoulder harness; she'd sniggered as he had apparently requested a pink one. They arrived to learn that he was off for his fitting with Jimbo tagging along, and Mandy and Wilf waited in Jack's room. Wilf switched on the TV, flicked the channels and got to BBC News 24. The running strap line got Mandy's immediate attention, *The Head of Armed Forces, General Charles Fawcett, found dead*. It looked like a suicide.

Mandy turned to Wilf, 'Do you have a secure phone to Del Boy?'

He nodded, pulled his phone and punched some numbers and handed it to her.

'Del, this is Mandy... you have, well I knew he wanted a pink one... yes I am sure he will appreciate that Del, but that's not why I am ringing.' She listened as Del correctly guessed the reason for her call and told her that Jack had already phoned and put forward the scenario that the General's death could be Len's doing.

Mandy blew out her cheeks and expelled the air slowly through tight lips.

'What control do you have on the scene Del?'

He chortled down the phone. 'Unfortunately local plod has been all over it, and we think the so-called suicide note may have been deliberately leaked to the press.'

Mandy thought for a while. 'Mind if I guess what it said Del?'

Del responded for her to be his guest, and she related that it had to say something like, "The Military is being decimated by the cutbacks and is in trouble in the command structure, through the ranks, blah, blah, disaster, blah, blah". Del confirmed she had not the wording but the sentiment and he'd heard it would appear in the next day's Sunday papers. It was on the internet already, probably courtesy of Len. He was quiet.

'What was the time of death Del?'

She listened as he chortled down the phone again. 'It was when Len was with you in the hospital. Jack said Len was good and he is; two police officers as an alibi.' The phone line was quiet again and she remembered Del's ability to leave the air still, to give time for someone to talk. Not many people can sit in silence. Most police interrogators knew this technique but few could keep silent themselves. Jack could, she had seen it in operation and quite impressive it was too. Ironically, it was the only time he was quiet.

'Okay Del, I will talk it through with Jack when we get home. Is there anything else we should know? I'll be honest with you, my money, if you pardon the pun, is on a financial hit.'

He was quiet again and Mandy matched him. Del eventually lost that particular game, 'I think we can expect the financial hit as well. Len is in the red zone, as Jack said, and his behaviour at the bedside last night was proof of that. ' Then he laughed.

'What's so funny Del?'

'Len kissed Jack before leaving, Mike was all upset...' and he laughed more, verging on giggles. Mandy resolved to tackle Jack on that one later and said goodbye to Del; a senior MI5 officer who could hardly control his sniggering.

Jack returned about an hour later and she lost her resolve to deal with him when she saw his broad childish grin, reflecting his success in getting a ridiculous pink shoulder brace. Wilf stepped outside and began chatting with Jimbo in the corridor. Mandy took in the look of Jack in his enormous pyjama bottoms, just a pyjama jacket draped over his shoulders.

'Mary and Joseph Jack, just look at you; I know I'm going to have to dress you, but how?' She was giggling and he was wobbling his head, almost in time with his belly. He waited for her to stop laughing and she waited for his belly to stop moving.

'A nurse will be here in a minute to show you how to dress me.' He was trying to be serious. This made Mandy splutter more giggles, and he joined her. They hugged, minor jolts of pain flaring in his shoulder as she laughed against him. He loved it when she laughed, it was worth a little pain and he would happily bear it.

The nurse did eventually come in and immediately shared jokes at Jack's expense as she demonstrated how to release the clips of the plastic cast and to get him dressed.

'The cast is just to hold the shoulder steady for a week or so, the bullet cracked some bones on the way; the wound will heal quickly enough' she said.

They discussed, in front of him, the removal of his pyjama bottoms but his look stopped them. The nurse eventually left and he stood there not knowing what to do; he had a shirt draped over the brace and an elephant's pyjama bottoms. Mandy looked him up and down, chortling mildly.

'Well go on then, ask me,' she said.

He stood still and thought through the possible booby traps that lay ahead of him, but his mouth was in front of his brain, and he asked, 'Are me Morecombe and Wise shorts dry?'

She burst into such a roll of laughter that Wilf and Jimbo rushed into the room, which made her laugh even more. Jack looked at his colleagues, shrugged his shoulders and yelled in pain; making all three of them laugh. Jack looked on, wondering what you had to do to get a bit of symphony around here and was greeted by more thunderous guffaws, Mandy nodding, confirming he had just spoken that Malacopperism thought out loud.

Mandy had brought him up some trousers and his tan brogues. She had dried them out as best she could as she knew he would want them regardless. He was grateful and they left with Wilf and Jimbo, who announced they were assigned to the pair of them for the duration; Del's orders and not to be questioned. Jimbo did not look at all happy about the arrangements. Mandy thought that although it was an inconvenience, she would not complain about having these two bodyguards around. She was though, concerned about Colleen and Michael, not wanting them to be vulnerable. She needn't have worried as later that morning they announced that they were off for a trip into Europe on Sunday; a last jolly before Med school started. Jack looked amazed, impressed and surprised.

Michael, unfazed, explained to Mandy that he had actually talked this over with his dad back in March, who had also helped out with some cash, which clearly he had forgotten. 'Clearly,' she said, putting her head to one side and looking at Jack as his face indicated a memory recalled, then instantly forgotten again.

Chapter 12

Southsea is charming and in places picturesque, almost bijou. It is a tightly packed, comfortable and well-off residential area of Portsmouth; a cramped jumble of beautiful and not so beautiful houses, generally squashed together but managing to nestle comfortably and never appearing jammed, offering a cohesive and soft feel. It made it a nice place to live, even densely populated as it was, but densely populated with 'nice' people, some of them not so dense. It was also quite extraordinary, in that it was encapsulated on the south and curving to the east by a broad and expansive common that sat before the ancient fortified seafront; and to the west, it nestled cheek by jowl with restaurants and pubs that could become distinctly lively. It was as if the residences turned their backs on all of this and hunkered down in their comfortable, cheek-by-jowl, relationship. It was edged on the north by a railway line.

Where you lived in Southsea depended on whether you were likely to be disturbed by nocturnal noises of the human kind, or desired that proximity. Where Jack had his house was not on a regular pedestrian through-route, and as a consequence was generally quiet. Any noise seemed like an intrusion. Mandy had marvelled at his intolerance of the "feckin' birds" in the morning, but had a natural acceptance of any drunken revelry that should occasionally pass by the house late at night. She guessed this tolerance stemmed from the fact that not so very long ago it would have been him revelling drunkenly.

Not far from Jack's house, in one of these desirous enclaves, snaked a serpentine road. The wriggly lane, overhung with mature trees, was inadequately lit with electrified old gas lamps that looked charming but offered no practical illumination. To compound the gloom, the street was heavily shadowed by high walls enclosing a jumble of chocolate box houses. One such, was a flint encrusted house that had more than its fair share of garden; the jewel in the residential Southsea crown, even more so in this premium zone. It was spoiled only marginally by the rowdiness of the nearby pubs, whose inebriated revelling patrons were currently spilling out onto the pavements to smoke and display themselves on a balmy summer Saturday night. A cacophony in anyone's books, but this cacophony did provide a semblance of cover for a planned assault on this incongruous flint house.

Combine this environment with the recent practice of fireworks at any time of the year, not just the traditional *Guy Fawkes Night*, and it meant that Jack slumbered through the noise of aerial bombshells and crackerjacks, with just the occasional, "Feckin' kids" comment to Mandy. She was not particularly surprised when Jimbo tapped on the bedroom door shortly afterwards.

'Jack, Mandy, we have an incident.'

He handed a phone to Mandy who was clutching the quilt to her breasts. She gestured for him to drop it on the bed and leave them. She switched on a light, picked up the phone and nudged Jack to wake up. He was awake but didn't feel like moving, it hurt when he did, which she understood had to be difficult for a fidget arse. The shoulder harness was only for moving around during the day was impossible to sleep in.

Mandy ignored the chorus of moans from Jack and spoke into the phone. Jack quieted; the quilt had dropped from her breasts, and he was not in the least bit interested in the phone call.

'Del Boy, yes, thanks for Jimbo and Wilf but there is no need to ring in the middle of the night to check its going okay.' She was showing a little of her famed impatience and Jack's self- preservation radar went to Red Alert, so he listened carefully, pretending to be going back to sleep just in case he needed cover, managing an occasional salacious peak at her beautifully pendulous breasts. He was secretly pleased with his multi-tasking capabilities.

'Why were we not told about this Del?' She listened and Jack moaned, more hedging, trying to raise himself from his pillow with a series of accomplished and certainly well practiced oomphs and aaarghs. She looked and shushed him, and she received the hurt child face in return, which transformed into a full blown adult version when it did not receive the sweet kitten response sought. He was being ignored as Mandy swung her legs out of the bed, rubbed the minimal sleep from her eyes and focused.

'That would be Central not our Nick, but I will call Jo and get it...' she paused, 'Okay you have, I should have known. Do you want us there?'

Jack was up now. The reality was that his shoulder was not that painful and he sensed he had reached that familiar stage where he could live with the pain, like it was a part of him, which of course was really another form of denial. Mandy was still on the phone listening to Del and watched as he did all the things he was not supposed to be able to do and that he had insisted she do. One handed he put his boxer shorts on, he had his shirt on, reached behind and with hitherto unnoticed dexterity flicked the snap buckles. The harness was secure. He noticed her looking and immediately winced, nearly fainting.

He received a full on frown, followed by a smile.

'Okay Del, yes we're up and will liaise with Jo.'

She hung up and he winced his way over to her and she completed his dressing, in and exaggerated and overtly sexual manner, which he appreciated and which she noted stopped the wincing, but not the mincing.

'Okay, skip the Stratford upon Avon and let's get moving. Seems that was not fireworks we heard, and it wasn't "feckin kids". Del thinks we may have found out where the gun runners are going.'

They went downstairs and fire up the laptop. Del Boy appeared on the screen; he was with Jo Jums. Jack marvelled at Skype and accepted it so long as someone worked it for him.

Mandy spoke, easing Jack to the side. He looked at her and she ignored him as he tried to push her back to get his face on the screen.

'What do we have Jo?'

It was Del's turn to feel rejected now, not lost on Jo.

'It seems that James Bond here...' she flicked her head at an irritated Del Boy, '...has been keeping a whistle blower banker tucked up nice and insecure in Southsea and didn't tell us. Remind you of someone Mandy?'

Del managed to poke his face in for a laugh from behind Jo, 'Bit of a blood bath Mandy.'

'The Banker?'

'Brown bread (dead) as Jack would say, along with a number of bodyguards and assailants, in fact it's hard to imagine anyone got out. And before you ask, no Len.' Jo said.

'No, he will have a cast iron alibi somewhere,' put in Jack, 'we'll be along in a minute.'

'I don't think so.'

'Sorry Jo, what d'you mean?' Jack reacted.

'I mean you stay indoors. Who's to say there isn't someone waiting, expecting you to turn up; so stay put.'

Del Boy poked his head around Jo. 'Couldn't have put it better myself, get yourself to the station in the morning and stick with Wilf and Jimbo.'

* * *

Mandy batted Jack's good hand away as she lifted off his harness to put a clean shirt on him. He was being juvenile and she was not in the mood. She was brought up sharp.

'Darlin', can you hold off a minute please, you're hurting me.'

She looked up at him and became aware of what she had been doing. She kissed him and returned to her task with gentler ministrations, looked back up to his face.

'What?'

'Nothing, just stay indoors.' And she kissed him again and told him she loved him. That was all she needed to do, ever, and she saw this in his eyes. She often wondered how it was with Kate. He adored her but she had heard that they had a stormy latter few years; presumably Kate had always ended up saying she loved him and he forgot everything that preceded the making up?

They went downstairs where the bodyguards had made themselves at home, washing the dishes and arguing like an old couple. She wondered about how her life had been completely transformed in the last few months; living, or sometimes camping with Jack, worried about Jack, and now she was also a spook and possibly a target, like Jack.

'Didn't think to do any breakfast for us then?' she said to a startled pair of spooks; so much for being on red alert.

Jimbo did look guilty but came back with Jack's new phone held up. 'Thought you might go into the station for a full English; we were not going to do Jack's muesli.'

A fair point she thought, even she would not do Jack's muesli, and took the phone from Jimbo. She scrolled to messages:

> *Hi Bat-Bat and Dobbin*
> *Had to step in again*
> *But not me in your backyard*
> *Looking into that*
> *Bit of house work needed I think*
> *Never cry over spilt red wine*
> *Mor.*

Before she could ask, Jimbo confirmed it had been sent onto Del and Jo. Jack had been listening whilst watching the TV, 24 hour news, reporting the suspicious death of a prominent banker in the City of London, not Southsea. Jack called out, 'The wine was a Pomerol, a nickname for Jocelyn Balls, Chairman of Cedric James a small merchant bank; ring any bells Amanda?'

'Len's bank.'

Jack walked from the living room to the kitchen, and explained to Jimbo and Wilf that Len had been a solicitor with the City of London Merchant bank, Cedric James, eventually leaving under a cloud due to erratic behaviour.

'We may need to rethink that. Len will have wanted the whistle blower to spill his guts, so to speak, but not like last night. I think he heard and reacted.' Jack looked at Wilf, 'Pass that onto Del will you, along with how people found out about my whistle blower...Mandy and I will have a Jean special in the station canteen.'

'One of us will drive you both; we are with you until this is over, okay?'

Wilf decided to stay and monitor the house and Jimbo was point duty.

Chapter 13

Just up from St James's Palace are a number of closeted alleys. In old London they would have been called runnels, places that you entered only if you were as poor as a church mouse, a bad lot, or stupid. Nowadays they were trendy places; quaint, full of Dickensian character. Daylight struggled to penetrate and the gulley in the centre of the paving of Crown Passage still resembled the channel that carried away the night's waste in mediaeval times. In modern days it just tripped the inebriated, some of whom would of course be considered human detritus, even in this very salubrious part of London's West End. The area did however have some good pubs and these were as atmospherically gloomy as the alleyways that afforded them access, and this was considered a part of their charm.

A brief and stimulating walk across St James's Park, and around the corner to Pall Mall and Whitehall, made this an ideal and discreet meeting place for the power-seeking and the powerful. Far enough from Downing Street and Parliament to make it a relatively anonymous meeting place for relatively anonymous power brokers. Today though, the lunchtime tipple was less relaxing, and the stroll across the Park had not stimulated so much as served to energise paranoia. The MP, a government chief whip, and the Prime Minister's Cabinet Secretary, a very senior Civil Service Mandarin, avoided the red wine; it reminded them too much of Pomerol. They had a pint of London Pride each, but this only served to stir the stomach rather than settle the nerves; they were frightened men and it showed. Although it was a hot day, it was cool in the Red Lion and though the ale was traditionally warm, that was not what was causing them to sweat. They sat at high tables, their jackets off and placed over the back of the pub stools, revealing moist armpits that ordinarily they would cover up. Vanity had no place here today; this was about survival, about feeling trapped and scared.

Typical of these types of individual, they shared an intelligent and superficial bond, a tacit camaraderie, but inwardly they looked for their own prospects of prosperity, or in this instance, survival. They did not really care about Fawcett or Pomerol other than how it would affect them. When they set up their *Star Chamber* it seemed safe. They arrogantly felt they were bullet proof. Their mission, if ever there was a need to explain, would of course seem logical to all right thinking people.

They supported the government of course, it was the right colour even if it was tinged with yellow, but it was not a strong yellow apart from the backbone, many said. It was not the yellow that people believed and had voted for before the coalition was formed, which was perceived as redder than yellow; but now combined with blue it became a muddy brown which, though not ideal, suited the *Star Chamber's* aims. They could live with this coalition, but these current Ministers were not behaving like the puppets or the blind mice they were supposed to be. Hypocritically they thought these Ministers were more doctrinaire in their own right, following a course of action only marginally less disciplined than their own stance, and their plans were beginning to unravel; what to do?

Lionel joined them, 'Pride please.'

They looked confused, as if maybe they should have a different visage, then realised he would join them in a pint of London Pride. The Cabinet Secretary, not such an impressive man out of his Whitehall Mandarin comfort zone, jumped towards the bar just a few feet away and jostled to get the barman's attention. His edgy manner demonstrated a man not only fearful but patently unused to having to make his own way with ordinary people around him. He thought about a whisky chaser while he was at the bar and then thought better of it. Lionel would be watching; he felt sick. He looked at himself in the mottled back bar mirror, and it reflected back how he felt; the prisoner sentenced to death, a hollow feeling in his stomach, his life passing before his eyes. Looking at his reflection, the Cabinet Secretary even noticed his own weasel look, sensed his limp hands that now leached a clammy sweat. The barman seemed not to want to touch his hand either as he flipped and slammed the change on the counter.

The Mandarin jumped, reacting to the bang on the counter, and looked in the mirror to see if his company noticed. They had; a wry smile from Lionel, but the MP looked ashen.

The Mandarin returned to the high table and placed Len's pint onto a beer mat, the shake in his hand visible. Len held the Mandarin's hand firmly to the table.

'There, is that better?'

Len's cold voice and steely piercing eyes reinforced the fear in the Secretary and the MP. Len lifted off, sat back and sipped the beer and rolled it around his mouth. This was ale and he had observed that Jack savoured this drink, especially his favourite London Pride. Lager he drank fast. He had learned a lot about Jack, his mannerisms, his expressions, and he practiced them; was pleased with his performance, and thought Jack would like it too. He put his pint down.

'Tut, Tut, Tut.' A rebuke received in silence as Len let the tuts sink in, secretly enjoying the palpable fear, wondering if the other pub patrons could pick up on it, sense it. They say you can smell fear but this was just body odour from their foul armpits. Len adopted the Jack silence technique and after a few interminable minutes the MP blurted out, 'It wasn't me!' and looked at the Cabinet Secretary.

'Well it certainly wasn't me.'

More silence ensued and Len drank some more of his pint and thought it was disgusting, but London Pride was one of Jack's favourites; an acquired taste he assumed and he was prepared to acquire it.

'I know, I dealt with the miscreants,' Len said, and once again he allowed the obvious to sink in, enjoying the reaction on their faces which they could not disguise.

'Do you want us to get replacements?'

Len nodded slowly.

'The reserve list. I presume you have kept them warm?'

They nodded this time.

'Then get to it.' Len tried to finish the pint but gave up. This was something he needed to practice if he was to become working class, along with Jack's accent of course; he would leave the cheese and onion crisps for another time as well.

* * *

Jimbo pulled up at the police station and Mandy and Jack climbed out of the back of the black Ford Mondeo; anonymous and discreetly powerful. They headed for the front entrance and could see Hissing Sid observing them from his fish and chip counter. Jimbo whispered something to Jack, who laughed and made a hand gesture that Mandy resolved to ask him about; she had seen it before, it was a little like the handshake that men friends of Jack did. She knew it wasn't Masonic; Jack would not go within a country mile of such a thing. Samuels had shown her once and it seemed to convey something, she felt it, felt the powerful masculinity, but that was all. She dismissed it for the time being, it probably was one of those things men did that had neither rhyme nor reason anyway.

'Aaaahem.' A throat cleared from the very top of the stairs.

Jack looked at Sid and whispered, 'The General?'

Sid nodded. 'And he would like to see you both.'

They harrumphed, smothered a laugh and trudged their way up the stairs, Jack marginally behind Mandy, taking up his dirty old man station.

'I know what you are doing,' and she wiggled her bottom for him. Mandy looked up and could see the General leaning over the top landing. 'We will be there after we've checked into the CP room General,' she said.

This seemed to satisfy the volunteer Big Society Chief Constable,

Colonel Horrocks, retired of the Coldstream Guards, nicknamed the General, and he clanked off on his tin legs. Jimbo had caught them up as they went into the CP room, and all chairs swung to face them as Jack called out, "ally-ally-in", something they used to say as kids Jack had told her.

'This is Jimbo, my body man,' he called out and swung his hand in Jimbo's general direction.

'And mine Jack.'

'I'm your body man sweetheart.' He looked at her lovingly.

Alice Springs was in front of Jack now and pecked him on the cheek, hugged him and stepping back, looked at him lovingly, noticed by Mandy.

'How are you Jack?'

'I'm okay love,' looking around to see if Mandy was riled, she wasn't and seemed for the time being, to be all accepting. She'd changed he thought, matured, and he liked maturity in a woman.

'Okay Jo Jums where are we?' Mandy asked, taking charge.

Jo spun in her chair. 'Briefing at twelve, go and see the General please, he's been on and on all morning for you both.'

Jack nodded, but Mandy seemed put-out, following Jack through the door to the staircase. Running to catch him up, she tugged his sleeve and gestured with her head to follow into her office; he did.

She sat on her desk, arms straight out behind her, propping the lean. She looked at him, crossed her legs – this was to be a nonchalant interrogation. Jack missed the "Nonch" signals, hadn't even got to the "alant" bit yet; he had ants in his pants.

'Right, what's up? '

He looked at her. 'It's my phone. ' He handed it to her and it revealed a text message:

> *Bat Bat and Dobbin*
> *Listen to what the General says*
> *He's not speaking out of his arse this time*
> *Listen, and keep your heads down*
> *And follow the dogs*
> *Mor.*

'Okay, let's go and see the General then,' she conceded.

The General was slightly taller than Jack's six foot four but Jack had argued it was because he'd arranged for his tin legs to be made longer. Also in Jack's view, he was a typical martinet military man, but after a few days of Jack Austin railing against military authority the General appeared to disintegrate. That is what Jack said, but Mandy thought it may have something to do with Jack and Mandy rescuing him after being kidnapped by Norafarty. He had been drugged and his legs taken and then returned with a ransom note pinned on the bum of his city boy trousers.

The Chief's PA looked up, she was expecting them.

'He said to go in.'

They did, and the General was standing in front of his desk, erect, a shiny but lived in face shaved to within an inch of its life. Shiny shoes, more city boy trousers with razor sharp creases, shirt and tie, shiny collar. It would be fair to say the man was stiff but Mandy thought maybe he needed to be with artificial legs, and wondered if they were shiny too.

Jack shook the General's hand, holding it and the General's gaze; communication complete. Mandy tried some of the same, nothing, just a polite smile that nearly fractured the General's unyielding face. Mandy had to hand it to Jack, he always said that most people were redeemable and he had found something in the General, who was now indicating for them to sit at the small circular conference table that formed an extension to his desk. Jack looked under the desk and elicited a polite laugh from the Chief Constable; this was where the General had been found, under the desk in the foot well, drugged and with no legs.

The General was not only stiff physically, he found it difficult to talk, especially to Mandy (and she thought more than likely all strong women). He tried to start but faltered. Tried again, this time beginning with an "Aaaahem" which clearly helped, because he got going. Jack was reclined in his seat looking at the ceiling. The General had no choice other than to exchange eye contact with Mandy.

'I hope that you will bear with me.' He stopped; they let him gather himself. This was something important and Jack brought himself upright and focused his eye on the General, who switched his eye contact with seeming relief. Clearly he felt more comfortable with men.

'I know I said I would resign and ask for Sitting Bull (the former Chief Constable) to come back, but this was declined by both Sitting Bull and eventually the Home Office. I began to wonder if there was some other motive'

He really had Jack's attention now, 'Is this something to do with your membership of the Military Star Chamber?'

He looked shocked and Mandy looked lost.

'Yes well, we do not call it a Star Chamber but *FORCE*. It's a retirement club for very senior military officers, but you make a fair point, it acts a lot like a Star Chamber.'

Mandy had her explanation but not how Jack knew.

'I was aware of this because when we were not getting on, I arranged for a bit of background on you.'

The General sat back and seemed to relax a tad; clearly one of the hard bits had already been overcome.

'It is not illegal you know.'

'I know, it's a bit like the Masons in the military.' Jack looked like he wanted to spit feathers.

'Yes that would be it,' the General said, not seeing anything distasteful.

'Are you worried that there may be a breakaway faction or another higher level that is maybe a little too active, not just pink gins and a bit of wallop?'

The General was nodding, and Mandy wondered what "wallop" was as Jack leaned forward conspiratorially to the General. Mandy followed him to the desk surface.

'It is known you know,' Jack whispered.

'How do you know? The Club invites memberships from senior ranks who are close to retirement. The experienced members can advise the current main men, who hope that they will be accepted into the fold when they eventually retire. From *FORCE's* point of view, it means we can influence the current military command policy.'

'Ironic really when you think that you replaced a highly experienced Chief Constable.'

The General nodded. 'What you need to understand is that the current incumbent senior officers desperately want to be allowed into the club when they retire, so they often reveal closely kept strategies for opinion and feedback, and act on the advice as well; did so myself when I was still in.'

Mandy was cottoning on, and probably faster than Jack.

'Are you saying that they are exercising too much influence and that there may be another agenda? They want you to stay as Chief Constable in Portsmouth, where we seem to be having some serious political problems?'

The General nodded, and Jack looked at him and then to Mandy - he was seriously impressed and seriously worried, but mainly impressed. She smiled at him and carried on.

'Was General Charles Fawcett, recently deceased, on this committee?'

The General nodded.

'Yes, and I have been asked to sit in his place. It is my feeling that Fawcett tried to arrange your death Inspector. I need to find out more, but it is well known in the higher echelons of the military that I am anti the cutbacks in the forces. I am worried that I may have given the impression I was more radical than I actually am. A further irony when you think about your attitudes, Chief Inspector.'

'It just may be that we are cut from the same cloth General,' Jack said, tapping his finger nervously on the table. There was a prolonged silence while the immensity of the information was taken in. Jack stood and strode to the window, and Mandy knew he was looking at the top of their tree and pictured it in her mind's eye. He turned back, took another chair beside the General and moved it so he sat right next to the military man who was clearly not comfortable with this proximity.

Jack stroked his unshaven chin. 'Are you saying what I think you are saying?'

The General looked confused, he obviously thought he had been clear, but Mandy knew Jack would want it spelled out for him.

'Jack is just looking for absolute clarification General, he's a stickler for detail.' She wondered if her nose had grown.

'Oh, I see. Well I see this as me being asked to step up into *FORCE*, and to advise the replacement to Fawcett at the very top level. I understand the new Head of Armed forces will be a Navy man, whom I also know from living down here; Admiral Chit Wesley.'

'What do you know of this Wesley, is he malleable, will he go to extremes?' Jack asked.

'I do know he wants to be in the club when he retires. It's a big thing for us senior ranks Jack, don't underestimate it. The motto is *Nobody listens like the dying; nobody speaks the truth like the dying* - we see retirement akin to dying.'

Jack grinned, he had said something similar himself and could see the correlation, could understand the sentiment.

'Tell me the rest, there really is another level isn't there?'

'Nobody outside *FORCE* knows for sure, but logically there must be. There must be a panel that sits representing the forces that control the country, or at least feel they should control the country; military, political, and of course financial. What I am saying is, I am scared and I cannot stop what's happening. I will be invited and if I decline, then I think I will not live long, even though I may be useful as Chief Constable. I think it's that serious.'

Jack didn't even stop to think.

'Then you must accept General, because it is clear that all that has happened here is related. It's no coincidence that all this is happening in Portsmouth, nor is it a coincidence that you were asked to be Chief Constable and that you remain in the post; likely assisted by some Mandarins in the Home Office or Defence. What we need to do is think this through, plan the best way to get what we want out of this situation and to protect you, which I think we can by the way.'

The General looked relieved and sat back, but his body language conveyed doubt; he was not sure how this could be done. If he could not think of a way, then how could anyone else? Typical military thinking Jack had surmised.

'When and where is your next meeting General?'

'It's at the Royal Naval Officers Club, Wednesday evening.'

'Is that where you expect to be formally asked?' The General nodded, and Jack reciprocated a nod to say okay and stood, playing with the chair back.

'Mandy and I need to think on this for a bit, so in the meantime carry on as normal, not that anything around here is normal.'

The General stood with patent difficulty and went to shake Jack's hand.

'How long have you been out of the Army?' Jack asked as he shook the proffered hand.

'Just under a year, and yes I know all of the personalities; home from home you might say.'

'Any others think like you?' Jack maintained the grip and Mandy noticed the General was colouring.

'I am not sure; certainly there is a lot of concern. You have to understand the devastating effect that a gap in recruitment and replacement of hardware can have for the development and efficiency of our forces, and how vulnerable this will leave us in years to come.'

Mandy had heard Jack say this only a few days ago and thought he was spot on again.

Jack released his hand. 'I think I do understand General.'

Chapter 14

'Well I didn't see that one coming but it explains a lot,' Jack said.
They had returned to Mandy's office and stood together, looking out
the window at their tree. A stiff breeze seemed to have developed in
the short time they had been with the General. The tree was waving
vigorously and combined with the still strong sun, the leaf shadow
pattern was energetically dappling their eyes; it was both mesmerising
and disturbing. Mandy was enjoying it but Jack was finding it a lot
like flashing strobe lights. He felt dizzy, gripping Mandy's shoulders
to steady himself. It all happened so fast and he made a dash for the
corridor and the toilets, bumping his shoulder as he went.

Hustling after him, she heard him bash into one of the toilet
cubicles and he was being sick by the time she followed in. Nobby
was embarrassed at the Superintendent's presence, desperately
finishing his wee and trying to do up his flies at the urinal stall. She
waved a reassurance to Nobby as she stood at the cubicle door, Jack's
retching resonating around the glazed tiled wall of the men's toilet.

'Is Nobby still there?'

'Err, yes Jane.' Nobby's embarrassed reply.

'Clear it with Jo Jums...retch...but I want you and Alice...spew...to
find out about the dead dogs in the harbour.'

He coughed, wiped his brow.

'Have there really been dead dogs found, if so whereabouts,
what sort, and is there a pattern? Speak to someone...retch...in the
Harbour Masters office...retch...about tidal patterns, currents and
see if we can trace back to where they were thrown in. Can anyone
tell us what they might have died from? Nobby, tell Jo...spew...to get

Mike to speak to Seb please.'

'What made you think of that Jane?' A distant voice.

'Jo, that you? Mandy'll tell yer.' He rummaged in his pockets for his phone. His shoulder was hurting like mad, whatever adrenaline or chemical in his body that made the pain acceptable, had clearly gone; the pain was excruciating.

'Can't find my phone.'

'Jack, can we have this conversation in the CP room, Mandy's office or anywhere else but the bog please?' Jo said, irritated.

'Jo we will. We then...' he blew air into the toilet bowl, it sounded like a tornado, '...need to talk about what we let the press know, brief Spotty on a press release. We'll have some more stuff from Len soon.'

Jo was not about to allow herself to be lectured by a dipstick talking to her from the bog. 'I'm not doing anything until you clean yourself up, it stinks in here; I don't know how you stand it Mandy...' she said nasally, fingers clamped to her nose, '...and who is Seb?'

'For fucks sake Jo, do what I ask; how fucking difficult is that?'

This echoing sharp retort from the toilet bowl was a shock and Mandy waved Jo and Nobby away.

'I'll help him and we'll be there in a few minutes. Jo, ring Mike please.'

Jack heard shuffling feet and a groan as Mandy got up off her knees, rubbing his back as she did so.

'Come on let's get you cleaned up. I think we may skip breakfast this morning, don't you?'

He managed a chuckle, but it was forced and still echoed into the toilet bowl. She'd heard this called the porcelain telephone before, could now see why. He flushed, stood, turned and he was on his own. Fucking brilliant he thought, and was leaning towards a major sulk and the wash basin when Mandy returned with her handbag. She had a pack of wet wipes, pulled some out and began wiping his mouth and face.

'Rinse your mouth out Jack.' She then produced a travel toothbrush with a small cartridge of toothpaste and he looked amazed.

'Wet wipes, toothbrush, no wonder you need a big bag,' he managed to remark.

'The toothbrush I have always carried, we work strange hours sometimes. And the wet wipes I started carrying when we got to know Meesh; with kids you need these things.'

He was out in the main toilet area and leaning his body weight through one arm, propped onto a wash basin and trusting in its strength. He turned, felt around and examined his face in the mirror, not really seeing. Mandy could, and she saw the shattered look on the wrinkled, ravaged face, reflected back at her. 'Bloody amazing,' he said to his reflection; she didn't question his thought process as he managed a smile.

Mandy ran cold water into the adjacent basin, told him to step over and to splash his face. He bent awkwardly, she could see his shoulder was hurting from his bodyshape and leaned over and splashed his face for him, gently caressing his skin. He responded with a sigh and then a guttural groan. She kissed his neck, he liked it, her body had moulded itself to his from behind and he sensed the pain in his shoulder fade ever so slightly. He pressed back into her and looked up at her smiling face in the mirror. She could see a mixture of emotion in his one eye, a hint of a smile, a dried tear, and now a definite glazing over as she kissed his neck some more. She dipped her hands into the water and rubbed his face. She pressed into him again and he responded. She allowed one of her hands to drift to the front of his trousers and covered him, gently squeezed.

Jo reappeared.

'Well I can see you have made another remarkable recovery Jane. I have everyone gathered for your meeting.' She emphasised "your, meeting".

Jack jumped, stood quickly and the back of his head bumped into Mandy's nose. She let out a yell and her hand left Jack's trousers and went immediately to nurse her nose, leaning into the adjacent mirror, looking to see if it was bleeding.

'Christ's sake Jack, look what you've done, get your arse into that room and get this meeting going!' Mandy howled. She looked at him in the mirror, his face now a forlorn look of ugly hopelessness that she could see may be justified in this instance, but decided to apologise later when they were alone. 'Come on, you're better now.' She batted his backside and she went after Jo, who had disappeared, not wishing to witness any carnal or retaliatory actions.

Jack followed Mandy and Jo into the CP room. The team, including the Sissies, were all there, gathered around the jumble of tables. He wasn't sure if he expected sympathy or just a normal, "Okay let's get down to business", but he did not expect to be greeted with an outburst of energetic laughter that appeared to be all but uncontrollable, except for Connie who at least had the decency to stick with a titter and to conceal that behind her inscrutable hands. His feelings were mollified in part when he saw that Mandy, still rubbing her nose, was equally perplexed. She stepped to one side to make sure they weren't laughing at her, and satisfied they were not, she turned back to look at Jack and immediately joined in the jocularity, folding her body in two and leaning on the table, unable to control her fits of mirth.

'What? Never seen anyone with a pink shoulder harness before? You lot are so juvenile at times, I wonder we ever solve any crime,' Jack said, thinking that should do it, but it didn't, in fact the laughter increased in intensity. He allowed his lips to press together and he was reminded of the cartoonists who drew fed up characters with a wiggly mouth. Unconsciously he felt his mouth, to see if it was wiggly; it was, but then so was the rest of his face, so how could you tell?

Mandy saw what he was doing and still laughing, caught his eye and gestured her head to his crotch where there was a big water-stained hand mark; he reddened. Mandy had rarely seen him embarrassed before and she put a consoling arm around her man. She looked at Jack's face and he was crying.

'Oh feck wuss boy, what is it now?'

There was a gentle laugh at that, but it was tentative. Just about everyone had seen Jack cry at some time or other but this was different; he was not crying at the suffering of another person, he was crying for himself. Jo and Mandy were whispering to Jack, concerned looks on their faces, he was looking and crying into the middle distance.

After a little time he spoke quietly, gently to Mandy and Jo.

'Sit down please I want to say something.'

They looked reluctant but he looked equally determined, which Mandy preferred. There was quiet and Jack struggled, but then he spoke; the sound appearing to come from the back of his throat.

'When I was a young lad, I spoke to old people and asked what it was like to be old.' He stopped and thought to himself, they could see he was recalling a picture in his mind.

'I remember one man talked openly and honestly, profoundly, and it changed me. He said, "It's strange, that as I get older I see more, but I am faced with the dilemma that I can't do anything about what I see".'

Jack stopped and the tears reappeared, he coughed.

'Retirement, getting old, you see, it's like dying, a very slow and painful death and nobody sees so well as the dying, nobody speaks so honestly as the dying...but who listens?'

He shook his head, there was an expectant hush in the room, it was clear he had not finished.

'Many, many years ago, when we were tribal, boys as they reached puberty left their mums and went to live with the men in the men's house, girls with the women. There they sat, listened and learned. When I grew up the generations mixed, talked; there were rebellious youngsters of course but generations listened to each other. No more. This is what this is all about; nobody is listening to the old folk, to those retired or about to retire. Len has made this his mission, he has listened to me and he is acting on my behalf.'

Mandy shaped to get up and then sat back as he carried on.

'I have reflected lately that I've had enough, that I wanted to retire and fuck off. I'm an old fart so what can I contribute? But I can see that I have a team that listen and will openly share, and I am moved beyond words and filled with renewed hope.'

He stood on his own, weeping, a stunned silence around him. Alice rushed to him and hugged him and kissed his cheek, 'Oh Jack...' she sniffed and huddled into his good shoulder and bawled. He released Alice, turned to head toward the door, gesturing for Mandy to follow. He left the room with applause behind him, everyone on their feet clapping.

Mandy caught him up and kissed him full on the mouth and the claps were enjoined with an "Oooh er matron" as she steered him out the door, down the corridor and into her office.

Chapter 15

In her office Mandy tipped her toes, and with both hands on his face, she kissed him gently.

'I love you John Austin.' She held onto his face, remembering he had told her how much he had liked it the first time she had done this.

'Where are your pain killers Jack?'

'I don't know, I put them down somewhere and I can't find them.'

She allowed her toes to relax and lowered her heels, she still held his face. 'When did you last take them?'

'Last night.'

'So you are in pain?' He nodded.

'Lucky I love you because you are like a bloody kid.'

She stepped away from him; he missed her hands on his face. She picked up the phone and dialled, turned her eyes back to Jack as she spoke into the phone.

'Jackie, Jack has had an episode and he has also lost his pain killers, we have a breakthrough and can't leave. Can you come now please?' She put the phone down.

'Jackie's on her way, sit down Jack.'

She pulled the chair to the desk and he sat, propped his head in his hand, elbow on the corner of the desk. She noticed that it was darker in the room. The shadow pattern of the leaves had disappeared. She looked out of the window and the tree was rocking energetically; the breeze had turned to a strong wind and the sky blackened ominously and it matched her mood. She saw him looking at her.

'Storm brewing over Cherry tree lane Jack,' she said.

'Yes it is Mandy, and for once I don't feel helpless and alone, thank you.'

She was behind him now and was rubbing the tense muscles in his neck, careful not to press close to his left shoulder. She saw him relax and press back into her.

'That was a powerful speech you made in there Jack. I know I laugh about you and your still waters, but they do run very deep in you, rough on the surface, but deep indeed. What you said moved me and made me think many of the older generation must be feeling the same. I suppose you also referred to *FORCE* and the retirees influencing the high ranks? Do you suppose this is going on in Government and the Banks?' She had a light bulb moment. 'Of course, Len and Pomerol.'

He nodded but appeared to be drifting off, she was okay with that and carried on her ministrations, massaging the tense sinews in his neck, happy to marshal her own thoughts. 'Just recently I have experienced a strange feeling myself. I've noticed I am comfortable with work. I sense a direction, I sense that I might get involved in something that may just be of some benefit; I am not just clearing up someone's mess,' she said, as if to herself.

He stirred, 'Nicely put love...' he was quiet, but she knew this man and knew there was more to come, '...we need to talk you and I; about where we go from here. I've had some thoughts.'

She hemmed, content that this man was comfortable talking about the future, about him and her; still sometimes with a masculine superficiality she thought, but she had come to see she could not force a man to think like a woman, especially this one, and what would be the point. Her man knew himself, knew where he was and where and how far he was prepared to go; and she was prepared to reach out just far enough and share, preserving their own integrity at the same time.

'What are you thinking Amanda?'

'What a bozo you are and how sometimes just as I am thinking you are a definite twat, you say something that is so gut-wrenchingly profound that my heart melts and I remember why I love you.'

'Yeah, but I'm your bozo though.'

She sighed, time limit reached, profundity over for a while.

'Yes, you are that love, you are definitely my bozo.'

There was a tap on the door and Jackie poked her head around. 'Ooh I wouldn't mind some of that Mandy,' she said, flexing her fingers, massaging the air in front of her.

Mandy let her eyes roll up to the ceiling. 'Jackie you are getting as bad as him.'

But as she brought her eyes back, Jackie wasn't there, she was crouching in front of Jack and Mandy chastised herself for thinking she was glad Jackie was in jeans.

Jackie had Jack's hands and rested her arms on his thighs.

'No point in asking what you are doing in work is there Jack?' Jack slowly shook his head; he seemed quite calm and no longer disturbed by the close presence of this psychiatrist. Jackie looked up at Mandy. 'I saw the news about the shooting in Southsea. Christ, what is this place coming to? I take it this is all a part of what you are involved in?'

Jack spoke before Mandy could respond.

'I've been feeling really strange Jackie.'

Both Mandy and Jackie were shaken by these words from Jack. Jackie had accepted that he would be reluctant to talk about how he felt and was there to just gently nudge, and help where she could.

'How so Jack?'

'I can't put my finger on it, I feel out of control,' he said.

Jackie looked up at Mandy but talked to Jack, he wasn't looking anywhere but into himself.

'Can you tell me how you have felt, have you had the shakes?'

Mandy answered for him. 'No.'

Jackie gave her a serious shut your mouth look, and Mandy closed her mouth like a snapper fish.

'Answer me Jack'

'Yes.'

'When Jack, you never told me.'

'Mandy, please be quiet or I'll ask you to leave.' Mandy looked taken aback on several levels, but promised to be quiet.

'Is it happening often Jack?' Jackie asked and he nodded. 'That's okay, perfectly normal. I won't give you any claptrap about it shows you are on the mend because it doesn't, and I am sure if I say you need to be off work and resting it will mean nothing, am I right?'

He nodded again. 'We're close to nailing this Jackie.'

She nodded this time. 'What have you been doing to make yourself feel better?'

'When I feel it coming on, I go to the loo.'

Jackie looked up to Mandy, said nothing, but they agreed with facial gestures, this was the diarrhoea explained. 'How do you get through it?'

'I remember when I was in the field and was in a difficult situation, scared, I used to just think into my stomach and breathe deeply and it would calm me, stopped me being scared, stopped me overreacting.'

Jackie nodded again. 'Okay.'

She stood and picked up the bottle of water she had brought with her, pushed two tablets out of a foil pack and handed both to him. 'Painkillers only Jack, supersonic, take them. You will feel woozy after, but you need them to get you through this hump. I'll leave you some normal pain killers for later.'

He looked at them in the palm of his hand. Jackie was forceful.

'Take them Jack, now.'

And he took them, made like he was immediately woozy, and this got a laugh from Jackie and Mandy, who were secretly relieved at this daft attempt at a joke.

'If you are not going home, get a sleep in your deck chair, I want a word with your long-suffering partner here.'

Jack got himself up and Mandy thought he did look unsteady on his feet, as he trudged to the door. He turned and thanked Jackie, who gave him the warmest smile she had ever given him. Mandy could see that it worked, and she remembered him telling her how important things like touching and smiling were to him. He continually needed this reassurance she supposed.

'Not reassurance Mandy, just a natural human desire that we sometimes forget to do and give, and forget we need, and forget how much it can help; even for the strongest of people.'

'Did I...?'

Jackie nodded.

'You did, and now come to me because you need your share.'

Mandy did and felt the warmth of Jackie's embrace and felt her cares melt away, if only for the time being. They stayed like that for a long time. Eventually Jackie went to leave, she handed her Jack's tablets that he had forgotten again and they rolled their eyes.

'You need to watch him Mandy, I am seriously worried and I will call in tonight; I take it you're at his house?' She nodded. Jackie touched her hand. 'It will get better and in the meantime I am here for the both of you and for the record, I quite enjoyed that hug.'

'Get out of here.'

'Where, back to the Isle of Lesbos?' Jackie said, and that did make Mandy laugh and she watched Jackie descend the stairs and go through to reception, saw but could not hear a passing comment with Hissing Sid, probably asking after his family.

'Do you think so?'

'Jo, did I?' Jo nodded and flicked her head towards Mandy's office. Both women went in; neither sat, Jo paced, Mandy looked out of the window.

'It's going to piss down in a minute and if it is really raining, Jack is going to want to walk the seafront and get drenched and come home for a hot bath, and because he's not well I'll have to have the feckin' taps.'

'Blimey Mandy, with all of that going through your head, any room left to talk about police or even spook work?'

Mandy turned and smiled at Jo, 'Jack is amazing isn't he?'

'I've known that for a long time Mandy, but he is also not well, and I know you know that and I know that you know we need him, but watch out for him for all of our sakes.'

'He will not go home even if he's ordered to, he's a bozo and he worries me.'

They sat and Mandy briefed Jo on all that had happened, all that they wanted to release to the press to keep the public informed.

Mandy shuffled around in her bag and handed Jo Jums Jack's phone.

Jo read the message.

'I thought it was something like that so I got them onto it already, thought best not to question and didn't want him to throw up over my shoes. I phoned Mike who seemed to understand who Seb was; I suppose we will find out later.' They both smiled. 'You look tired Mandy; can you take off early today?'

'Not much sleep last night, what with the shooting. I will see if we can get off soon but Jack wants to brief the team and get it all going.'

'I would say that I could brief but it would be a waste of breath, and frankly he does seem to think on his feet and come up with some interesting stuff, often out of the blue. Don't know how he does it, but he's sound asleep at the moment so let's do it after lunch. They agreed and Jo left after Mandy briefed on the General's predicament.

Mandy swung in her chair, sensed the air pressure that threatened a storm and secretly wanted it to rain hard so she could walk and get soaked with Jack, but with his shoulder a bath would be out of the question but there were other ways to relax and they had unfinished business.

* * *

The General took a call, agreed nervously, and asked his PA to see if the Superintendent and the Commander would join him for a sandwich. The PA phoned down to Jean in the canteen and arranged for sandwiches after she had a confirmation from Mandy and the Commander.

'I can't help it, but I feel awkward, I hope you can excuse me,' the General said as Mandy settled herself at the conference table.

Mandy viewed the General in a different light these days, not quite through Jack's eye, but nevertheless more caring; an understanding existed between them now.

'We need to get past all of this General,' she said, impatient with the military man.

'Aaaahem, yes well, Jamie will be joining us, but in the meantime, how is Jack?' Mandy ran through all that was happening with Jack and his PTSD, how he is being closely monitored by Jackie and stressing how worried she was.

'I confess I am worried also, and please do not take this as any slight on your capabilities Mandy, but I will feel a lot more comfortable if Jack was around.' Mandy thought she must remember to tell Jack that his redeemable character philosophy scored again.

The Commander announced himself and held the door for Jean who entered and plonked a plate of sandwiches down, and after asking after Jack, she disappeared to spread the word; people were concerned. The General briefed the Commander.

'I have just taken a call and agreed to sit on the committee, so for heaven's sake tell me what to do.'

Jamie offered casual reassurance to the General but looked to Mandy who shrugged her shoulders but took the conversation on.

'General you have your first meeting Wednesday evening, which gives us a couple of days to think this through. If I have learned anything from Jack, it's not to rush decisions. I want to talk this through with him when he wakes up.' She thought it amazing that nobody even thought this was an odd thing to say.

The General had his hand up. Feck, save me from little boys she thought and laughed to herself, but didn't show it.

'I had a call from the Gnome Office,' he said.

Jamie laughed. 'Jack's getting to you General,' and both men chuckled and Mandy was warmed by this but felt she needed to assert herself.

'What did they say General?'

'They wanted to let me know that they were on the scene and they would support, but how did they know?' He flipped his hands to reaffirm his being completely out of his depth.

Mandy raised her eyebrows but it was Jamie who responded. 'The Gnome office...' and he chuckled some more with the General, '...they have their ways I imagine.' He winked at Mandy.

What was that all about, Mandy thought?

'I want to go down and check on Jack, but we have a couple of days to work out how we deal with this so if you will excuse me...' She stood, didn't wait to be excused just left, gently closing the door behind her.

Chapter 16

Mandy returned to her office, and was recalling the number for Father Mike when the phone rang. She picked it up, listened.

'Show him up will you Sid.'

Mandy went to greet Father Mike at the top of the stairs. He followed into her office and she indicated the PVC chair, wheeled her own chair to share the view out of the window with the priest.

'The tree?' he observed and she nodded, and they both watched as the tree swayed vigorously in the strong wind and the now almost horizontal rain, which pelted the window with the power of hurtling stair rods.

'How is he?'

'Have you not spoken to Jackie?'

'Yes, but I'm asking you,' Mike said.

'Well, he's asleep in his deckchair at the moment. The shoulder should heal quickly - he can get rid of the harness in a few days - but frankly, he is completely fucked up and I'm worried Mike, he hasn't even asked after his birthday.'

'He'll never ask after his birthday, those things mean nothing to him personally,' Mike said, rubbing his chin. She noticed he hadn't shaved, and he noticed her looking.

'It's been hectic since the shooting. Want to know what's happening?'

'Who's Seb?'

'Sebastian Sexton of the Sexton Detective Agency of Southsea.'

'Not sure I've heard of that one Mike?'

'You wouldn't have. Have you never wondered how Jack can just pluck solutions and theories out of mid-air, solve crimes?'

She could not contain her expression of wonderment because she had lately been thinking just that, and Jo Jums had hinted something similar just now.

'Please don't tell me I have another revelation to deal with?'

'Jack gets solutions from anywhere he can, his expertise is seeing the relevance and joining the dots I suppose, but we can let Jack off the hook here. Seb is a lad with Asperger's, on the autistic scale, who Jack has nurtured since a child in his own inimitable way. Seb would be about twenty-two now and does not like company, his dad set him up in a converted tool shed, and with his computers and singular mind he has a knack of solving mysteries.'

Mike allowed that to sink in and continued, 'Jack asked him to think about the dead dogs, to find out about the others and to see if he could work out, with times and tide tables, the currents and if there was a commonality as to where they may have entered the waters; which is why I'm here.'

'Why did he not tell me?'

'Because the boy wants anonymity, doesn't want to meet anyone. Jack and I are exceptions, although he would like to meet you, now that he knows how much you mean to Jack. But I warn you, it is a truly strange family and they live in a cemetery.'

Mandy wanted to say "What?" but couldn't find her vocal chords. Mike interrupted her unspoken exclamation.

'Seb has identified a zone where the dogs could have entered the harbour waters.' He picked out a chart from his priest's handbag, which she supposed if she was being benevolent was close to being a briefcase, but she wasn't feeling in the least bit well-disposed toward this man of the cloth.

'What else do you have in your handbag?'

'Ouch,' Mike said, 'well I suppose I do deserve a little of that, but give Jack and me a break for a while at least eh?'

'Shut up Mike and show me what you have.'

He stood and spread the chart on the desk top; she joined him and could see an area circled in felt tip.

'The northern top of the harbour, Portsmouth side, where the ships due to be scrapped are stored, a small and not much used wharf.' She knew the area and pictured it in her mind's eye. Jack used to like to cycle around that part and together they had walked Martin, before Meesh had adopted the dog.

'What do you think Mike?'

'I don't know, not my province, but if Len says follow the dogs then I imagine Jack will follow them, but Del says get someone else to do the actual following please.'

'We will, and thanks Mike. Can I keep the chart please?'

Mike nodded as he stood. He turned upon reaching the door.

'Stay safe Mandy and keep Jack close.'

Mandy folded the chart and headed for the CP room, called Nobby and Alice to her and stood at the Chaos Table. Jack was still asleep in his deckchair; she took a little time to look at him and then snapped out of her dream. Nobby and Alice were standing waiting and she saw Jo monitoring her clutch of chicks.

'It's alight Ma'amsie, I just want Nobby and Alice to go and look at the place where we think the dogs went into the harbour, look at it and report back, if that's okay?'

She unfolded the Harbour Chart as the two detectives nodded assent; Alice not able to disguise her excitement at being let out to play.

'Just look.' Jack had been listening.

'Okay Jane,' they both responded, gathering up their weatherproof clothing.

'D'you get any aerial photos with that chart sweetheart?'

'No, I suppose we should get some?' Mandy replied as he stretched out his good arm and Nobby gave him a hand out of the deck chair.

'Be 'andy...' he said and gestured to Connie and Frankie, '...but let's see what you find first. And Alice, give Kipper a ring, he knows the harbour tour guys doesn't he?'

Alice looked fazed for a short while, then twigged.

'Yeah, my cousin Boz runs tour boats from the historic dockyard, he goes all round the harbour.'

'That's what I thought, wouldn't 'urt to 'ave a chin-wag there since you're out on a jolly; see if he knows something?' Jack turned to the window. 'You know what I fancy love...?'

'A walk in the wind and rain, along the seafront, get soaked and then a hot bath?' Mandy said, interrupting his words with a face displaying mixed feelings.

She gestured for him to follow her, they were not really needed in the CP room and she was convinced Jack only went there for the social amenities. He sat in her office and she stood behind him and rubbed his shoulders, sensing again how far she could go. He winced; not far. 'The charts were from Seb, delivered by Mike just now. Tell me about Seb...' She stroked his face and kissed his neck so she would get the truth.

'Not much to say...' he started, leaning into the massage, '...except he's a kid with Asperger's and was troublesome as a youngster. Kate was his social worker, mixed up family but all very bright, dad in the City all week, mum very intelligent but underutilised, same old, same old, I suppose.'

'Dad in the City, still?'

'Want to know which bank he's with?'

'Just a guess,' she said, 'Cedric James?'

'Spot on sweetheart. Anyway, Seb got himself into lots of trouble and Kate got more and more involved. She arranged for him to be switched to a special school for gifted autistic children and he prospered, though he never returned to mainstream education. Kate thought he needed a male role model, other than his older brother, and since his dad was away most of the week she introduced me. I suppose you could say we hit it off, but mainly we exchanged a few words and sat contentedly in each other's company, sharing thoughts. I often sounded out theories about the cases I was working on, and discovered his analytical mind. His dad, who's not short of a few bob, bought him a state-of-the-art computer set up and he tore into it, loved it, excelled, and I took a lot of the credit for his ruminations and solving. Answering a few of your questions is it?'

She nodded. 'You suggested the Sexton Detective Agency though didn't you?'

'You know me well love. Yes I did and he liked it, but he only wanted to do the problem solving, no limelight, and all from his tool shed. His mum gets the evening newspaper and reads out the crimes to him and he sets about solving them, purely for recreation. If he hits on a solution his mum gets in touch with me; it's what eventually gave me the idea for the Community Policing squad.'

'Cemetery?' she said quietly, containing her amazement.

He laughed. 'Yeah, Sexton you see?' She didn't. 'His name is Sebastian Sexton; sexton is the name given for a gravedigger or a cemetery caretaker and Sexton House, in the old Eastney cemetery, came up for sale and Seb cajoled his dad into buying it; saw it as a sign. A largish house which came with a chapel and a big tool shed that once held the tools I suppose. They didn't have to maintain the cemetery as it is now defunct, but Seb likes to do it. He's set about straightening everything up, literally, so it looks orderly, and even installed a new storm drainage system, enjoying the civil engineering aspects.' Jack chuckled. 'His own Catacombs; apparently he always wanted some of them and money was no object, so...' He chortled some more and Mandy stopped massaging and stood back, amazed at the story.

'Anything else you haven't told me?' She was more curious than irritated.

'Well, there may be other things but I just don't think of them until it comes up, like the dogs in the harbour; jogged my mind, know what I mean?'

'I see...I think...and that is what happened whilst you were throwing up?'

'Yeah, that's it, right.'

She walked around to his front, hitched her skirt and sat astride him. Looked him in his eye and held his face.

'I said I will wait and learn as we grow together and I will.' She kissed him and noticed he was not fully focused. 'Woozy?'

He nodded and she got off him. 'Okay let's have a walk along the seafront; Jo can handle the briefing.'

Chapter 17

Wilf accompanied them on the seafront walk and he didn't look pleased at the prospect, and only mildly amused when Jack said he couldn't share the bath with them when they got back. It was the height of summer, but walking along the seafront was raw, bitterly cold - the rain saturated wind whipped off the full Solent tide, sending surf crashing over the sea wall and along the promenade. The combined wind, rain and spray stung like needle pricks on their chilled cheeks and Jack loved it, revelled in it, nosed himself into it, challenging the elements. Wilf didn't and walked behind, using them as shelter. Mandy snuggled into Jack and had come to quite like the experience of these elemental walks, except she preferred the getting home and the bath bit better.

They stopped and leaned on the promenade railings as if to look out onto the Solent, but it was impossible; visibility was virtually non-existent, even if you were brave enough to lift your face into the biting wind and rain. Mandy could feel rivulets of water running off her hair and down her neck. She shivered and Jack pulled her to him, hugging her tight with his good arm, and planted a kiss.

'You look gorgeous,' he said.

'Can we go home now? I'm freezing.'

'Said you should have put your vest on,' he replied, and still hugging her, his laughter lost into the wind, they turned and headed inland across the bandstand fields, through the cut in the ancient ramparts and down into the lea of the Castle. Then onto Castle Fields, where they found a temporary shelter from the gale force south-westerly.

* * *

While Jack, Mandy and Wilf made their way home, Nobby and Alice wended their way through like two drenched lovers. Leaning into their sluggish walk along the bleak north western harbour shoreline, they huddled, wind and rain swept. At this far northerly point, it was open across the wide harbour and the south-westerly hit them full on. They walked under the motorway flyover and along the water's edge, discreetly surveying the areas outlined in felt tip on the chart. The path eventually led them to the far side of the sports centre and they could see the shipping graveyard in the haze of the storm; ghostly images of old ships, listing, some broken and fractured, all rusting.

Trudging heavily into the wind, comfortable in their physical closeness, Nobby told Alice how he had always been fascinated by the yards, and as a lad he had wanted to climb through the dead ships, especially the old submarines, now long gone. He even had nightmares imagining the skeletons of drowned sailors still on board.

She looked up into his slim, well framed face and smiled, a warm nurturing love for him. She imagined he had said something nice but she couldn't hear, the wind whistled around her ears and the rain made her squint, so she just had a blurred image of him, a lot like the rusty hulks stuck fast in the harbour mud. They eventually made their way around to the scrapping yards and broken down warehouses, the crumbling wharfs of the old fuel depots. They found some temporary shelter and huddled together, looking out to the open water; the tide was high.

'Dad used to come here for Calor gas when I was a kid,' he told her directly into her ear, 'this yard used to be full with orange and blue gas bottles. I can still remember the clanging sound they made and the smell from the heater we had in our kitchen, the condensation driven from the heat.'

Alice was not all that bothered about these memories, she wanted to look further.

'Shall we go in?' she asked. Nobby shook his head, but she was off and he had to run to catch her up. He folded his arm around her again, mildly irritated that he was impressed by her cavalier nature. They nosed their way around the tip of the shallow, disintegrating wharf, looking out across the harbour to the south and west, their focus a large hulk, listing, rusting, only some twenty metres or so off-shore, looming large and ghostly in the fuzz of rain. They stood huddled and looked around, then made their way across a barren and broken concrete apron and approached the big shed that bordered the end of the wharf wall. The high and wide sliding doors were locked but opened a crack, and they could hear the wind as it sped and whistled through the narrow opening. They took turns peaking in but saw nothing, just blackness. It smelled of something not particularly pleasant, and Alice, still not past the sickness phase of her pregnancy, felt she might retch.

'Oi you two, get orf wiv yer.' It was a tall, scrawny, middle-aged man, not pleasant looking, a skeletal face with jutting cheekbones, charcoal five o'clock shadow, hook nose and red stained vampire's eyes that beaded onto them, conveying a brutal menace.

'I'm sorry, we were just looking around, it's lovely,' Nobby said.

They appeared an innocent couple and the man appeared disarmed.

'What're you ducks?'

Nobby carried on undeterred, 'We love it out here whatever the weather, don't we love?'

Alice nodded and pushed their enquiry. 'What d'you do here? You remember when it was a Calor gas depot don't you babes?' Nobby nodded this time.

The man was still taken aback. He was used to people being intimidated by his look and manner, but this couple seemed unfazed.

'It's a temporary dock now, too far up the harbour to be any practical use; used only occasionally, scrapping an' that. I look after it for the owners; keep people like you out, so bugger off or I'll get the dogs out,' the man said, winding himself up.

'You keep guard dogs?'

'Two Rottweiler's and not friendly like,' he said forcefully, amazed he had not scared this couple off.

'Can't hear them,' Alice said, stamping her cold feet, rubbing her hands and blowing steam through her nostrils.

'What?'

'Said I can't hear the dogs, they can't be that frightening!' Alice laughed, nudging Nobby. The bloke was getting wet through, not being dressed for the rain and wind, unlike Nobby and Alice in the wet weather gear Nobby had collected from his sailing club.

'You'd know about it if they saw yer; they're in the compound.' He pointed, and Alice made to move in that direction. 'Oi, what're you doing?'

'I'd love to see them, I love dogs, come on let's have a look and then we can go,' Alice said.

The man looked resigned and led them to the chain link fence, curled at the top with a barbed wire roll. Initially they saw and heard nothing. The guard kicked the fence and out of nowhere, two of the fiercest, biggest, and meanest looking hounds Alice had ever seen came bounding out and leapt at the chain linking. Foam oozed between steaming, bared teeth that made her think they might be rabid; their ferocity patent. Nobby and Alice took an involuntary step back, although common sense said they were protected by the fence.

'You've seen-em, now fuck off.'

They needed no second telling. Nobby thanked the man pleasantly and they left and made their way back to the station. Alice said she would have a chat with Uncle Alfie about the place tonight. Nobby would go with her, she knew; they were inseparable now and she liked that.

* * *

As Mandy, Jack and Wilf broke from the lea of the Castle and the fortifications of Castle Fields, so the westerly wind reasserted its pace and the horizontal rain hit them from their left. The elements were so forceful it was hard to see a pace in front of you. Mandy wrapped her arms tightly around herself, a hand tipped to deflect the rain from her eyes as she hurried to cross the expansive common, intent on the relative shelter of the Southsea streets. She heard Wilf whinging close behind her and looked back. There was no Jack, and she felt like she did when momentarily she had lost one of her children in a shop; panic, fear, visions of all the terrible things that could happen. She recalled the anger and relief when she found them and now she could not see Jack she sensed panic for a grown man.

Wilf picked up on her signals and swung his head in all directions. 'He was just here, where could he have gone?' He dashed back out into the open, crossed the road, dodging traffic and ducking the road spray, and ran back onto the common. Jack could not be seen. He pulled his phone out, his panicked look was frighteningly bizarre, water streaming down his face and entering his steaming open mouth as he spoke, expectantly looking up every now and then as if he would miraculously see Jack standing there.

Mandy started wildly running and Wilf called out, but it was useless in the wind. He chased her, saw her running in all directions, zig-zagging illogically, as if avoiding a sniper's fire. He looked back to the edge of the housing estate, looked to two towers of flats and their upper windows and parapets, illogical but necessary in the light of recent events; he couldn't see any threat and resumed chasing Mandy knowing that Jimbo was calling the cavalry. He soon caught hold of her.

'Stop!' he shouted.

She turned to him, panic scrawled across her tired, soaked and freezing face, stark white teeth shining brilliantly in the murk of the wet afternoon.

'Wilf where is he?'

'I don't know...let's retrace our steps...' He gripped her hand and tugged and they trudged, eyes trained into the wind and rain, seeing nothing. Then Wilf saw a man waving at them from the

Castle Fountains. They ran towards him, and as they neared so they could see a sopping, obedient dog, clutched by the prone figure of Jack, awkwardly leaning against the pond wall. He was clutching the animal as if his life depended upon it, the dog in a patent protective stance.

'My dog ran off and found this man and now they won't leave each other; I don't know what to do.'

Mandy went to Jack and the dog growled through bared teeth. She stood back, wary.

'Jack,' she said, looking around to see a police car approaching down the pedestrian boulevard. She became aware of the colourful flowers; pansy's she thought? Predominantly yellow, purple, blue, and incongruously she thought of her swirly gravy dress that Jack liked, at the same time marvelling at how the plants were miraculously surviving the wind and rain. But then the police car slewed and parked, taking a few of the resilient flowers with it.

Jack spoke. 'Hello there. Felt like a sit down, he's a lovely dog, Martin, I've missed him so much.'

She looked at Wilf, then the dog owner. She pulled her warrant card, 'Police, what's the name of the dog?'

'Charlie, he's a border terrier.'

She recognised the dog as the same breed as Jack's dog Martin, and that dog and man were locked together.

'Right Jack, let's be having you then. I'll call Gail and we can get Martin down to see us, how about that?'

'This is Martin silly,' Jack replied through chattering teeth, and the dog looked like he was not disputing the fact.

The dog owner, a tall and well-padded surly man, was cold, wet and agitated. 'Look mate, that's my fucking dog and his name is Charlie, not Martin.'

Jack looked up for the first time, saw two police cars parked and a third coming down where he regularly walked and used to walk with Martin, and he looked at Mandy like he didn't recognise her. He did Jackie as she ran to him in just a jumper, jeans and trainers, having climbed from the third police car. She was in front of him now and Charlie the dog was calm, accepting, he felt no threat to his rescued man; Jack appeared to relax with Jackie.

'Hi Jack, we need to get you into the dry, will you come with me please?'

He looked up. 'Alright, can Martin come?'

'Let's get you home and Martin can follow okay?'

He nodded, and started to get himself up. 'Felt like a sit down, its lovely here, the Castle, the fountains and the flowers.' Jackie had his hand and was putting an arm around him as he stood and prattled on.

Mandy shuffled to them. 'Jack, what's up love?' He looked confused and turned to Jackie for an explanation.

'This is Mandy Jack, do you remember her?'

Both women saw the panic in his eyes as he shook his head. Mandy cried, Wilf put his arm around her and Jack broke away and punched him full on the face and pushed him into the fountain waters, immediately following up, stepping into the water to hit him again.

'Jack! Stop this right now!' Mandy shouted. Wilf spluttered and they could see blood from his nose immediately diluting and then disappearing into the waves of the pond.

Standing beside a spluttering and splashing Wilf in the pond, both fists raised, Jack shouted to the heavens, 'Fuck off the lot of you, fuck off...!' He made to run but was held by a uniformed policeman, also soaked, one foot in the pond. Jackie joined them in the pool and began whispering in his ear. Mandy was fighting emotions of concern, panic and intense jealousy, but Jackie had calmed Jack and began shuffling him towards the police car, finally easing him into the back seat.

The man began dragging his dog by the lead. Mandy remarked on the image. 'The dog doesn't want to leave Jack; he has this way with animals.'

The patrol car left and Mandy stood there, bedraggled, cold, wet and sobbing. Wilf did his best to comfort her as he phoned, she could just hear his mumbles, the rain saturated wind still whistling about her red raw ears, picking up her straggly hair and causing it to bat her cheeks. Wilf closed the call and pulled her with him to a patrol car and they both got in, the door thudded and there was a stunning silence, she could hear only her own deep racking breaths mixed with the spray of the fountain and the rain hitting the car's side windows.

'Get Mike, Wilf,' she said, her breath steaming up the windows.

Wilf punched a number and spoke to Mike, short and to the point, and ended the call. 'He knew already and will meet us at the house,' he said, and told the patrol officer the address. They knew anyway, had dropped them home once after both had celebrated a bit too hard one night. Mandy smiled at the patrolman.

The officer turned around and looked kindly at the Superintendent. 'He'll be okay Ma'am; he's had to put up with a lot lately.'

'He's put up with a fucking lot? I've put up with a fucking lot, so shut the fuck up and drive.' The officer kicked the car into life; it slewed, the pansies helpless, and eventually the car picked up traction off the pavement and then bounced onto the road.

Mandy spoke to herself, 'Where's she taking him?'

Wilf did nothing, said nothing, they were outside Jack's house already, it was just around the corner and they saw the other patrol car parked and Jackie disappearing through the front door, gently pushing Jack in front of her. Wilf got out and went around to Mandy's door, held it for her; she stayed still for a moment. She apologised to the patrolman then got out and slowly made her way to the front door that Jimbo held open for them.

As Mandy passed through the lobby and into the kitchen, she noticed Jackie was rubbing Jack with a towel, but more than that, she noticed the only two people not dripping onto the tiled floor; Del Boy and Dr Jim Samuels. Jackie spoke first.

'Take this towel Mandy, I need to talk to Jim.'

She took the towel and went to Jack, who still looked like he wondered who she was. She began to rub his hair, she was crying and Jack looked at her, she dabbed his face and noticed they were both shivering. 'Come on let's get to the shower and warm up,' she said and pushed and steered him up the stairs, straight into the wet room. She started the shower, felt it get hot and stood Jack under it still dressed. She needed to get him warm. She went out and returned with towels and their robes, stripped him off and threw the clothes into a corner. He looked marbled, white and blue, like a stone statue. She rubbed vigorously with a spare towel and slowly she could see colour and sensed the feeling returning to him. The water cascaded over them both as Mandy stripped and discarded her own clothes. Instinctively, he began to massage and warm her in return and she responded, enjoying his touch.

'You know, you are really beautiful; what's your name?'

She felt like bursting into more convulsive crying, but held off.

'It's Amanda and I love you Jack.'

'Jack?'

'Yes, Jack, and I am Amanda.'

There was tapping at the door. 'It's me, Jackie, can I come in?' She came in anyway. 'How is he?'

'He doesn't know who I am or his own name. Oh Christ Jackie, his biggest fear is Alzheimer's, what's happening?'

Jackie, still dressed, joined them under the shower, the incongruity of it all lost on the two women.

'This is nice, what shall we play?' Jack said through a boyish grin.

Mandy and Jackie looked at each other and laughed, it seemed not unreasonable at the time; it was feckin' funny.

Chapter 18

Rather than go to the police station, Nobby phoned and briefed Jo Jums on what they had found and said they wanted to probe further, to meet with Alice's Uncle Kipper and the cousin who ran the harbour tour boats. Jo was clearly pre-occupied with the imminent press briefing and she told them to "Go to it".

They did and relished the prospect, this was quality time together. Only Alice thought how it would be when she couldn't do this with the baby. She decided to adopt Jack's Church of Egypt for a while, but knew she would have to talk this through with Nobby soon – knew also he would dread the conversation. She looked across to him and he was, of course, oblivious; just like Jack.

* * *

Mandy and Jackie cradled Jack and steered him to the bedroom where Samuels gave him an injection and he went straight to sleep.

'A sedative, he will be out for about three or four hours. Time enough for us to talk this through. Mike has arrived, shall we go down?'

Jackie and Samuels left, Mandy sat on the bed holding Jack's hand for a while longer, then tucked it under the bed covers, stood, leaned over and kissed him and still in her robe, hair wet and tangled, she went downstairs; she didn't give a toss. Wilf had used the other bathroom and was now dry and in a change of clothes; Jackie was in one of Colleen's robes. They sat around the dining room table as

Jimbo served hot minestrone soup and Mandy thanked him whilst breaking garlic bread and sprinkling parmesan. Jimbo smiled but was clearly concerned; he had known Jack for some time and he liked Mandy, he wanted everything to be alright for them.

'What time is it?' Mandy asked.

'Six thirty,' Jackie said, and Mandy blushed as it dawned on her that they had been in the shower together, and she had been naked. Jackie smiled and winked.

'Oh shut up Jackie, it's not funny.'

'No it's not,' Samuels said.

'Is it Alzheimer's?'

Samuels and Jackie shared a restrained chuckle. Mandy felt comforted that both Jimbo and Wilf looked as worried as she did. Samuels answered in his accustomed direct manner.

'No Mandy, but we are worried about Jack. When he wakes he should be relatively back to normal. I have discussed this with Jackie and we think that maybe the effect of the wind, wet and cold, probably combined with the pain in his shoulder, took his mind back to the harbour waters and that particular recent trauma. It's not unusual in these circumstances for the brain and body to switch off, that's why we think he just wanted to sit down. Thank God for the nurturing instincts of that dog.'

'Animals like him and he likes animals, he wants to take me on a date to the feckin' zoo for Christ's sake,' Mandy said.

They had no answer to that and resisted even a tame laugh.

'We also think that his mind switched to something he could cope with, he recognised the dog as Martin, Jackie as a doctor, not you - but then he wouldn't because he was experiencing child-like symptoms. When you nurtured him like a mother, he responded, correct?'

She nodded. 'But what happens now? Will he be able to think, and what are we going to do about the General, and Len?'

'We don't know, it's suck it and see time...' Samuels left it hanging. Mandy was not content. 'What are you not telling me?'

Eventually Jackie filled the subsequent silence. 'If he were any other patient we would admit him to hospital.'

'What, a looney bin?' Mandy said, shocked.

'Well, we tend not to call it that these days, but a psychiatric unit where we could help him along, bit by bit.'

'But you're not going to do that are you?' Mandy said.

'No we're not.' Samuels replied, in a matter of fact manner. 'Jackie is now fully briefed as to who we are, who Jack is and his full history. She is going to stay with you and we are going to get through this. We will give it two weeks and if we have not got it done by then, we will arrest Len and anyone else we feel we can and close the Op; get Jack sorted. I promise you that Mandy, faithfully. You will be married and he will be well, he will also get his medal; bet you thought I'd forgotten. I know Jack has but you haven't, have you?'

'No,' Mandy replied sharply, recalling that Jack had been recommended for the George Medal and it had been mysteriously put on hold. She thought originally it had been a prejudiced General who had frustrated the award, but had later found out it was Samuels and MI5 who were worried Jack had gone 'rogue' and was actually working with Len to bring the system down. They thought they could deal with Jack, but not the embarrassment if he was guilty and if it was just after he had been given a medal by the Queen.

'So, we wait and see?' Mandy said, fixing Samuels an unfriendly stare.

'Yes,' Samuels replied, and quietly, with Del Boy, Jimbo and Wilf, he made his way to the front door and left.

'How about you Mandy, how are you?' Mike asked.

'To be honest Mike I don't know. I was so shocked to see him like that, I'm not sure it has truly sunk in and I'm worried for him, and me.'

'You always think of people like Jack as bullet proof, but he is human like the rest of us. Jack I admit has a higher level of tolerance than most, mainly because he lives in denial a lot of the time, but his body and his mind shut down today; that's all. Thankfully we're convinced it's temporary and actually refreshingly normal, but you need to look after yourself as well.' He stood. 'I'll take my leave, might treat myself to a shave and I'm just on the end of the phone, though you are in good hands with Jackie.' He winked.

'Feck off Mike,' both of them said.

* * *

Alice made a call to her Uncle Kipper and they agreed to meet later that evening at her Aunt Mabel's, one of Kipper's many sisters. Kipper was the youngest and the only boy of eight kids; mothered and mollycoddled just did not enter into it for the local villain. Kipper was there early. He liked Alice, and he had been close to Alice's mum since she had got herself pregnant. Although the roguish crime family, as Jack would have called them, were not at first pleased with Alice's choice of career, they respected her for it and had taken warmly to Nobby, her filth husband-to-be and father of the forthcoming child.

Jack had explained to Nobby that the Herring family were a product of their environment, that Nobby should recognise that these were actually warm-hearted people, just a tad south of the line for honesty, but not when it came to dealing with people. "You can see what they're thinking and they say it; get a few more like them in politics and we may get out of the shit" Jack had said. That was why Jack liked Alfie Herring and many of his family, and why they liked him, even recognising that every now and then he had to nick one or two of them, it was a part of their lives, in and out of prison and other peoples' houses and such like.

Kipper was a short and stout man and always wore a suit, shiny material, the ensemble completed with a skinny tie and soft, small, Italian leather shoes. He had presence despite his thinning hair and portly shop manager look, and he was respected, had to be to have lasted this long because he was at least Jack's age. Kipper's face showed it, whereas Jack always argued his face, in contrast, maintained a youthful visage.

'Nobby lad, how yer diddlin, Alice tells me you've found an 'ouse in Sowfsea and it's all going frew,' Kipper said, shaking Nobby's hand.

Nobby acknowledged Alfie and agreed they were lucky to find a really nice Southsea terraced house with a pleasant garden for the baby and at a price they could afford. He was unaware that Kipper had arranged for the house and fixed it up for his niece and her future filth husband. Alice and Kipper decided this was something Nobby didn't need to know just now, maybe never. "Just luck I suppose", Nobby had said. Jack saw, but decided it was one for the Church of Egypt.

Aunt Mabel, the female equivalent of Kipper, wobbled out with a tray upon which sat a teapot with a woolly cosy that looked like a retired knitted, Rastafarian hat; green, yellow and black bobbly wool.

'Got this off Sammy, you know the black bloke at the market. He said it was an 'at, the dozy bastard, it's a fuckin' tea cosy,' Mabel explained to Nobby, who couldn't take his eyes off the tray.

'Oh,' both Nobby and Alice said as they sat in the overstuffed settee. Kipper squashed himself into an armchair, lifted his leg and farted. They all laughed and retched together, it was one of Kipper's foibles; you had to accept it. Nobby says his mum still tells everyone about it happening when they first met the family, and remarkably she laughs as well. His dad told him later that Jack had told his mum to laugh, so now she does; Nobby thought it was strange, but Alice didn't.

The tea was so strong it just about made it out of the pot, and Mabel poured into her best china cups from the market, lined up on a spindly legged coffee table in the centre of the room. It had a glass top that protected a picture of a country cottage and garden, incongruous in this gloomy, criminal North Portsmouth terraced house; was it only him that saw this Nobby thought? She poured like a canteen lady, non-stop back and forth, filling the cups, saucers and the cottage garden. Nobby followed Alice's example and poured the saucer tea into the cup. Alfie noisily drank his from the saucer, looked at Nobby.

'S'alright son, the Kings of Ireland used to do this,' he said, and laughed, as did Alice.

'Right then me ducks, what d'yer need your Uncle Kipper for?'

Nobby was speechless as Alfie used his teaspoon to fish out the end of his overly dunked biscuit, then eating it off the spoon with exaggerated slurps of pleasure; he imagined the Kings of Ireland did that as well.

Alice stepped in to save Nobby from further embarrassment.

'There have been some dead dogs found in the harbour and we believe this has a connection to some of the stuff that has been happening lately.'

'Oh shut up sweetheart, what can a couple of dead dogs 'ave to do with those terrorist Muppets blowing up, and the banker being shot? No more than they all deserve mind you, if you ask me.'

Nobby found his voice, shuffled forward in his seat, causing the settee cushion to fart and Alice to wobble and to react, steadying her rattling tea cup in its saucer. He put his cup and saucer onto the brimming coffee table, rested his elbows on his knees and cupped his chin in his hands and looked Alfie right in the eye, something he had always done and a trait secretly admired by Kipper.

'It's more than just that Kipper. Jack thinks there is a conspiracy and it's being played out in Portsmouth.'

'Nobby!' Alice said, shocked, 'that's enough; you mustn't tell Uncle everything.'

Kipper looked hurt, but sat back to watch and see how this lad dealt with his precocious, strong and feisty, favourite niece.

'Alice, we are going to ask Alfie to help us and he should know what he's getting into; it's what Jack would do.'

He didn't wait for a response and carried on talking to Kipper, who winked at Alice as she sat back and looked longingly at her Nobby.

'You see, Jack thinks that all that has been happening is some malevolent force, tipping things over the edge to get a reaction from ordinary people, to make them force the government back to more socialist values, reinforce the welfare state, you know what I mean; backtrack on the cutbacks, and so on. Yeah?'

'Haven't a fucking clue what you're talking about Nobby, but if Jack says so then it's good enough for me; what d'you want me to do?'

* * *

Mandy, Jackie and Jimbo were at the table - it was just after ten in the evening. Mandy and Jackie had a glass of wine each but neither felt like drinking. Jimbo had water and it was coffee for Wilf as he monitored the computers and CCTV by the washing machine.

'I'm feckin starvin', not one of you thought to wake me up for dinner then?'

They turned to face Jack who was at the bottom of the stairs, all three mildly shocked.

'I think I might get your dressing gown Jack, you must be cold with nothing on?' Mandy said, not sure whether to laugh or cry.

'Thanks love. Jackie, you're here?' He stayed on the stair and Mandy squeezed by, looking back to Jackie as she passed.

'I'm having a glass of wine Jack just on the off chance I might see a hunky naked man who might change my mind about being a lesbian. Still waiting though.' Jimbo laughed, and Jack could hear a muffled chortle from by the washing machine.

Mandy sidled back down the stairs and put the robe over his shoulders, threaded his right arm in and wrapped it around as she did the belt up. 'Thanks love.' He kissed her. Mandy looked round quizzically to Jackie who just shrugged her shoulders as Jack stepped off the stairs and took a place at the table, pulling a chair aside for Mandy to sit with him.

She went to take the chair and he moved it as close as it would go and she allowed his leg to rub hers and followed it with her hand.

'Okay darling?'

He leaned back as if trying to focus. 'Yeah? Why, shouldn't I be?' The lack of focus was now replaced with a quizzical look.

'No reason.' But she looked to Jackie again.

'Okay what's going on, you keep looking at Jackie. What happened while I was asleep?' He noticed the serious look on the face of Jackie, and Jimbo rose from his seat and went to join Wilf; he was no part of this.

'You had an episode Jack,' Jackie said.

'Nice one girl, you almost had me going then,' Jack said nervously.

'Jack, I told you that you might have what we call episodes and we cannot predict what they might be or when or where they might occur, but you had one today. Mandy remembers pulling you to her just as you got to the Castle and you winced in pain. Maybe the combination of the weather, the cold and wet and that pain made your mind and body recall the harbour incident; being shot, the shock of the cold harbour water, who knows?' Jackie flicked her hands to indicate it was just a guess. 'You began to relive that. In some cases like this, the mind will switch off and go into safety mode; we think yours did this afternoon.'

Jack looked at Jackie; Mandy could see he was trying to see if he could recall anything. He couldn't.

'Shit-a-brick,' he said, puffing air in an exaggerated sigh.

'Couldn't have put it better myself,' Jackie said, smiling warmly.

Jack picked up on Mandy's concern and rested his hand on top of hers, looked deep into her eyes.

'Don't worry love, I've a good trick cyclist and I think she may be recommending sexual therapy.' He looked up at Jackie, 'what d'yer fink Doc?'

'Oh Jack, don't make light of this I was worried. You didn't know me. You didn't know Samuels or even Del Boy, just Jackie.'

'Samuels and Del been here have they?' He made a facial gesture to indicate his surprise, or perhaps that was annoyance. Mandy nodded and sniffed. 'Father Mike here too?' She nodded again and carried on sniffing. 'Well then, I'm sorry, and thank you Jackie. What do I have to do to get better?'

Jackie leaned into her answer. 'Work through your traumas, starting with your eye I think. I'm going to take you through them all and we are going to look at the trigger points. When we identify them, we can work out strategies so you know what is happening, when it happens. The berserking is bollocks of course and we will trace that as well why we're at it, there is something else there, and we will find it and you will work with me.'

'What will happen?' Jack asked, concerned, and Mandy shared that concern and looked beseechingly to Jackie.

Jackie gave him and Mandy a warm and radiant smile in response. Jack melted, he was good at melting and was secretly relieved he could still do it; Mandy was still on tenterhooks.

'You will get better, it's what happens; we get better,' Jackie said.

Jack stood. 'Good, that's that sorted then, I'm tired.'

He walked over to Jackie and she lifted herself from her seat to meet him, opened her arms and embraced him and he muffled into her dressing gown, 'Thank you Jackie...' he looked at her, '...I'll be there for you to help me; time to get straightened out eh?'

He turned to Mandy, she hugged and kissed him and he spoke to her, 'I love you Amanda, let's get me bonce right, then we'll get married; can't have you marrying a bleedin' looney.'

She nodded and rested her head on his chest, his heart was racing; he was scared. She looked at Jackie who noticed everything.

'I'm going back to bed,' he said.

'Shall I bring you some soup?'

'Nah, I'm not hungry anymore.' He trudged up the stairs. He had been shocked by what he had learned and not a little worried.

Chapter 19

Kipper was struck by the thought of adventure, he scented fun in the air and all on the side of the law; very novel. He had helped Jack several times in the past and always thoroughly enjoyed himself, if not always emerging unscathed or uninjured. He didn't care about the reasons, and politics never bothered him, he would help Jack for the sheer hell of it.

'Let's go see Boz and see what he knows,' he said, standing and rubbing his hands together.

Nobby looked to Alice for clarification.

'Boz is my cousin. He runs the tourist boats.' Alice looked to her uncle. 'Where will he be, I'm not sure Nobby is ready for the Mother Ship yet?' The Mother Ship being Alfie's local pub, a notorious criminal pub, and coppers, except Alice of course, were definitely not welcome.

'No worries, he'll be down the 'Ard. He runs night-time tours in the summer, but not much business tonight I would guess what wiv this filfy wever; no offence Nobs lad.'

Alice giggled. 'Give him a call and let's go see him then.'

'Doing it now babes.'

Kipper got out his old phone and laboured over punching the numbers in. Alice got up and went to the kitchen where she subtly poured the tea down the sink. Nobby laboured with his and Alfie watched as he did and took great pleasure in it; gave him the thumbs up and they went to the front door.

Nobby thanked Mabel for the tea, hugged her and won a friend for life. Alfie patted him on the back. Alfie climbed in the passenger seat of Alice's little old mini, complained, but was grateful Nobby had at least taken the back seat. They set off for the Hard.

The Hard was the Historic Naval Dockyard area of Portsmouth, a mixture of new and old, charming and not so attractive buildings skirting the landward side of a wide boulevard that fronted the harbour mud flats. The old dockyard wall and buildings closed the view, where the spidery masts of Nelson's *Victory* could be seen poking over signs announcing Henry the Eighth's Hairy Nose (as Jack would call the *Mary Rose*), the Victorian *Warrior* battleship proud and sentinel at the entrance to the historic dockyard. The area had character and was full of characters, and not all of them would qualify for Sainthood and tourist grants. It was a mix of the old Waterside Families and the Portsea Estates nearby; if you were in, then you were in, if you weren't then it could be fun but a little hairy, a lot like Henry's nose.

Nobby was relieved to be with Kipper, who was being heartily welcomed by the patrons of the beautiful old pub, *The Ship Anson*; the landlord fussing and surreptitiously checking, had he transgressed the unwritten law. Alfie put the man at his ease, reassuring him that he was here to meet with his nephew, Boz. The landlord summoned up a round of drinks and followed them to where Boz was lounging and reading the Evening News. Alfie flicked his lighter and set fire to the newspaper, giving the Landlord apoplexy and not a little shock for Boz.

'What's your fucking Game Kipper?' Boz said, as he leapt from his seat, and along with the Landlord, commenced treading out the fire, to the sound of Uncle Alfie's machine gun laughter, the nervous general mirth of the other patrons, and a giggling fit from Alice. Nobby remained stunned.

They eventually sat around a table, Boz having now also seen the funny side; the landlord returned to his position behind the bar and nursed his irritated ulcer.

Boz was a large brawny man, all of six four, so muscle-bound Nobby thought he would have trouble walking. He looked to be in his early thirties, jet black hair, the colour of Alice's, the beginnings of a leathery, old salt face, but young and good looking in a way; though with the appearance he could turn ugly if you upset him. When he laughed though, he looked like a soft rabbit and he was truly a gentle giant with Alice; a strong relationship, and one of familial love. Nobby was welcome, Alice was his passport, and he shifted a little closer to her, just in case.

Boz knocked his pint back and Nobby leapt up to get another round and Alfie approved some more of the man Alice was marrying. Alice began explaining to Boz why they were there. Nobby, looking back from the bar, was frustrated at the prospect of missing the conversation, but the landlord instantly supplied a tray of drinks and snatched Nobby's money and helped himself to a generous tip.

Resigned, Nobby returned to the table and joined the conspiratorial tête-à-tête, squashing his head into the quiet exchanges taking place just a few inches above the table top, the odour of generations of stale beer clouding his nostrils. Just as Nobby had adjusted his body position, so Boz, Alfie and Alice sat up straight, and he was left crouching over the table as they laughed at Alice's daft filth bugger. Nobby managed an embarrassed chuckle, Kipper farted, Boz laughed, and Alice remarked that she preferred the smell of charred paper and stale beer.

'Sorry, but apart from Kipper farting, what happened just then?' Nobby enquired politely.

Alice patted Nobby's hand. 'Boz is reluctant to talk too much, but he's aware of something happening at the old wharf we visited.'

'What though?' Nobby replied.

Uncle Alfie stepped in as Boz was oozing agitation. 'Nobs lad, shut it. I know you're mustard for a filth but leave this to the professionals, eh?'

Reading Nobby's frustration, he tapped his nose as Jack does, but the gesture seemed not to smooth the Nobby feathers and Kipper made a mental note to check with Jack on the nose tapping.

'We'll find out okay son? Boz has a number of so called mates what fight dogs on the wharf, but that's not the bleedin' point. Boz has been told that somefing else is 'appening and I'm not in any

of it, and this my son is my Manor, so I'm right royally pissed off.'
Kipper turned to Boz.

'I fort you fort the dogs in the country, 'ow comes nobody told
me this was happening down 'ere?'

Boz sensed that the level of interrogation had ramped up and
was worried.

'I just found out meself, I called Squirrel before you got here.'
Boz's face looked like he thought he'd gotten away with it and
Kipper let him know he had.

'We 'ave some serious shit 'ere and I wants a word with Squirrel,
so get him out of his gaff and 'ere now.'

Kipper sat back and quaffed at least half a pint and smacked
his lips. Boz picked up his phone and made a call, the conversation
taking place below the table and judging by the length of the call
and the crouched animation of Boz's whispers, Nobby thought that
Squirrel was not fancying coming out and leaving his nuts.

Kipper grabbed the phone and any previous covert pretence was
gone. 'Get yer fucking arse down 'ere Squirrel or I'll tear yer tail off.'
He hung up.

Boz grabbed the phone back and dialled again. 'I'll tell him
where we are shall I?' Kipper and Alice laughed, Boz grinned into
the phone and Nobby looked like he may have shat himself.

The other customers settled, pretending to be having a lovely
time and not in the least disturbed by Kipper's outburst.

* * *

The Cabinet Secretary and the Government Chief whip were
joined by Vice Admiral Chit Wesley and David Sexton, redressing
the balance on the recently depleted committee. They all looked
nervous except for Sexton, whom they all knew to be a cucumber;
his cool manner and reputation for ruthless cold dealings in the
financial markets with Cedric James Bank preceded him, and had
been one of his principle recruitment qualifications.

The room was darkened as normal. They awaited the tap at the door, the new boys having been briefed and waiting patiently. Out of respect they had a couple of bottles of Pomerol and talked about this becoming a tradition. They liked things like this and each of them projected their imagination into the future, the tradition established, when they would be individually lauded for their part in the work they were doing and the behaviours they had set and established. Had Jack been there he may have seen this as a form of denial. Well, that's what Len thought as he stood at the door looking in, noticing the palpable fear as the men stared into the depth of polish on the table, knowing he was there but also knowing they were not supposed to look. Except for Sexton. Sexton did look, slow and deliberate, and even smiled - if you could call the thin lips, fixed straight and horizontal with just the hint of an upturn in the corners, a smile.

Len looked on and approved of the choices made. It was an uneasy hush as his heels began to tap dance towards the table. The chair scraped louder than was normal and the ensuing intake of breath was audible; was Lionel angry? He poured his Pomerol into the crystal goblet; he swirled, sniffed and held the glass to the intense central light, sipped and nodded his approval. He paused and then in hushed tones said, 'You do not take the initiative, you do not anticipate what I want. I take it the lesson is learned?'

Len looked around the table at the bright white faces, hints of an embarrassed bloom on cheek tops, on faces suspended in the halo of light, and he nodded to them, to reaffirm his words. The reflected light accentuated the grotesqueness of their visages, a stark brilliance of shiny skin, deep shadowy nostrils and eye sockets and the blackness of half opened mouths.

Len had the knowing response he wanted and pulled some folded sheets of paper from the inside pocket of his suit jacket. They radiated the brilliance of the white light as he smoothed them in the centre of the table. 'Let's see if you can do this right shall we?'

He stood and his shoes tapped their way back to the door and he disappeared into the peripheral gloom. The whirring of the lock could be heard, and he became visible again as the light from the outer room bathed Len's upright, svelte figure. The gloom was all too soon restored as Len left and the door mechanism whirred and locked shut.

* * *

Nobby kissed Alice goodnight at the door of her Mum's house. Alice's mum, Jolene, ruled the house with a rod of iron and the stepfather was in awe of this commanding and still attractive woman. She was shapely like Alice but shorter. The likeness to Kipper was there in the stance and body language and Nobby had witnessed that power when he had asked if she was aware where Alice's dad was, so he could be at the wedding. There had been a serious drawing of breath from Jolene as well as her daughter. Sam, the stepfather, was visibly agitated but had no grounds, or was it backbone, to express himself; he went to the pub. That suited Jolene just fine.

"We don't mention dad here, it upsets Sam", Alice had said. Nobby thought it was more Jolene that seemed to get upset but he did leave it.

Nobby kissed Alice goodbye and she watched him go. Even though it would be shutting the stable door, Jolene never let him stay over, but they would have their own house in a couple of weeks and this comforted the both of them.

'Nobby, don't go!' He stopped in his tracks and came back, expectant, excitement written across his face.

'What is it love?' He took her in his arms thinking she would sneak him to her bed.

'Let's go and look at the warehouse, see what's 'appening?'

'No Alice, we would need back up and the go ahead from Jo on that one, besides, I would like to talk this over with Jack, get his take.'

'Oh fuck Jack, come with me; I'm going to go anyway.' She had lost the coquettish look and exchanged it for a more *devil may care, and fuck you if you don't do what I want*, look.

'No Alice, we do this properly.' She reluctantly accepted, kissed him goodnight and he walked to the waiting taxi with a sense of trepidation. The cab took him back to his car at the police station.

Chapter 20

Mandy was asleep. Jack felt he had slept enough, it was close to midnight and he fancied a cup of tea with Jimbo. Wilf was asleep on the settee and Jackie had Michael and Winder's room. Jack felt remarkably well considering, and was enjoying a laugh with Jimbo when the phone rang. Jack leaned back, looked at the clock on the wall in the kitchen. He answered the call, listened then spoke.

'Calm down Nobby, talk slowly.' He listened some more, Jimbo could hear Nobby was shouting.

'Jimbo and I'll be there, have you called this into Jo Jums?' He listened. 'Well do that now son. We'll meet you at the main turn off for the warehouses; whatever happens, don't go in on your own, got that?'

He hung up, looked at Jimbo, thought for a minute.

'Get hold of Mike and tell him we may need a bit of armed back up.'

He described the situation to Jimbo, leapt up and scooted the stairs two at a time, slowed and tippy-toed into the bedroom, but Mandy was awake and sitting up, arms folded; she made him jump.

'What is it Jack?'

He dressed as he explained that Nobby had left Alice at her home after they had learned that there may be a dog fight at the old warehouse tonight. She had wanted to go but Nobby said no. 'He went back to the Nick and called her to apologise and after a row with Alice's Mum, she found that Alice was not in her room; the stupid mare's gone on her own.'

Mandy was up and getting dressed herself. 'What're you doing?'

'You're not going on your own, are you mad?'

'I might be, I don't know.' He paused to consider, but got side-tracked wondering what face he had on; Mandy confirmed for him, it was his eeejits one, he humphed, he thought it had been his side-tracked one; it just goes to show.

Mandy had her sensible head on, 'We have to do something. Nobby's calling Jo?'

'Yes, and Jimbo's calling Mike, then coming with us,' Jack said.

'Armed back up?' She was hopping, putting socks on. She squeezed into her jeans, buttoned up and was ready and they took off down the stairs. She noticed he'd left his harness off and he wasn't wincing; mincing yes, but that was normal for her tart of a fella. However, whatever pain he felt didn't stop him looking at her backside, tight in the jeans; she sighed, he was okay, for now.

'Del says you're not to go Jack,' Jimbo said.

'Did you tell Del to fuck off?' Jack replied.

'Well in a manner of speaking, and he told me to go with you. I'm ready.'

Wilf was up and on the computers. They made their way down the back garden and into the garage and Jimbo's car. He reversed out and set off north. Jack's phone went.

'Mike…Shit, okay, call Kipper, tell 'im what's 'appening.' He closed the call.

'No spook back up,' he said to the darkness in the car as he speed dialled. 'Jo, we've no back up, can you call armed support pretty please? Brief 'em to hold back and come in only on my command or if they hear me crying; I've a bad feeling about this.'

Moments later the phone rang again. He listened and closed the call. 'Tactical can't get there for half an hour. Jo's on her way in,' he said.

'I have some kit in the back Jack, vests as well.'

'How many?'

'Two sets, Wilf and me.'

'Mandy, you'll have to stay back and run the Op okay?'

Mandy understood the logic. 'Okay, but you wear the vest and let Jimbo look after you,' she said. He was quiet. 'You okay Jack?'

'Mmmm.' He tapped his fingers, it wasn't Dr Who, he was scared. They were pulling up and Jimbo nodded towards an agitated Nobby, under a streetlight, bouncing on the balls of his feet.

The black Mondeo drew up beside him, they got out and Mandy got into the driving seat and set her phone up, called into the nick while they were getting suited.

'Barney is Jo in yet?' She listened, Jo was on her way and Barney put her through to Nylon in the Ops room. 'Nylon have you been briefed?' She nodded to herself as she listened. 'I will be running the Op from this phone okay?'

She closed the call and saw Jimbo, Nobby and Jack, walking down the short road like they were meeting the bleedin' Clancy's at the OK Corral. She eased the car into gear and silently rolled to follow them, carried on past the entrance to the compound, turned, parked, switched the lights off and opened the windows. It was a humid night; sweat trickled down the back of her neck. She could hear the pained noises of stressed and distressed dogs. At least the weather had calmed; just a fine misting of rain, no wind.

The three men came to the driver's side. Jimbo and Nobby had vests but not Jack, all three had handguns.

'Jack where is your vest?'

'Blimey you sound like my Mum!' he tittered, but it was a nervous titter, whether from the potential action or Mandy's look, it was difficult to tell; the money was on Mandy's look. 'I'll stay back to form a visual link to you.'

She sighed. 'Okay, be careful all of you. Nobby, no gung-ho, and Jimbo you know Jack will be shite with that gun don't you?' Jimbo nodded but was focused. 'Okay get going.' They left and she called it in; it had started.

* * *

Kipper had summoned Plug and the Jaguar was full - Kipper, Boz, Plug and Squirrel, who squirmed with cold dread in such company, as well as the fear of what might be going to happen. Plug had been involved with Kipper in the terrorist and Crusader incidents. He was a telegraph pole of a man, with a natural physical strength that dominated his miniature brain. He had a skull shaped like a horse and the front top set teeth protruded and hung down so much, you felt like giving him an apple. The overhanging top jaw and crooked teeth made him look like Plug out of the *Beano's Bash Street Kids*; hence his name. He was however a useful man to have on your side in a fight. He had no fear and was rarely bested, and tonight was important to him; he loved Alice.

Boz drove Kipper's Jag like he was getting away from a bank job, which was one of his other known skills, after pootering around the harbour spinning stories to the tourists; a lot like he would do with the police if ever he was caught. Squirrel was like his name, a ratty, ginger haired weasel of a man, small in stature and presence, no moral code, a known informer but never on the Herring family; he had a modicum of intelligence.

Squirrel twitched, Kipper, Boz and Plug were relaxed and had already called at a house to collect tools of the trade, all of them pump action and sawn off. They were focused, no words were exchanged, not that Plug ever joined in any conversation. All that could be heard was Kipper muttering under his breath what he was going to do to his niece when he got hold of her. They passed Mandy in the black Mondeo, turned and pulled up behind. In the rear view mirror she saw them get out and rolled her eyes as she saw what they were carrying. Leaning out of her window and in a hushed voice, 'Kipper, I'm not sure that the sawn-offs will be needed.'

'Mandy, get some serious back up babes, I know the guys in there. I've been doing a bit of looking into this since Alice and Nobby left. Now, where are Jack and Nobby, and more to the point Alice?'

'Jack should be just around the corner there.' She pointed to the very dim glow of a corner light hanging off a portacabin, the light projecting a halo globe in the fine drizzle. 'He's with Nobby and a colleague, Jimbo.'

'Jimbo's here? Brilliant, he weighs in for at least three men.' Kipper looked at his crew and explained that Jimbo was a spook. Mandy looked, listened but contained herself; she could ask how Kipper knew Jimbo another time.

'I've been hearing the dogs but it's been quiet for nearly five minutes,' she said, as they left her and strolled towards the warehouse.

'God give me strength,' she said to herself as she went to answer the phone that was on silent and vibrated in her lap; she thought of Jack, tummy butterflies told her she was scared for him.

Chapter 21

Alice had crept to the perimeter of the warehouse and peered through the crack in the main sliding doors. She saw a pair of dogs hoisted and being shown to the crowd, a crescendo of shouting and arguing ensued. She tried to ease one of the doors; it was too heavy. She had already seen dazzling halogen lamps suspended over a makeshift ring, and those lamps were swinging in a breeze coming from somewhere. She concluded there must be a side door and squelched her way through puddles around the perimeter of the building until she saw the projecting shaft of light from a propped open side door.

The noise of fighting dogs and cheering men began again and was relieved the noise of her progress would be masked. She got to the door and could clearly see the fighting ring only some ten metres away, surrounded by aggressive men, two deep, waving fists of money. The smell hit her sensitive nostrils - dog shit, blood, animal and human sweat. She eased her phone from her pocket, flicked to camera mode, no flash, and began snapping just as she felt her backside lift into the air and she was flung into the warehouse, somersaulting and landing on her back. She was winded and dazed and from the floor she saw the man who had been on guard that afternoon lean over, recognise her, pick her up again heave her through the crowd and into the ring with the dogs.

Jack, having seen Alice creeping around, had followed. Nobby and Jimbo had unfortunately circled the other way, just luck he supposed, but he was able to see the man grab Alice's backside and toss her into the ring. He heard the roar from the appreciative crowd, the howling crescendo from the dogs. He raised his gun, charged through the door and fired a shot into the air. He hit the head of the guard with the butt of the pistol and jumped into the arena and shot the first dog that directed itself to him. The second dog had Alice by the throat, she was backing away, punching the dog on the skull but the animal had a lock. Jack chased them down and fell onto the hound and Alice, and with the gun at the dog's temple he fired. The noise deafened him but he was resolute. Alice's face had been savaged and blood was gushing from a neck wound. He put his hands around it but it was useless, blood pulsed through his fingers.

He stood and felt a searing pain in his shoulder, but the men were closing in on him. He fired over their heads, but being such a terrible shot he hit one of them. It was probably a good thing as it did cause them to falter; Jack looked deadly serious. They began closing again and were then halted by more firing, pistol shots and a loud report from what could only be a shotgun. The closing men froze. Jack could just make out Kipper's booming voice within the ringing of his ears, but not what he was saying. The men stood rigid in reaction to Kipper's voice, then began falling like ninepins as Plug and his whirling windmill arms began slicing through the crowd. Slowly sense returned and the crowd of men started running in all directions; Kipper, Boz and Squirrel pumped shots at legs, and men fell. Jimbo and Nobby also fired at the running legs. Plug had Alice in his arms, running for the door, crying, wailing and calling out for help; at least that was what Jack thought he was saying. He reached the sliding doors, and had begun shouldering them apart when they were peppered with a hail of machine gun fire. Plug reacted in an instant, diving and rolling with Alice.

The front yard was now completely ablaze with floodlighting. Jack looked out; intense white light, fencing, barbed wire sparklingly illuminated, and machine gun flashes from the harbour. Jack backtracked and joined up with Jimbo. Through the melee and carnage they sneaked to the outside, via Alice's side door. From this angle they could see the machine gun muzzles flare from the old scrapped ship. The guns were strafing the forecourt, oblivious and uncaring of what might be hit. Jack eased out and Jimbo followed, snatching at Jack's arm, pulling him back.

'Kin ell Jimbo that hurt.'

'Sorry Jack, stay behind me.'

They moved and eased themselves around the edge of the fenced compound to the relatively dark, far side of the wharf's edge. It was low tide and the hulk was stuck fast and listing to the north, away from them. The machine gun fire ceased for a short time, people taking stock. Then the eerie quiet was shattered, a return fusillade was directed at the ship as tactical set themselves up.

Jimbo eased himself off the wharf's edge, sensed the ooze of the harbour mud, feeling to see if he would be able to walk with a sound footing and found he could squelch some progress. Jack followed and they set off towards the hulk, soon to be swallowed up by the darkness, their feet sucked by the mud. A searchlight swept across the edge of the rust bucket. As they closed, they could see the gunmen leaning over the side and firing intermittently. One was dangling, didn't look at all well, probably sea sick Jack said, and he could hear Jimbo snigger. The firing land-side had ceased and Jack got his phone out and called Mandy in a whisper.

'Ambulances love, Alice has been hurt by the dogs and a bit of a bloodbath inside, and before you say, it wasn't me, okay.' She started to reply but he stopped her. 'Listen, Jimbo and me are out in the harbour, by the old ship. There's a rubber motorised dinghy to the rear and we think the men on the ship are going to make for that. Get the Harbour Police and make sure they're armed.'

Mandy acknowledged and went to work making her calls. Harbour Police were already on their way, always armed, and she briefed them. She already had the ambulances and had fielded calls from Del Boy and Jo Jums. Jo Jums had arranged for more tactical and they now had the place buttoned up. Her principle concern was that they had not been able to get Alice out and then she saw Nobby running with a body over his shoulder. The firing started up again and was immediately answered by a deafening coordinated salvo from the reinforced tactical units, now spread across the harbour frontage. The rusty ship took the hits, and sparks crackled into the black sky. The firing from the ship ended just as Nobby got to a waiting ambulance. Mandy was out of the car and she could see the paramedics working. Alice's face and throat shocked her. The doors slammed to the sound of Nobby crying, calling to Alice.

Squad cars were pulling up, as were the major incident vans. Lights were erected and soon the road outside the warehouse was a flood of light and buzzing activity. She answered her phone. 'Jack, the firing has stopped and the men on the boat will be making their escape...'

'Ship love,' he interrupted her.

'What?'

'It's a ship not a boat.'

'Fuck off tosser, and be careful,' she said, and then in a hushed tone, 'Alice looks bad, she's on the way to hospital, finish this now Jack and come back to me.'

Jack closed his phone and put it into his trouser pocket. He looked down and could feel the water up to his calves. Further on it was up to Jimbo's knees.

'Tide's coming in,' Jack said unnecessarily.

Jimbo nodded, getting a knife out. He waded to the dinghy where he sliced into the inflated sides and rear, leaving the two prow buoyancy tubes, so it gave the appearance of still floating to those coming down a steel ladder fixed to the inclined hull. They could hear the thrumming of powerful engines of an approaching boat, a light swivelled across the hull and ladder and the men climbing down. Gunmen still on top fired a salvo at the police launch. The light doused immediately and the patrol boat could be heard to swing in the water, but the engine noise increased in volume as it continued to approach, this time from a different direction. A second boat could now also be heard and Jack began to relax, and as a consequence the pain in his shoulder flashed like an electric shock.

Two of the men had reached the boat and toppled into the water as the stability was gone. Jack noticed Jimbo silently float towards the men as they scrambled to get back in. He chopped the neck of one and used the butt of his knife on the other. Both were stunned and Jimbo snapped plastic cable ties on their wrists behind their backs, professional, smooth and efficient. Jack phoned Mandy, reported on what was happening and told her to let the patrol boats know to watch out for Jimbo and him in the water. She acknowledged and ended the call.

The first patrol boat was on them now and Jack could just see the grey and black of the hull as it picked up some reflected light off the water; the tide was rising fast and Jack sensed a reciprocal rising panic in himself.

Two more men came down the ladder, simultaneously firing at the patrol boat. Jack raised his pistol, fired and missed, but the sparks off the ladder made the man he wasn't aiming at fall off and crunch into the hull of the dinghy; they heard a snap and he was still. The second man aimed at Jack but before he could fire, was hit by a knife flung by Jimbo; he fell and was swallowed up in the inky black waters.

That appeared to be it. Jimbo saw Jack making for the ladder, the water was up to the MI5 man's chest and Jack's waist as the patrol boat eased in.

'MI5 officer and Portsmouth CID, we are going up the ladder to investigate,' Jimbo shouted. 'We'll need two officers and powerful torches.' Jack heard Jimbo taking control as he waded to the ladder and stepped onto the first rung, pulling with his right hand and feeling the twist in his left shoulder as he rose up.

'Shitehawks that hurt.'

'Jack, you've done enough, get onto the patrol boat please and leave this to me now,' Jimbo ordered.

'Feck off Jimbo, I'm halfway up now.' And Jack found the climb surprisingly easy as the hulk leaned over at nearer sixty degrees as opposed to the vertical, and the rounded hull flattened toward the top.

Jimbo called out in a whisper, 'Watch as you go over the top, they could be waiting.' And then back to the patrol boat, 'Douse the light.' The searchlight went out. The second patrol boat could be heard easing around the other side of the listing ship as Jack eased himself up to peek over; there was an immediate burst of automatic fire.

'Semi-automatic pistol Jack, stay back.'

They stood there hanging on the ladder. 'What shall we do Jimbo?'

'Shut up I'm thinking.'

'What you thinking?'

'How I could have been bodyguard to the Queen, now shut the fuck up, I'm listening.'

Jack listened but could hear nothing. Jimbo had better hearing, his ears were still ringing from the shot to the dog's head. He was starting to look back at Jimbo when he sensed a bullet fly past his face and a man fell from the ship's side, brushing past Jack; there was a splash.

A shot rang out, a thud, and then a call from the deck, 'All clear to come aboard, this is Officer James.'

Jack poked his head over the ship's side and saw a police officer, flak jacket and peaked cap smiling as the searchlight hit his face. 'Hello Jack, at least we aren't fishing you out of the harbour today.'

'Siderney is that you?' and Jack did a mock *Sid James* laugh, then a *Kenneth Williams, "Stop mucking about"*.

Officer James smiled, which was more a pained grimace at the mention of his nickname, 'Welcome aboard Cap'n Birdseye,' he called back and Jack could hear laughter from the officer's body radio. Jimbo was beside him and more officers were scrambling onto the sloping deck, swinging powerful light beams as the ship was checked out.

Jack answered his vibrating phone. 'Hello love, we seem secure here, what about on shore?'

'Alice is in a bad way Jack, they're operating now, she has a tear at her throat which is serious but they can deal with it, then its facial stuff,' Mandy said, and then she was quiet, the enormity of the situation becoming a reality.

'How's Nobby holding up?'

'He phoned just now, I said we will be up just as soon as you get ashore. It's quiet here now but quite a few gunshot wounds. I think you could be busy with interviews Jack.'

'Can't someone else do them Amanda?'

She laughed. 'No Jack, they are going to want to interview you.'

Jack laughed, pleased to hear her laughing. Jimbo was back on deck, waving a hand to Jack. 'Hang on a minute love, Rambo wants a word.'

Jimbo called across the deck, 'Jack, we've been down into the hold and it's an arms cache. I think Del Boy has an answer to some of his questions.'

'You hear that love?'

'I did Jack, should I ring Del Boy?'

'Ring Mike. How's Kipper and Plug?'

'They've disappeared. Boz got a knock on the head, said something about a squirrel and Plug seems inconsolable about Alice. I think we will find Kipper at the hospital.'

'I'll have a butchers at the arms stash then we can go to the hospital as well. I take it Jo is up to speed?'

'Yes Jack, as you would expect another exemplary performance; she's briefing the Commander now and we have agreed to meet up in the morning.'

'What, ten?'

She chuckled. 'You seem a lot better Jack.'

Chapter 22

Kipper was at the hospital and sat beside Nobby, both men leaning forward in their plastic chairs, heads in their hands.

'It's Alice, always been bleedin' impechous,' Kipper said.

'I thought she'd calmed down with the baby, but she was just bubbling below the surface.'

They looked up. Alice's Mum was back from talking with the nurses. 'They still don't know nuffing, you fink they would pop their heads in or somfink?'

'Sit down love.' Kipper patted the seat beside him. 'They'll tell us when they know, don't fret, eh,' Alfie said, trying to reassure his sister.

'Oh Alfie, my girl, and she was getting married.'

'We can still get married, when she's better,' Nobby answered probably more vehemently than he intended.

Jolene looked at her brother, and Alfie explained. 'What she's saying lad is Alice won't want to get married if she's scarred. She'll be finking you won't want er...' he paused, '...will yer? Many wouldn't,' he said, shaking his head.

Nobby looked shocked. 'Alfie how can you say that?'

'I say what I fink. I know a lot of men wouldn't go near a girl what was scarred.'

'You fucking tosspot, I love her and not just the way she looks.' Nobby stood and stamped across the room to look out the big windows, to see nothing, just blackness and the wind strengthening and starting to drive the returning rain.

He saw Alfie's reflection behind him.

'Sorry Nobby.' Kipper put his arm around him, stretching up and from behind. It was a comical sight; a squat, portly old villain, hugging a tall, slim and relatively smart copper.

'You're alright Nobby my old son...' The two men looked at each other, the tall one with a look of mild surprise, the other one smiling, '...for a filf that is.' They both laughed then stopped abruptly, remembering where they were and what was happening.

'You have to laugh, it helps, and she isn't the type to want yer moanin' and wailing over her.' Jack stood there sopping wet, with muddy and stinking trouser legs, the bottom department of those trousers sagging like there was something equally unsavoury contained within, and judging by the smell, there could be as well; Jack had after all, been very scared.

'Jack, she was asking for you in the ambulance...not that she was making much sense,' Nobby said.

'How is she Nobby?'

'They can mend the gash in her throat, looked worse than it really was, missed the vitals. The facial stuff is bad though. They have a specialist surgeon starting the cosmetic job now, but she will need a lot of follow up work.'

Jack nodded. 'The baby?'

'We don't know, they've not said anything. She was worried what you would say, going off like that.'

'Me?' Jack looked surprised.

'Yes Jack, not sure if you've ever noticed but she worships the ground you walk on,' Nobby asserted.

'She does that Jack,' Kipper said, smiling at his discomfiture.

'She'll need a lot of comfort and reassurance Nobby, and Kipper you'd better change your clothes, you smell like a battle zone,' Jack said.

Alfie didn't care. He looked to Nobby. 'Jack and I'll be there for her and you son.'

Nobby noticed Mandy for the first time, and he went into her outstretched arms, staying in her embrace for a few minutes.

A surgeon in blue scrubs appeared. 'Nobby?'

Nobby looked up. 'That's me.'

'Are you the father?' Nobby nodded.

'I'm sorry, she has lost the baby. We have a specialist with her now and we think things will be okay. We did all we could but...' he tailed off, then started up again, '...as far as her other injuries go, we have dealt with the neck wound and she will recover fine. Her face, I am sorry to say, will be badly scarred and will need a lot of cosmetic follow up work, but they can do wonders these days. She wants to see you but be prepared, the injuries are serious and though still woozy, she will be very sensitive; mostly she seems sorry to be the cause of so much pain for you. She's in recovery now and we will be moving her to ICU, just for the night we think; okay, shall we go?'

Nobby followed the surgeon and Jolene looked mightily pissed off.

'Oi mush, what about me, I'm her bleedin' muvver.'

'Yes, she was asking after you. She wanted to see Nobby first.' This seemed to mollify Jolene, but Jack could see that the surgeon had just made that up; you can't kid a kidder.

Chapter 23

It was organised chaos at the station; frenetic action, tension and excitement pervading the halls. Jo held sway, marshalling the troops, one of her strengths in a crisis. She allocated her officers tasks to mop up the aftermath, using uniform teams seconded from Cosham and Central to make up the numbers.

Kettle and Jed were at the hospital marshalling their own allocation of uniforms to secure the walking wounded. They reported three fatalities to Jo, no identities as yet, some seriously wounded but mainly shotgun wounds to the legs for a lot of them. Curious Jo thought.

Bookshop and Bombalini were coordinating with MI5 on the arms find, she knew that Bombalini was feeding back to Europol and MI6, as the source was identified in Europe and had been tracked on the cross channel ferries, but nobody knew where they were going and for what. Jack had suggested military involvement but that was still in the realms of speculation, and Jack's speculation at that. They had some of the protagonists and there was a good opportunity to get some serious intelligence from them. This was being handled by MI5 and the Harbour Police, much to the relief of Jo Jums. She knew she would get the feedback anyway and could do without the hassle of those particular territorial and jurisdictional rights.

Wally was on site with the uniforms, liaising with the RSPCA on animal welfare. She had heard already that Jack had shot two dogs in the fighting ring and one was only wounded. That dog had been humanely put down. She wondered how Jack would feel about this; she knew it eventually would strike him and made a mental note to talk to Jackie. She knew also Jack hated this type of dog, the pit bulls, and often talked about the growing number of the breed in Portsmouth, even talked of his suspicions that pit fighting may be happening. But even he did not blame the dogs but the characters that had them, bred them, strutted the streets with them; intimidating in their shared hostility and arrogance.

Via Father Mike and Frankie, she had sorted the intelligence priorities. She saw now why they had wanted a team on the ground. Ordinarily they would have spent the first few hours arguing a turf war and who should be running the investigation. With Jo Jums on board and presumably Jack before her, this was no longer a problem. Smart she thought to herself, very clever Jack.

* * *

Jack was irritating Mandy outside ICU, moaning and wiggling his wet trousers, trying to keep the cold soggy material off his skin. Jolene came out from seeing Alice.

'Jack?' Mandy looked at Jolene and thought she could see where Alice's good looks came from. She also noticed an exchange between her and Jack.

'Jols, how is she?' Jack said.

Jolene gestured with her head to follow. 'She's proper awake now, quite upset and she wants to see you. And Jack?'

'Jols?'

'A word wiv you first please?' Jolene said, accompanied with an obscure head gesture.

'S'okay Jols, you can talk in front of Amanda...'

'It's personal Jack.'

'Thought it might be, I have no secrets from Amanda.' Mandy looked to see if his nose grew, it didn't and she relaxed a little as a consequence.

'It's more a secret of mine, but if you're sure?' Jack nodded. 'Okay, you asked for it. Alice is your daughter and she knows it...'

Jolene gabbled, speaking rapidly in her Pompey tones, '...has done for a while, it's why she went in the filf, why she has always wanted to be near you.' You could hear a pin drop. 'I know you've never known it, but there's a bond and you've sensed it, right?'

Mandy answered for him. 'I've seen it, and it explains a lot.' Jack turned to both women, still speechless, his mouth half agape, not sure how he was feeling.

'The fing is Jack, she's about to tell Nobby. He's been asking who her fucking dad was, on and bleedin on, the tosser, and he's now insisting that her dad be told, that he would want to be 'ere wiv 'er. She'll tell him Jack cause she's not 'erself. She knows what you just did for her in that dog pit, and now, 'eaven fuckin' 'elp us all, she wants somfing more. She's finking crazy Jack, she's bleedin' mad wiv it.'

Jack still looked stunned but Mandy knew her man and could already see the tears welling. She put her hand over his and squeezed. 'Go in Jack. Would you like me with you?'

'Jolene, why didn't you say?' he said, ignoring Mandy.

'You fucking dipstick, you was a serious filf and I was part of this family...' She waved her arms about, as if this was all the explanation that was needed.

Jolene knew Jack and he was of course satisfied with that explanation, but Mandy wasn't, she was doing maths and she looked at Jack.

'You were married.'

'Separated, Alana was three, I wanted to be by the sea after I retired from MI5, and Kate wanted to stay in London.' Jack flicked his hands recalling the despair. 'After about three years or so, she'd seen a job she wanted in Portsmouth Social Services and got it,' he said, shaking his head and looking at the floor. 'She didn't come down for me. I'd bought that house already and it was special to me, I loved it. Kate wanted to move somewhere else but I said no; she never liked it there.'

'My God and I thought that house was you and Kate,' Mandy said.

'I know, I saw but didn't know how to say.'

Jolene broke up the trance between the two. 'Jack she wants to see yer.'

He nodded, 'Okay; Amanda?' She put her arm into his crooked elbow, squashed him to her and he yelped.

'Oh sorry, I'd forgotten about your shoulder.'

He hadn't, and it was hurting like mad. He kept his jacket covering the wound that had reopened; he could sort that later. They made their way to the bed, Jack's shoes squelching on the polished floor and the nurse scolding at the state of him and urging only two at a time, as if they didn't know that. Jack talked her out of it, telling her he had something important to say and it needed the three of them.

Smiling at Jack, the nurse decided to ignore his state of dress and the rules.

'Just a few minutes, seeing as you're a regular here.'

They quietly chuckled, except Jack who was holding back his sobs. He had made eye contact with Alice, her head and neck swathed in bandages, just a pair of red fulsome spanner lips and intense blue eyes, just like Jack's Mandy thought, and dulled only slightly by the painkillers. She also thought she could see it now, the girl following after him all the time, her height, her behaviour, couldn't understand the kissing but saved that for later. Mandy had always sensed a connection between them. Jack of course sensed something but left it at that, never pushed; feckin' typical. He approached the bed. Nobby was standing on the other side and watched his every movement. Mandy stood back, ready if needed, but she was a spectator here. Jack pulled a chair up but didn't sit, looked away for a short time, leaned and nicked a grape from the next door bed and sucked on it. She willed him to bite the bloody fruit. He looked uncomfortable, didn't know what to say; a gobstopper grape.

'Dad, I'm sorry.' The tears were falling freely, dampening Alice's bandages as her dad's own tears made the tortured journey down his wrinkled and ravaged cheek. Jack gulped and choked on the grape, coughed and looked into her eyes, took the grape out and put into his pocket. His body language and his eye were saying all that Alice needed, but Nobby looked like he wanted an explanation and was likely to insist. Mandy tugged Nobby's arm and he went with her. She took him outside where Jolene was waiting, Nobby looking back at Jack, looking for confirmation of an absurd notion.

Jolene approached, unsubtly blousy.

'Nobby, Jack is Alice's dad and I've just told 'im.'

Mandy turned to look at Jack; he'd still not sat down and was just looking at Alice, hovering over her.

'I'm going back to Jack. Nobby can you give us a few minutes please?'

Nobby went into Jolene's shoulder. 'We lost the baby,' he said and cried.

The blousy, brassy, warm and loving tart with a heart, hugged the lad before her. 'I know love, I know. I'm so sorry.'

Mandy broke the trance between dad and daughter.

'Hello Alice, are you happy about having a dickhead as a dad?' The corners of Alice's mouth turned upwards, the hint of a smile, and she winced as Mandy continued, 'Well, I can see you've inherited his wincing, you poor girl.' They both laughed and Alice's eyes brightened. 'Can I say welcome to the family?' The eyes glistened and the tears increased the intensity of the glassy blue, just like his she thought. Jack immediately dabbed them with his handkerchief.

'Jack put that filthy thing away!' Alice laughed again. Jack sniffed, used his hankie, it looked okay to him. Mandy looked at him, his face looked ravaged but had an energy too, a mixture of pleasure and worry, a strong hint of shock, and a rigid streak of pride.

'Jack, I'm sorry...'

'Don't you dare call me Jack, its dad now.' She laughed and more tears flowed. 'You need to meet your brother and sister and I need to have a serious word with Nobby, interfering with my girl. Too late to get you into a nunnery I suppose.'

'The baby Jack...dad...I lost it.'

'I know and I was going to be number one Godfather and Grandfather which would top Kipper I suppose, but shut up and get better...you will have time and Nobby's a good lad.'

'He won't want me like this dad.' She tried to raise her hands and he noticed for the first time they were bandaged; defence wounds he surmised.

'He's not that superficial Alice, you know that don't you? What you're thinking is in your own head, not his.' Nobby was back, he looked at Jack and clearly didn't know what to say. Jack signalled for him to follow. He did and Mandy left them to it, and sat on the chair he had pulled up and not sat on.

'I'm sorry Mandy, I knew and have wanted to work with him all the time since I have known. I wanted just to be close to him.'

'I know Alice and you have a good dad, but you do know he will embarrass you and become a right royal pain in the arse now he knows don't you?'

Alice nodded and was in pain. 'Mandy can you get a nurse please, I'm hurting.'

Mandy stood, looked around for the nurse then pressed the buzzer that was hanging there.

'You will be okay Alice and please don't worry about a thing, you did what Jack would have done and look how he's gotten away with it all of his life. I will make sure you are okay, but please, never again, yeah?' The nurse was there. 'She's in pain nurse.'

The nurse acknowledged and showed Alice the morphine controller and pressed it for her. Jack was back with Nobby. They'd had their man-to-man chat, she would have to sort that later Mandy thought, burst Jack's bubble, inject some sense into Nobby and find out what psychobabble Jack had imparted as masculine wisdom from upon high.

'Alice, darling, you poor love.'

Jack looked back and could see the Commander with his arm around his son, Dorothy now at the bedside opposite Jack; this is good for Alice, Jack thought. The nurse looked like she was ready to give up on the rules.

Mandy shushed the nurse. 'We are going now Alice, I need to get Jack checked at casualty, he thinks I can't see the blood stain under his jacket. We will be up tomorrow okay?'

Alice nodded and Jack looked like he wanted to kiss her but didn't know how, where, or if he should, in the end he whispered to her, 'I'm right proud you are my daughter. We have time to make up, have you been to the zoo yet? I'll teach you to whistle...can you whistle?'

Mandy tugged Jack on his good arm and they left, Alice laughing as her dad wiggled his fingers like saying bye-bye to Meesh. Mandy looked at him and was proud too, it felt good that they loved each other, but couldn't help wondering how many more revelations were still to come.

Chapter 24

Dawn, and it was wide awake club for the both of them. Mandy could hear Jimbo downstairs briefing Wilf on the nights events; Jimbo had remained on the scene with the harbour police.

They got up with overt wincing from Jack and rolled eyes from Mandy, and they went down in their dressing gowns. Jack could smell his coffee pot and was immediately charged, as though the caffeine was entering his body through his olfactory organ. They sat at the table in the dining room and a shuffling and dishevelled Wilf brought coffee for himself and Jack, and tea in mugs for Jimbo and Mandy.

'What have we got Jimbo?' Jack was straight in and Mandy wondered why she ever worried about him.

Jimbo rubbed his red eyes. 'Not massive...' he drank some tea, relished its warmth and strength, '...but nevertheless enough of a cache to cause some mayhem.'

'Anyone talking?' Mandy chipped in.

'Not yet, they've been shipped up to London.'

'Same type of guns used on the Banker?'

Jimbo nodded again, sipping more of his tea. 'It's the source alright, and Del thinks we can get Cyrano to pull the drugs bust in now; we have enough on them all for the arms as well, so standby for some serious pats on the back for CP and Cyrano's team.'

The drugs bust was a result of Jack's suspicions (and Seb's confirmation) that some of the recent events were being funded by drug money. They had discovered drugs being shipped into Portsmouth within the frames of bicycles carried on the backs of domestic vehicles using the cross channel ferries. MI5 wanted to hold off on the bust in order to follow the drugs trail and find the source of the gun running.

'So much for staying under the radar. We will get some Intel from Len I suppose, once he knows we have the drugs and arms sewn up, so watch this space. I will need to talk with Mike and Del on what we release to the media.'

'I'm not sure Del's your man there Jack, he's not overly keen on the plan you set in motion, felt you bamboozled it past him with Samuels,' Jimbo said. 'Are you going into the station?'

'Yeah, except I'm dropping Jack at the hospital first,' Mandy replied.

Jimbo nodded and Wilf went off to the spare room just as Jackie came down.

'Jack, how are you?'

'You mean apart from him becoming a father last night?' Mandy chortled.

Jackie turned to Mandy, looking stunned; Jimbo had the same look and Wilf reappeared.

'I knew you were good Jack but that's Immaculate Conception stuff isn't it?' Jackie could not contain herself, 'Have you mentioned this to Father Mike, you could have some serious flack coming your way.'

'Watch it,' Jack said, 'we hold very strong views on that sort of talk in the Church of Egypt.'

Wilf laughed from the stairs and turning to trudge back up, he said, 'Tell me later, I'm shagged, congratulations Jack...and Mandy I suppose.'

Jackie looked to Mandy for an explanation, knowing it would take an age to get the salient points from Jack, if ever. Mandy did explain and jaws hit the table, except for Jack who looked like he was ready to strut his stuff, peacock fashion. Mandy and Jackie went to the kitchen to brew more tea and coffee and were making toast as Mike came through the back door; no knock, he just barged in. It irritated Mandy, but Jack encouraged this notion of the old days, "in and out of people's houses" or some such clap trap.

'Morning girls, congratulations Mandy, where's the new dad?'

'Figured you would find out, not much gets past you does it?' Mandy said.

'Direct line love.' Mike looked heavenwards, collected a demitasse, nicked a bit of buttered toast and bounced into the dining room, chomping as he went.

They could hear the hail fella well met mirth and accompanied back-slapping from in the kitchen.

'Have some toast before we go in Jacks, it might be the only chance we'll get; they look hungry to me,' Mandy said. Jackie was already eating some buttered toast whilst spreading marmalade on another slice for herself. 'Jackie, what about Jack?' Mandy pressed for answers to concerns that had plagued her sleep and now her waking moments.

Jackie gulped some tea. 'Watch and see...I hear he was in the water again, cold, wet, shots fired and pain from his shoulder I would imagine, and he survived. I want to talk to him about that, see how he felt. It's a case of working through all of his troubled areas and when he can see that it's okay, he will be okay, and slowly he will mend. I'm not sure that it's standard therapy to go back into the line of fire, but then again, I'm not sure how we will keep him out of it, short of locking him up.'

Mandy took it all in and nodded, looked like she was considering the locking up bit, and they smiled at each other; a shared thought.

'Should have stuck with me Mandy, I'm a lot less complicated!'

Mandy hugged Jackie. 'Thanks for everything Jackie and I'm sorry I can't give you what you want.'

'Give her what she wants Amanda?'

Jack, like Mike, had bounced into the kitchen like feckin' Tigger. 'Feck off plonker, and take this toast with you,' Mandy said, and handed Jack a pile of toast knowing it would all be gone by the time they got in.

'What a turn up, Alice being Jack's daughter,' Jackie said, securing more toast for herself.

'I knew there was something but couldn't put my finger on it. The strange thing is Jack knew something as well. Ever since she appeared at the station he'd taken a liking to the girl, pushed her along, guided her - and I suppose, protected her. Look at what he did with Dorothy, getting her off Alice's back about Nobby. Not sure how Nobby will feel about Jack as a father in law!' They giggled.

'Number one father-in-law,' Jackie said, and they giggled some more.

* * *

The team, not unexpectedly, were exhausted, red eyes rubbed raw. Jo felt like she had grit under her eyelids and longed for her bed, but knew this would not happen until a lot later in the day. She had briefed the Commander and settled the nerves of the other nicks in Portsmouth, their senior officers would all be getting calls from the Home Office and things would eventually go back to normal.

She looked up from her desk.

'Mandy! Didn't expect you yet, how are you and how's Jack? Actually, where is Jack?'

Mandy laughed at the flurry of questions. 'We're all okay and Jack is at the hospital with his new daughter.'

'I heard, what a turn up. Did you see that one coming?'

'Not that in particular, but I always sensed something between them, didn't you?' Jo nodded, but secretly thought it was Jack being a tosspot bloke.

'Jo, I presume you have everything in hand, I suggest a meeting at midday, then get your team to their beds, do the press briefing then get off yourself.'

'I will Mandy, but there's a lot to tie up, and we still don't know how to deal with the General and his Star Chamber meeting.'

'Jack will think of something, rest assured.'

'How is he Mandy, I mean really?'

'Really? Fuck knows. One minute he's a fart in a trance and

next he's storming boats and shooting dogs... I'm off to see the Commander and the General. If dipstick comes in, let him sleep please.' And she flicked her eyes to the vacant deckchair.

* * *

Dipstick was sitting with Alice, who was asleep. Nobby had just left; he was going to get shaved and showered and go into work. Jack had tried to talk him out of it but he was adamant, and Jack knew he should let him work until he dropped. Jack also knew he would probably get into trouble for doing that but he was good at hiding, wasn't he?

'No dad, I agree with you, he needs to work, needs to be doing something, and yes you did say it out loud dad. It feels nice to be able to say dad after all this time, dad.' A sleepy voice but a welcome voice to Jack's largely ineffective jumbo ears.

'Does it love? Then keep saying it, because it's music to my ears as well.'

'I'm scared dad.'

'About Nobby, that he will still want you?'

'Yes.'

'Well you can relax on that one sweetheart, the boy's a diamond. Even before I knew you were my daughter, I would never have let him near you if I didn't know he was good enough for you.'

'Really dad?'

'Yes darlin', I've always had a soft spot for you. Couldn't understand it, thought it was sexual at first but that felt odd, couldn't explain that. Why did you kiss me in the pub?'

'Oh dad, I'm so embarrassed at that, and it was odd for me too, but I have always wanted to sit on your lap, to kiss you and smell you. I don't know, I just did and I'm sorry.'

'Don't be love, we're set straight and we'll go on from here. I've spoken with Alana and she'll be up the weekend, you can meet your sister and her bloke Josh. Michael and Winders are in Europe, so you'll have to wait for that one but if he phones in, I'll tell him. He will love it, trust me, they both will.'

'You sure?'

'Of course, they'll be delighted and you have Meesh to meet as well, you already know Martin and you do know that Dolly will be here any minute don't you?' He saw the glassiness in her eyes. 'Just you concentrate on getting well, you're to worry about nothing else. We will get you the best people and you will be looking good again in no time, trust me on that. You do trust me don't you?'

She nodded; it was painful and she winced.

'Good,' he said and turned, sensing someone behind him. 'Hello Len, Dolly.' He rose from his chair, walked past Len and hugged Dolly, then shook Len's hand.

'Alice, you know Len of course.'

Alice didn't know what to say, but she didn't have to say anything, Len did the talking, fluctuating between his now more practiced estuarine and his natural public schoolboy accent.

'Blimey this is a right turn up, you being Jack's daughter. How are you my dear?'

Jack was proud of Alice, even in this state she was in good Austin copper mode.

'Fuck off Len, this is all your doing you know,' she said.

Len turned to Jack, who was beaming pride at his daughter's intelligent response; a chip of the quite young, good looking block.

'It's okay mate, she's in a bit of a two and eight.'

He turned to Alice and Dolly. 'I want a brief word with Len, why don't you two talk about me and I'll be back in a minute.'

Len followed Jack out of the ward like he was off on a jaunt with his best pal. He got a smile from the nurses behind their desk and Jack thought, the smarmy git.

They found a coffee vending machine and stood by it. Both men would never drink the stuff dispensed from a machine like this, but it was a good place to stand.

'How d'you like the publicity Len?' Jack asked.

'I'm not responsible for the dogs Jack, I promise. I knew it was going on of course, but I wanted you to find the arms dump.'

'I know Len. So what d'you think about the coverage? I think it's doing the trick.'

'Yes, yes Jack, it's very good, but what happens next?'

'Next step is the big one, back-tracking by government in response to public opinion and we have to give them a route out of their own shite, something that will allow them to save their political double faces. You need to press a few of those buttons you've been holding onto, the military and some more leaks from the financial institutions, just to spice it up and nudge it along. I thought I had that one taped but someone got to him. You dealt with that, nicely handled by the way.'

Len beamed again, he was enjoying himself; this was the best time he had ever had with Jack, and by a coffee vending machine!

'I have a few more irons in the fire. Have you had breakfast Jack?' Len said, trying to look casual and leaning on the vending machine but frequently looking to see if it stained the shoulder of his tweed jacket.

'No,' Jack replied, 'I fancy a greasy spoon, ever been to one of them Len?'

'If that is what you would like Jack, then I would too, a new experience lubbly jubbly!' Len rubbed his hands together and it was all Jack could do to contain his laughter.

'Hang on a mo, I want to say goodbye to Alice.' He went back into ICU, put his arm around Dolly and leaned over to kiss the eyelids of Alice.

'Gotta go darlin', I'll be back as soon as I've done what I have to do wiv Len, love you sweetheart.'

'Thanks dad.'

'No, I was talking to Dolly.' The three of them laughed, he leaned further over and whispered to Alice, 'And so it starts darlin', time to wind you up like the rest of me kids.' He kissed Alice's ear, hugged Dolly, and went to join Len.

Chapter 25

Mandy finished her meeting then drove to the hospital to see Alice and to make sure Jack had a lift. Dolly was in the ICU waiting area while they moved Alice to a side ward. They sat together, exchanged pleasantries, the shock of Alice being Jack's daughter and shared a laugh.

'Jack with Alice?' Mandy casually enquired.

'No, he went off with that chap you call Norafarty,' Dolly replied matter of factly.

'What, Len? Bugger that turnip, where'd he go Dolly?'

She shrugged her shoulders. 'Sorry love, he didn't say. Just said he'd be back up to Alice when he'd done what he needed to do.'

'Dolly, I have to go, give my love to Alice and say I have to go after her drip of a dad, she'll understand.'

'So do I babes, I'm sure he'll be okay though...' Dolly's reply drifted as Mandy dashed off, jogging down the corridor, her phone ringing out in one ear and various staff members admonishing her in the other. "Fuck off" seemed to do the trick, as she got through to Mike.

'Mike, that feckin' turnip has gone off with Len and I don't know where, was Jimbo tailing him?'

'Stone me, no,' Mike came back, 'Jimbo's on his way to your station now, Wilf's back on the computers. I'll phone Wilf. Where do you think they would go?'

'I haven't a clue and I don't know what to do,' Mandy said despairingly.

* * *

'Jean, can I have two full English's, toast and girl grey tea for me and Len, alight darlin'.'

Jean trotted off on the balls of her feet, a huge grin splashed across her bird like beak, watched by all the other copper patrons who had to stand in line at the counter for their breakfast. Jack was the only one who got the maitre d'hôtel service in the police canteen, and was waited on at table. Add the fact that they always had apple crumble and custard at lunch time because it was Jack's favourite, and there was a head of steam of resentment building that Jack was aware of but couldn't be arsed to do anything about.

'Good, now we've ordered, what about the politicians?' Jack said, 'I take it your Star Chamber has someone on it, and they have juice on the right people? Why don't we do the Members first and then let's talk Whitehall Mandarins.' Jack's face displayed a light bulb moment. 'D'you know what, I love apple crumble but I might just ask Jean if she can do a mandarin orange upside down cake, you'd like that Len.' He signalled to Jean, who of course left the frustrated queuing customers and came running.

'Jean sweetheart, Len and I might be around for lunch and I was wondering if you could do a mandarin orange upside down cake for afters?'

'Oh Jack, I could do that, would you like custard as well?'

He looked at her askance, wobbled his head and said nothing.

'Righto, custard as well,' she said, and her sparrow's bum wiggled its tail feathers with excitement.

'Jean, I love you, you know that don't you, and can I 'ave a lump to take up to me daughter in hospital please?' Jean looked concerned, confused and worried; clearly news had not reached the canteen yet of his new daughter, although that would change anytime now as Jean was headed directly for the canteen phone, frustrating the queuing coppers even more.

Just as Len was ready to get talking so the two big plates of fried eggs, sausages, bacon and tomatoes, beans, black pudding, along with toast and a refined, perfume tea, was banged down in the closest Maude, Jean's number one assistant, could come to silver service. She hugged him and cried into his cheek, 'Jack sweetheart, I've always loved that Alice and she's your daughter; can see it now, we all can.' She stood back and gave Jack a playful pinching of his cheek. 'She has the cheek of the devil, and that devil is you Jack Austin.' She blew him a kiss and trotted off to the canteen telegraph; the customers could wait for a bit longer as the apple crumble was rubbed off the chalk-board, to be replaced with mandarin orange upside down cake. Jack looked around and all eyes went down to the floor; normality resumed. Jack had a rep.

Jack tucked into his breakfast and Len tried to. He watched how Jack did it, breaking the eggs and dipping in his toast, HP sauce splurged and mixed into a mess. Len mimicked him, trying not to be revolted, and made a mental note to visit some greasy-spoon cafes to practice, along with the pub and London Pride, the thought of which made him feel even queasier. He swallowed a mouthful and held it down, breathed through his nose, then cleared his mouth with tea.

'I have already started the wheels for the MPs and the Whitehall Mandarins,' he said, desperately fighting his natural gagging reflex. 'We should get some reactions soon. Obviously I have a new boy from the City and I need to break him in, the military chap looks good for a few laughs though.'

'Good stuff Len, tuck in my son. I love to wind the military up, any chance of a bit of a dib?' Jack watched Len try to tuck in and enjoyed the thought of him being sick later and the look of confusion about what "dib" meant.

* * *

Father Mike had spoken with Del Boy who was furious with Jimbo and Wilf, but most of all with Jack.

'Find him, how hard can that be, a one-eyed feckin'cockney

barrow boy dipstick pirate.'

Mandy was in a greater quandary, and decided to go back to the station, phoning Jo Jums from her car. Jo was already organising her team to get out to Jack's favourite haunts. There was no movement and Jed asked, 'What are Jack's favourite haunts?'

'I don't know, he must have some?' she turned from her phone, 'Nobby where would you go if you were Jack?'

Nobby could hardly keep his eyes open. 'Well Ma'amsie, if I were him and knowing how Len wants to be like Jack, I would take him for a fry up breakfast.' He chortled to himself.

'What is it Nobby?'

No, it's alright it's just a thought...' And he chortled some more.

'Nobby for Christ's sake, I am rapidly regretting the kindnesses I have bestowed on you this morning after disobeying my direct orders last night,' Jo said in her Mumsey voice.

'Okay, okay, sorry, I just wondered...' and Nobby fluttered his hands as he chuckled, '...it would be just like Jack to take Len to the canteen downstairs.' They all laughed, all except Jo who picked up another phone and called Jean in the canteen. She listened and hung up and immediately went back to Mandy.

'The dipstick is in the feckin' canteen downstairs, having a fry up with Public Enemy Number One.' They could all hear Mandy laughing on the end of the phone, through humour or relief they didn't know. Jo Jums reassured Mandy she would contact Mike and call the hunt off. 'Have you had breakfast? Only you might want to join the loving couple.' Jo quickly hung up before the anticipated expletive riddled repost.

* * *

'I hope you saved me a sausage Len, because Jack never shares his fry up.'

Len stood for his gentlemanly greeting, shaking her hand; she'd fended off the European kiss.

'Hello Mandy, can I get you a chair? Please join us.' Mandy pulled up her own chair and could see Jack hurrying his huge mouthful so he could get his defence in quickly.

'Slow down Jack, it looks disgusting enough on your plate without having to watch you eat it.'

Len laughed and Mandy gave him the stare and he harrumphed a gulp, to Jack's great amusement.

'Guess what love, Len dropped by,' he said, figuring that would defuse the look Mandy had.

'No kidding Tonto.' She was defused, any residual ire that remained was mainly because she realised he could always defuse her with his eejit smiles and banter.

'Darlin' I really like his dickey dirt, got it in Jermyn Street didn't you Len?'

'I did, I get them made but you can get some off the peg that are jolly nice.' It looked like Len kicked himself for speaking posh.

Jack smiled, he'd noticed of course. 'See, I need to get some more round the houses as well. I have to go to jolly old Harley Street soon, we can take a detour to St James's can't we dearest lovely Elizabeth?' He was pleased with his *Pride and Prejudice* quote.

Mandy was immune, knew also that the Harley Street appointments were no longer an issue as Dr Samuels was content to let Jackie treat Jack, but just prior to this it was an ultimatum from MI5 that Jack get himself sorted, and they had arranged for him to see Dr Samuels in Harley Street. She also knew when to follow a suggested lead from Jack.

'I think we can do that, have we got some dates sorted?'

'Got to do that, I also thought when we're up there we could meet Len, lunch or even dinner after the theatre, better still a Prom concert, I love the Proms; that be okay, eh Len?'

Len radiated happiness with just a shade of mild displeasure that Mandy would be joining them, but he thought he could deal with that.

'Jack I would love that. I will sort out some lovely seafood restaurants. We could have lunch at an Oyster bar, with champagne, you can see your trick cyclist...' he waited for Jack's approval at his use of slang, got it with a nod, '...then we can paint la ville rouge.' Mildly displeased that he had let the estuarine, working class accent and idioms slip again. He clapped his damp, camp hands together with joy, didn't see Jack nick one of his sausages but Mandy had. She also knew Len would be grateful.

'How long you down for Len?' Jack asked, chewing, and Mandy averted her gaze back to Len.

'I'm going back to town in a minute, unless you decide to nick me. Are you going to do that Jack?'

'Not today Josephine, I'm having far too much fun. What you doing tomorrow night?'

'I've nothing planned.'

'Brilliant, fancy winding up some stiff military raspberry tarts?'

'What do you mean?' Len asked, befuddled, thinking cakes.

Jack chuckled and leaned back in his chair, as if visualising a humorous situation.

'The feckin' General has been asked to join some fart-faced committee for retired military eeejits...' It was like Jack had another thought. 'Bet Pugwash will be there, and other military bigwig martinets. Come on Len, let's wind em up? I'd love to see Pugwash's face when he sees you.' Jack shook with laughter and followed this with some major wincing, feeling his shoulder.

Pugwash was Captain John Littleman RN, formerly the Big Society twat, Chairman of the community policing committee, with whom Jack had had a serious altercation. This was exacerbated when it was leaked to the national news media (by Jack of course) that Portsmouth CID called the Captain, Pugwash, after the old cardboard cut-out kid's cartoon of the 1960's. Jack had even heard that the Navy guys called him Pugwash as well now; his life's work complete.

'Stop being a baby with your wincing and yes that sounds like a hoot, are we going to be at their table?' Len replied, excited.

'Brilliant Len, I'll see if I can wangle something. Shite this is going to be brilliant, you eating that bacon?'

Mandy rolled her eyes as Jack fished his fingers around in Len's beans for the neglected bacon. She stopped him wiping his fingers on his trousers and passed him a paper napkin. He blew his nose on it which, after a short while, Mandy reasoned was better than him getting his handkerchief out, but then he handed the full, squidgy green tissue back to her.

Jack saw Len off from the car park, waving like he was seeing off a dear and close member of his family. Mandy waited in reception and tapped her foot, watching through the glazed screen, having to listen to Hissing Sid laughing and enjoying the performance from Jack, and then Mandy's clear irritation at Jack's energised state as he returned.

'Jack, am I supposed to go along with this farce tomorrow night?'

He made his way past her to the stairs. 'Come on love,' he beckoned her and she followed. He allowed her to pass and he took up his dirty old man station, watching her backside as it ascended. She knew better than to tackle him on anything while he was concentrating. She went into her office and he followed, they both stood by the window. It looked like being a beautiful day, the atrocious weather of yesterday forgotten and the sky exuding benign warmth and good feelings. He put his good arm around her waist, sidled to be behind her, snuggled his chin into her neck; it felt smooth so soon after a morning shave. Her irritation was slowly replaced by fluttery butterflies as she responded to his pressing against her.

'Jack what are you up to?'

'I'm trying to stop you being irritated by me.'

'Okay, well you've done that,' she laughed. 'Now what are you really up to?' She turned to face him, they kissed, lightly at first then the intensity increased, it seemed like a while since they had engaged with passion. She even thought the lustre was wearing off for him, but he did have a bullet wound in his shoulder. She had to try to stop these irrational thoughts, the nagging feelings of doubt.

He pulled away. 'I think I know how to end this.' He left the statement hanging as she responded to the knock on the door.

'Good, you are normal, we need to talk.'

'Jo Jums, certainly, fire away.'

'Well I was rather hoping you would start Jack, maybe tell me what really happened last night, but I suppose I am mainly intrigued, a DCI having a fry up with public enemy number one in the police canteen and then waving him goodbye and not nicking him?' She waited but got no reply. 'Jack, please tell us what you are thinking?'

He sat down in the PVC chair, Mandy sat in her swivelley comfy office chair and swivelled, while Jo leaned against the wall. Jack told them, left out a few of the juicy parts he would have to keep to himself for the time being, and left Jo and Mandy to cogitate while he went to see the General.

'Did he say "cogitate"?' Jo said, wondering whether to be amazed at his expanding vocabulary or the fact that he got something right.

Chapter 26

'Well I didn't see that one coming but it explains a lot,' Jack said.

'Jack, can I really do that?'

'General, my old China, you've been done up like a kipper, very cleverly snared. Your sense of duty has been abused, but as you said yourself the other day, "You're fucked if you do and fucked if you don't", so let's go out fighting eh?'

The General nodded, looked like he wanted to pace the floor and was sure he never said "fucked". Jack gave him his hand and helped him up. They both went to the window, Jack waiting for the General to meet him there and steady himself.

'Don't tell anyone,' Jack said, 'and react surprised at seeing Len and me turning up tomorrow. Invite us to join you as a natural course of events, a senior police officer and a West End, London Solicitor. Make it as natural as you can, then leave the rest to me. I want to talk to a few of your comrades in retirement and arms. Back me up, okay?'

The General looked nervous, reluctant, but Jack had put it to him very clearly. He was well and truly trapped and his own vanity had been the catalyst, as well as the government rhetoric convincing him of his duty to the Big Society. Sadly the shine had become somewhat tarnished.

* * *

'Mike, report what you want to Del Boy but we are closing in. I want you to take Mandy to the Gravediggers tomorrow evening. John Sexton always comes back to his family for Wednesday evening and he is likely to want to spend that evening in Jonas's pub.'

He explained for the benefit of Mandy, that Jonas was the eldest son of the banker, Seb's guardian older brother. When they had bought the cemetery and Sexton House, John Sexton had also bought the pub opposite the cemetery for his other son, who set up a micro-brewery, and his middle daughter, Pansy, and her partner Angel, ran the Gravediggers bed and breakfast.

'I've spoken with Seb and he will have spoken to his dad by the time you get there. So relax-a-cat; he brews a good pint and I recommend the seafood stew,' he said to Mandy, and smacked his lips at the thought of it.

* * *

'You should really have custard with this.' Jack was feeding mandarin orange, upside down cake to Alice. She was enjoying it.

'I saw that dad.'

'What? I have to test it. What sort of dad would I be if I didn't test it for you?'

Mandy had dropped him off, parked the car and made her way to the ward, and was watching from the door of the small side room. She smiled and thought to herself how easily Jack had slipped into his role. She allowed herself a brief fantasy of what it would have been like if she had had children with Jack. She yearned for him and it was like her love was not being requited. She recognised it for what it was; she was jealous. Up until yesterday she had Jack to herself, shared momentarily with his children, Meesh and Martin; but she could see him working hard to make a bond with Alice. She knew she had to work on this one; more stinking thinking.

Leaving the hospital, Jack phoned Jo from the car.

'You don't need us back do you Jo?'

Mandy looked at him.

Jo was naturally irritated. 'Well apart from all the unanswered questions no. I'm going to have to do the news conference at five thirty and don't know what to say; so no, you go off and relax.'

'Jo Jums, I have to spend some quality time with Mandy. Brief the press on the dog fight only. Clear the rest with Del Boy, but if the subject of the arms gets raised, pass it off to the Gnome Office. And Jo, I want you to labour that there is a lot happening and we are undermanned, the situation last night could have been a lot worse than it eventually was, blah, blah.'

'Okay Jack, we've had feedback from Len, so the team is busy following that and Jack...'

'What love?'

'I'm sorry for being selfish, you need to nurse your wounds, have some time with Mandy and get used to having a new daughter.'

'You forgot something Jo.'

'What's that?'

'Len, he loves me too you know.'

'Feck off Jack.'

Jack had his hand on Mandy's leg while she drove. 'We have so much to talk about, but I want to take you to bed and I will need you to be very gentle with me. I've booked The *Bistro Montparnasse* for us for tonight; it's just you and me and your scarlet dress if you wouldn't mind my darlin'.'

* * *

The press conference was noisy and heated and well handled by Jo Jums, all the points were covered, no balls were dropped and they were out and away after just a half hour. Jo wrapped up her stuff, the CP room was empty. She looked around and surveyed her territory and felt a sense of great pride and thought, thank you Jack. Then left to get stuck into her husband.

* * *

It was midday before the CP room began to fill up. It was routine stuff on the boards for the day, if you could call all that had happened routine. Jo Jums addressed the team

'Okay guys listen up,' Jo called the meeting to order, 'Jack and Mandy will not be in today, they are up to some really stupid stuff tonight so we may be needed to help out, but in the meantime let's get started on the admin and square away events so we are ready.' There were murmurs of displeasure at the admin, tinged with jittery nerves at the potential for excitement, not knowing what it was or would be, but if Jack was involved it could be good.

* * *

The weather had completely redeemed itself from the foul offerings of Monday. The sun beamed behind the edges of the curtains in their bedroom and they felt a vague guilt that they should be out enjoying it, but the sinful pleasure of a day in bed had won through. Jack had warmly suggested Mandy should stay in bed, he would bring the breakfast (that was a late lunch), and Mandy relished the thought until she heard the tray crash on the stairs.

She got up and went to see what had happened, knowing in her heart that she should have done this anyway.

'I don't suppose it occurred to any of you bozos to carry the tray for one armed, one eyed Dick here?' Wilf and Jimbo withered under her stare.

The logic seemed only then to dawn on all three of the men as Jack was toying with the toast on the stairs with his bare toes, watching it tumble down one, and then two steps, like a slinky. She decided not to even try to fathom what was going through their minds; she thought she heard Jack whisper "goal".

'Leave this to us Mandy. Wilf, you get some more breakfast and I will clear this up.'

'Thank you Jimbo, sense at last. Come on Jack.'

He followed, enjoying the sight of Mandy in her silk things, knew there was a name for them, but it was irrelevant; she looked gorgeous in them. They shared a noisy shower and she marvelled to herself how her inhibitions had all but dissipated. She looked at Jack as they caressed under the cascading water; nope, he'd never had any.

As they dressed later, Mandy could hear Mike downstairs.

'Mike's here, go and talk to him while I finish off.'

'He's here, how'd you...?'

'Just one thing,' she said smiling.

'Hearing aids?'

'Hearing aids. And Jack, are you not wearing your shoulder harness this evening?'

'No, it's feeling okay and I want to be a little freer tonight.'

She didn't know whether to believe him but dismissed it, secure in the knowledge that his nose had not grown. She laughed to herself but felt the familiar butterflies, this had shite written all over it, but relaxed as Jimbo would be monitoring Jack, and Wilf was on her and Mike. Another spook, Tony, was looking after the house. She marvelled that all of this seemed normal to her.

She watched her eeejit of a man disappear around the bedroom door, doing his Charlie Chaplin leg flick as he went. She loved him and loved also that he had stood at the door to watch her face as she processed the latest information, only leaving as Chaplin when she stuck her tongue out. She ignored the very rude hand gesture, only slightly titillated – save that for tonight.

'Mike, you meet Len, I'm off with this vision of loveliness,' Jack said. Mandy stood on the stair, making half twists of display, whilst looking to see if they had got the butter stains out of the carpet; they hadn't and the tea marks were still there as well.

'Multi-tasking love – good,' Jack said and she smiled, ignoring the stained stair carpet and enjoyed basking in the warmth of Jack's admiring looks.

'It's only jeans and a blouse.' But she could see the love in Jack's eye and also enjoyed the circumspect glances from Wilf, Jimbo and Tony.

Jack argued with Mike that he would drop them off and then take the taxi onto *The Pembroke* pub in Old Portsmouth. It was a testament to the strength of the Father that Mandy and Mike said goodbye to Jack and Jimbo, and watched them disappear into the pub. As the door was slowly closing behind him she heard, "Len, what you 'aving? General didn't know this was a watering hole of yours?"

'You know he would rather be with you and having a pint of the glorious Gravediggers ale and seafood stew,' Mike said.

Mandy just hemmed and focused on what she had to do.

Chapter 27

'Gawd blimey, this the whole military high command? ...'cept you Pugwash of course.' Jack folded over laughing. 'I 'eard you guys were having cut backs, a bit like us, but this takes the ship's biscuit, ward room shut is it, no pink gins?' Jack roared more laughter.

The General looked nervous and Pugwash was fuming, the glowing light from the bar bringing out his rusty features, highlighting his clenched jaw. The Captain was a tall and slender man with absolutely no presence, a receding chin contributed to that, and Jack always thought that if Pugwash had not been an arrogant martinet shite, this would serve his simpering manner well; a veritable modern day Uriah Heap, just lacking in the 'umble.

The General clanked to a stand, to proffer a handshake and to get Len and Jack a drink, he was tugged on the sleeve by a slight man with perfectly coifed fair hair. The General introduced Admiral Chit Wesley who stood. Jack leaned over the table, his hip brushing Pugwash's face, disappointed that he never could manage a fart when he wanted, and was reminded of his Uncle Davey who could summon one on demand.

'Bet they call you *Shit Wesley* eh?' he said, willing his bowels to comply.

The Admiral shook Jack's hand but could not stop looking at Len, who completely ignored the new Star Chamber member, then falteringly he replied, 'No, it's Admiral.'

'Bit like Star Trek eh?'

The Admiral looked to the General and then to the other stuffed shirts sitting around the table, seeking assistance; he got none.

'Why are we having a drink in this pub again Colonel?' he asked the General.

He got no reply, was forced to be introduced formerly to one Lionel Thackeray, or the "Shyster from London" as Jack called Len. 'Did Pugwash up like a kipper, eh?' And Jack and Len shared a guffaw as Jack slapped Pugwash on the back. 'Still, all water under the ship's bridge now eh, Pugs?'

As Jack stirred shit, Len supplied pints of ale to the table.

'Shove up Pugwash, alright if we join you Herr General?' The General spluttered, also as instructed, but acquiesced with an "Aheeemm".

Len squashed in, and now all of them were on their third pint of strong ale. Len started to look squiffy, as did the others, except the General (but he would wobble when he stood anyway).

'Well this is nice, so what's happening then? Len's down for a case and so we got together for a couple of pints and thought we'd have a curry. What you chaps doing, fancy a Ruby?'

More spluttering from the General, Admiral, Pugwash and the two other officers that the General had not got around to introducing; it was difficult to see if they were all embarrassed or flushed with the ale.

'Colonel Walsh, Marines and Wing Commander Bertie Boakes,' the General said, finally introducing the other officers.

Jack looked at the men and encouraged them to drink up. 'Oi Shit, your round I think,' and shouted to the landlord, 'Bonkers, another round, the Admiral's in the chair.' Bonkers gave a Benny Hill salute and several of the punters on bar stools joined Jack in a discordant whistle, to welcome Chit Wesley to the bar. Jack followed, slapped him on his diminutive back.

'This is good eh?' and he raised his dead, non-existent eyebrow with his finger, bent and guffawed his beery breath right into the Admiral's nose, enjoying the recoiling response.

He watched as the Admiral passed the pints around to his fellow officers and then handed a pint to Jack. A few drinks later and Pugwash was more flushed than when Mandy had pushed him across a crowded bar and given him what for, and the General looked blissfully happy, the beer having clearly eased his nerves. The Wing Commander was flying, the Marine Colonel was looking sick and Jack thought he must be in the band; trumpet probably. The Admiral looked pissed as a ship's rat and seriously cheesed off.

'Right we must go, niiiize to 'ave a, met you, err, Inz-pector and you, Lionel or izit Len?' The Admiral slurred.

'Chit lad, drink up, I haven't bought my round yet.'

'No, no I must inthisssst, we have a dinner engagement in the Woyal Naval 'fficers Club and we are late.'

Jack was amused at the slurred defiance of the diminutive Admiral, then thought Nelson was small.

The General clanked to a wobbly stand. 'Fellow officers, we will retire to the club.' He looked at Jack and Len. 'I invite the Detective Inspector and the London Shyster...' he looked pleased with himself for that one, '...to join us. We can have a drink at the bar and honour will be satisfied. Bertie it will be your round, then yours Pugwash, and then a light repast. Are you up for that Jane, Len?'

Jimbo smiled, he had thoroughly enjoyed himself, even though he had only had a lime cordial and sparkling water. He sucked his lime and followed the revellers, helping the General along, who seemed to be surprised to see him. Jimbo winked and the General felt even more reassured.

Chapter 28

'I'll have a dry white wine.'

'They only have the ale that Jonas brews himself,' Mike said.

'What?'

'A half for Mandy Jonas and a pint for me please,' Mike called out. The statuesque man, with chiselled features and dark, almost black, sunken eyes, responded with a broad smile that softened all the previous edges. Mandy reappraised the man she thought originally to be a gypsy. He was handsome, a veritable Heathcliffe, which was appropriate as this pub was like stepping back in time. She felt the flutters of sexual attraction and Mike noticed; she frowned at his childish smirk.

'Righto Father,' Jonas said and went to the back bar and poured from tapped wooden barrels. The ale shone clear and deep, a dark amber refracting the light from guttering candles on the counter.

'Some place eh?'

'That's an understatement Mike. No electricity?' Mandy replied.

'Not in the bar, Jonas has it outside for the micro-brewery of course and the kitchen, but here it is meant to be old, Victorian I imagine, and if you don't like it then Jonas or any of the Sextons for that matter couldn't give a toss.'

She looked around her. It was like stepping back in time, two large fireplaces at each end of a wide but not very deep room, and a low ceiling. A roughly hewn tree trunk supported by beer barrels formed a bar top that had been polished smooth on the serving surface and reflected their own images, as well as the flares from candles and glowing gas mantles.

Jonas was back. 'Fish stew or beef stew?'

'Would it be a silly question to ask if you have anything else?' Mandy asked.

'It would.'

'Well, Jack said to have the fish stew, so fish stew please Jonas.' Again the smile, again the gleaming teeth, again the transformation, again Mandy's innards fluttered.

'Jack likes my fish stew,' the landlord said unnecessarily.

'Father Mike, how nice to see you!'

Mandy turned and there was a tall and well-built man, elegantly but casually dressed in pink chino type trousers and what looked like Len's attire, which it was; obligatory for posh knobs and bankers, and she knew what Jack's response to that would be as well.

'Yes but there's no need to say wanker. Mandy isn't it?'

'Mike I didn't...?' Mike nodded and John Sexton smiled the same smile as his son Jonas.

'I will get these Jonas, fish stew for me,' he turned, 'Beryl?'

Mandy then noticed the petite woman, almost in this man's shadow, obviously Beryl Sexton.

'I'll have the beef and a pint please darling.' She touched her son's hand and the giant responded with the melt.

'Shall we sit down? Jonas, bring the drinks and food over please.'

'Is Seb joining us Beryl?'

'No Mike, he would like to meet you though Mandy, so if you have some time later we can go over to his tool shed?' Mandy nodded, still taking in this unusual quirky but quaint pub, and a family who seemed incongruously matched and naturally comfortable in their environment. She had not even gotten around to the thought that she might meet an autistic lad, who seemed to solve all of Jack's crimes from a cemetery out-building, and the lad had "Cattycoombes" as Jack called them. Too much to process even for a proficient multi-tasker, so she sipped the ale and her mouth was hit with fruity sensations, just a hint of bitterness along the back edges of her tongue; a fizzle from still beer?

'My God, this is wonderful,' she remarked to no one.

Jonas melted in visage and presence, satisfied that he'd had the anticipated approval. He only served his ale, he only served fish or beef stew, and if that worried you, then you could fuck off; it's not like they needed the money. This was a hobby for Jonas; it kept him close to his family and facilitated his need and desire to watch over his vulnerable younger brother - and his Mum of course.

* * *

Jimbo watched and followed the ribald crew of military men, one ugly copper and an arch criminal lawyer, as they walked in the road, offering not very polite reposts to the motorists who dared to challenge their right to be walking where they wanted.

Despite the proximity of the Royal Naval Officers Club, just a short walk from *The Pembroke* pub, it took a good twenty minutes for them to get there and to gain entry past a recalcitrant steward. The Marine Colonel looked at Jimbo bringing up the rear, and recognising a shared military background waited to assist Jimbo past the exasperated steward. 'Paras?' he asked, and Jimbo nodded. 'Who you looking after?'

'The Inspector Sir,' Jimbo replied in a clipped military fashion.

'Well you have your hands full, and from what I have seen this evening, it is no wonder he's had so much trouble lately.' They shared a strained laugh as they walked through to the Club lounge and the Colonel got Jimbo a Ballygowan and lime and a stool at the bar. He joined his party, now furnished with pints of beer and sitting at a window table. The Wing Commander, "B,B,B,Bertie" as he was being called by everyone, had bought his round. Just the one from Pugwash to go Jack thought, and that should have them where he wanted.

Jimbo looked on and observed.

'This is nice isn't it?' Jack said, walking back from the toilets, overtly adjusting his bits and pieces. Jack looked around the table to see who actually did think this was nice. It would be unreasonable to expect Pugwash to be enjoying himself, but noticeably everyone else was. Jack targeted a seat, shuffled the stuttering Wing Commander around and sat next the diminutive Admiral.

'Shit, not enjoying yourself then?' Jack said and Len nodded to acknowledge he understood Jack's interrogation approach.

The Admiral was not enjoying himself and told Jack so, 'You Sir have gate crashed a private gathering, and I for one would very much appreciate it if you and your lawyer chum left. Now.'

'Don't be so childish Chit, Jack and Len are my guests, although Jack you will have to leave soon. I am sorry but the dinner really is private,' the General said, all as previously agreed; the evening could not look like a set-up.

The Marine Colonel was truly enjoying himself. 'Come on lads drink up. Your round Pugwash and then dinner eh?' The Colonel flicked his fingers and the irritable steward appeared and looked down his nose at Jack. Jack had seen this look many times before, his like, jumped up barrow boys, were not welcome here; so Jack tripped him up as he left and thought if only Jo could have seen that, it was a doozey.

The Colonel laughed and called after the steward, 'Cheer up man, and don't come back with that scowl.'

Jack winked at the steward and noticed Wesley supping his beer with difficulty. 'So what you up to then?' The Admiral spluttered and the Colonel had to wipe the front of his jacket. 'Blimey Admiral you're jumpy, what you plotting?' The Admiral was ashen, the alcoholic bloom had faded and Pugwash looked equally askance at Jack, like his backbone had crumbled. He subconsciously shifted his chair back, as if to distance himself from his co-conspirators; bravery personified.

'Sorry Shit, hit a nerve did I? It's the copper in me; I'm always looking at people as if they're up to no good. Bad form I know, so I apologise. The Chief knows me,' and he nodded to the General. 'Don't you Sir.'

'Jack, I do know you, and sometimes you go too far!' Also something they had agreed upon. The General had to assert himself and eventually abrade and dismiss Jack, with a request that he come to see him first thing in the morning, but not before Pugwash had bought his round; Jack and then the Colonel insisted. Len looked one degree under and disappeared to the toilets and Jack gestured with his head for Jimbo to take care of him. Pugwash did get his round and signed the chit brought to the table.

'A chit, is that where your name comes from then Admiral, "Chit" Wesley?'

The Admiral stiffened his lollopy, pansy body, patted his immaculate hair, and thus comforted, he replied, 'No, I was named Chit, my parents were stationed in India and it is an abbreviated Indian name.'

'Righto Shit, now you mention India, any of you boys up for a ruby?' They each declined and Jack stood, sinking his pint.

'Jimbo, let's get Len off the bog and you guys can get back to your pink gins and your plotting. Although I warn you, the General is Chief Constabule now and when I see him in the morning, I will question him.'

Colonel Walsh stood and escorted Jack to the lobby, catching Jimbo's attention.

'Jimbo, a moment please? Maybe you could get Len a taxi?'

Jimbo looked to Jack. 'Okay Jack?' Jack nodded, and Jimbo eventually steered a staggering Len outside to hail a cab.

The Colonel fixed his look on Jack.

'He lost his legs in a covert operation in the first Gulf war; he was a Para, as was Jimbo. Jack, I don't know what your game is but please be careful. I like you, and this is some serious shit. You know we have to do this, the military; you understand do you not?'

'I do, and if you have checked up on me, you will know I don't like the body count you military men call collateral damage. I'll tell you one other thing Colonel, if anything happens to the General, I will come after each and every one of you. He's a good man and straight, he thinks he was selected as Chief Constabule as some sort of reward or recognition.'

The Colonel stopped Jack saying any more as Jimbo returned. He signalled with a flick of his head and Jimbo stood back, a reaction not lost on Jack.

'Leave the military alone. And those Mandarin, civil service fucking bastards, leave that to the military as well.' The warning, which he was not expecting to be so blatant, registered. There was more to this than meets the eye, he thought.

Chapter 29

The dulcet baritones of the suave banker, combined with another two halves of Jonas's ale and a delicious seafood stew, had lulled Mandy into a reflective reverie and an extraordinary sense of well-being. She allowed herself a passing thought as to how Jack was getting on, when he intruded as only he could; the stuff of nightmares. A shocked drunken entry into the pub, Jack held up by the collar of his jacket by the very sober, and if Mandy was any judge, long-suffering Jimbo.

'I'm sorry Mandy; he insisted he wanted some seafood stew. I wanted a curry but of course...'

'It's okay Jimbo,' she said, pulling up a chair, 'pour him down here. How much has he had?'

'I lost count after seven pints Mandy, but it must have been eight because Bonkers bought one.'

'Who? Oh never mind,' Mandy said.

Jonas came over to the table with a bowl of fish stew and some hunks of bread, asserting, 'Fish stew, but no beer Jack, okay?'

'Yesh fankyou...' said in his country accent that was more like a drunken pirate.

John smiled, completely unfazed by Jack's drunkenness and ordered a beer for himself and Mike. Beryl took Mandy by the hand. 'Let's go and see Seb, he will be wondering where we are.'

Chapter 30

Jack had wanted her to meet John Sexton and she thought she understood why, but just what was she getting into tonight? Was Jack on his own mission after all? Was he singing his own song from their shared hymn sheet? Or was she just a part of his large orchestra and he was the feckin' soloist in a complex concerto? And why was she suddenly thinking in musical analogies? Jack had said something once at a concert, a violin concerto, Sibelius; what was it? He loved the Cadenzas, where a composer allowed the soloist scope within the score to develop his own virtuosic melodic overtures. Is that what jack was doing? Was Jack fiddle-arsing around or giving her a subtle message?

She focused again to find Sebastian Sexton stood stock still, rigid, looking at Mandy but appearing to stare through her, through the walls of his nerve-centre and off into the now dark night. Seb had the build of his mother, slight, marginally taller, probably five seven. A handsome lad, she already knew was twenty two. Knew also that he had Asperger's and this explained the detached manner of their greeting. Jack said to expect a lot of silence and shared thoughts. "Shared thoughts?" she had argued, and Jack had laughed and said she would see, and now she did. It was like Seb knew exactly what she was thinking and she, somehow, sensed his thoughts. For a lad on the autistic spectrum she felt a connection, and it must have shown in her face because Beryl touched her hand.

'Jack has made a good choice.'

Mandy felt ridiculously grateful and flattered. She wanted to tell Beryl to fuck off, thinking also about her drunken bozo, but found herself thanking Beryl. Then the thought - how can so much have gone on in this city and she has known nothing of it? How has she known Jack all this time, and known so little of the man?

Seb had not spoken and when he did, it was just, 'Good.'

Mandy had thought that ordinarily she would meet this family that had so much and resent them, and she knew this was a weakness of hers - she envied people who had the appearance of a comfortable lifestyle and an ease of living. She'd had to work so damn hard and couldn't see her life in any other way. Jack was the same and she always thought he would have been better as a market trader; she had even called him a jumped-up barrow boy in moments of frustration and anger. Actually, she thought this suited him and thought also, if he could have his life over, this is what he would like to be; singing to sell his wares, connecting with people before he sold them something. Had he sold himself to her, and if he had, what had she bought? And why did she not resent this family, or this woman Beryl? Was it because the woman clearly was devoted to her youngest son, and she empathised? Did she admire or feel jealous of the love that this woman had clearly assembled around her, the husband, sons and the daughter? All there as a family, running their lives seemingly independently but as a collective support system; Beryl must know that when it was her time to go, Seb would be well cared for. Is this what gave her the self-assured aspect, was it the knowing? What would that be like?

Beryl gently steered Mandy by the elbow to the door. She looked back and said goodbye, but Seb's back was turned and he was already at his desk, working at the computers. She noticed the Evening News opened on a desk to the side of him; it had red felt tip circles around crime stories, local mysteries. She had a crazy thought - has Jack ever solved a crime before? Now that she thought about it, he always seemed to just come up with ideas out of the blue, or he would disappear and then, when he returned, he would have an answer, with no explanation or deductive logic. Fuck me, I think that's it, he has winged his whole life, a turnip cockney barrow boy, an East End of London Spiv!

She was outside the tool shed now, walking down the Victorian patterned tiled path. The gate creaked gothic horror style and Mandy looked at Beryl.

'It's like an early door bell, we know if someone is coming and then we can see who it is on the infra-red CCTV.' Mandy swung her head to and fro but saw no cameras. 'They're there, rest assured.'

Beryl laughed, but was she laughing at the visage of Mandy, or was it the terrible wailing coming from the pub across the road?

'Oh Christ, feckin' *San Francisco*, and next it will be *Underneath the Arches*,' Mandy said.

'He sings it better than Tony Bennett,' Beryl said.

Mandy did a double take, knowing this is what people used to apparently say about Jack's Dad's, Uncle Pete, when he sang that song in the East End of London pubs. Beryl laughed again, and Mandy realised that this family knew Jack very well indeed, and she was marginally comforted but also mystified. Would she go through the rest of her life finding things out about Jack, and was she excited by the prospect?

The noise increased as Beryl opened the pub door, and even though there was an underlying and identifiable tune, it was in truth a painful wail. Beryl stood there with the door open and listened.

'He's not that bad, though in hindsight I think Tony Bennett and Uncle Peter may have the edge on him!' Mandy laughed as the two women stepped inside.

The pub had a few more patrons and they all seemed to be gathered around one the huge fireplace. Jack was leaning with his good elbow on the mantelpiece, holding court. The shelf was at his shoulder height, so his elbow and arm was horizontal and she thought he'd soon be horizontal as well; he had managed to get himself a pint of Gravediggers - how? He'd not spotted her as he sang to the ceiling with his eye closed, belting out "San Francisco" like it was going out of fashion, the gathered assembly doing the piano accompaniment, "dooodey doo dee do". It warmed Mandy to watch him and as he finished the crowd cheered and applauded and he shouted, "throw money, throw money", like his dad's Uncle Pete used to do, as he'd told her a million times before.

Then he saw her, beckoned her over and she almost sprinted to him, concerned that if he left the mantelshelf he would fall over. He brought his bad arm up, winced (which she knew had to be for effect because his whole body was probably anesthetised), and rested it over her shoulders, a leaden weight. He sighed his beery breath across her face and planted a very wet, ale sodden kiss to her lips. Before she could object he sang, looking deep into her eyes; was his eye focused? She couldn't tell.

'We've been living togevver nah for fortee years and it don't seem a day to much – ah...' he always ended each line with an 'ah' or a 'yah', *'...and there ain't a lady living in this land, that I'd swap for me dear old Duch – ah.'.*

He had tears in his eye as he sang to her. It wasn't *Underneath the Arches* that followed, instead he sung, *"If you were the only girl in the world - ah"*. He knew the words to this, he had apparently always sung this when his mum played the piano in the pubs. He sang right to Mandy, her body vibrated, the beery fumes almost causing her to pass out, even before the emotion with which he sang wrenched every fibre of her being, and the turnip then proceeded to tell everyone how much he loved this woman.

'Time to get you home I think Jack,' Mandy announced, looking to Jimbo to assist in the removal.

The crowd disapproved of Mandy's decision and called for more, receiving the Mandy stare in response. Jimbo appeared from the gloom of a corner and together with Mike, hoisted Jack back from the seat he had found, and assisted him to the door.

No longer responsible for standing or direction, he could now devote all of his energy to shouts of bonhomie and quips that he thought were really funny. John Sexton took Jack's hand, his other hand on top of his wrist, but he looked directly at Mandy and she felt the electricity of that look. He said, 'We finish this now Amanda, this one is for Jack...' he flicked his head in a laissez-faire manner, '... and the country I suppose.'

They stepped outside the pub and miraculously a taxi was waiting, but of course it was organised by Wilf who had been monitoring the perimeter all evening. 'Christ Jack, how much have you had to drink, I thought you'd arranged with the *Pembroke* landlord to have watered down beer?'

'What, and miss out on a good evening?' At least this is what they thought he said. Mandy wasn't about to waste her energy finding out.

'Let's get him home.'

Chapter 31

Jack woke, Mandy was not in bed and where she had slept felt cold. He looked at the clock, it was nearly midday. He allowed himself a big blow of air and then thought, I'll just have a bit more kip, five minutes, and he did.

'Jack.' He felt a nudge, then another nudge. 'Jack, better get up.'

'Fuck off Jimbo, it's my day off.'

'Oh, is it, I'm sorry Jack. Mandy didn't say when she left this morning.'

Jack opened his eye; the headache had gone but as he went to talk so his tongue stuck to the upper part of his mouth. Jimbo handed him a pint glass of water and he raised himself up, wincing, taking the glass and drinking it all.

'Cheers Jimbo, what's a hand?'

'What?'

'What's happening Watson; a foot?'

'What, apart from Mandy being mightily pissed off with you?'

'She is? I only 'ad a coupla beers and a bit of a sing-song.'

'A bit? Well no, that's not it. I would say it was because of all the demos that are happening around the country sucking up police resources. Or perhaps not that so much as Del Boy ranting that this was all because he had allowed you to release Len's diatribes to the Press. Or it could be the call from Samuels that she took at breakfast, asking why you had not replied about the George Medal invite. She found the letter behind the cushion of the settee. The ceremony that Samuels has accepted on your behalf is this Friday - two days time - and she hasn't got anything to wear.'

'She's got stacks of stuff Jimbo; I like her in that green dress.'

'The one she wore in Exeter?'

'Yeah that's the one, I like that one.'

'Yeah, I like that one as well. You're a lucky man, she's a handsome woman Jack, but at the moment I think you're on your own. Best get up, have a shower and clean your teeth thirty-three times. Wilf has some lunch, or brunch, for you downstairs.'

'Who took Mandy to work?'

'Tony'

'Oh, I'd forgotten him.'

'A bit like you'd forgotten the medal?'

'Yeah, a bit like that. D'you think Tony looks like Charles Hawtry ?'

'Who's Charles Hawtry?' Jimbo replied.

'Christ's tits, I thought it would be a good day today. We made real progress yesterday and I thought Mandy liked me singing, *If she was the only girl in the world* last night. Never fails that Jimbo, women are suckers for it and Jack Austin knows women.'

He looked up at Jimbo not having received the resounding vocal affirmation that he was expecting.

'Egg, chips bacon and beans, two slices and a big mug of tea; come on, or it'll get cold,' Jimbo said.

'Lubbly jubbly Jimbo.'

* * *

Mandy was in with the Commander.

'The General not in yet?'

'No, his missus phoned in, he was not feeling very well. Mentioned something about Austinitus.' Jamie laughed and Mandy groaned. 'What is it Amanda, you look like you didn't enjoy that, are you not diverted?'

'Oh yes Jamie, I am exceedingly diverted, I'm just up to my eyeballs in eeejits.'

'Ah well, I know what that is like. So we'd better move on without

Jack and the General.'

'Look Jamie, the demos, that's uniform really, let's not allow ourselves to get sucked into that now, we have so much going on.'

'The problem is that the media are calling for Community Policing to step in, not realising that it doesn't do what is says on the tin. How did it go with the General last night?'

Mandy looked at him and the Commander gulped. He knew when not to push something and that he may just have transgressed the unwritten law.

'When Jack wakes up, I hope he is able to remember how it went, but in the meantime I have a bigger problem.'

'You do, what's that?'

'Jack is being given the George Medal by the Queen this Friday, and he forgot to tell me. I found the letter stuffed behind a cushion on the settee and I have nothing to wear, and neither does Jack for that matter. I will organise a morning suit for him but then he will want to wear his tan brogues with it, because they have juice. I will argue that they do not go, and he will say that he could explain this to the Queen and she will understand. She knows about juice apparently?'

'Christ Mandy, is all of that going on in your head?'

'That and a whole lot of police stuff, so you see, I'm going to leave the demos and anything else like that to you and your uniforms; just keep Jo or me posted, okay?'

'Okay Amanda, bloody good news about Jack and the medal though, I thought that had been canned?'

Mandy gave him her best *God give me strength look*. Jamie looked like he was preparing for a full frontal onslaught and then looked relieved when she turned to leave.

'Just keep me posted Jamie please.'

Now that is what you call a near miss, he thought.

* * *

Jane
What a hoot last night
Weird hotel but a good experience
When are you up in London?
My treat
Mor.

'Mandy, message on Jane's phone.' Frankie waved the phone but gestured to the screen on the crime wall, the message was up there. 'Where is he anyway?' Frankie asked.

'He was so pissed last night I am hoping he will have sobered up for Friday when he meets the Queen,' Mandy replied, distracted by the message and finally only looking round in response to the silence.

'What? Friday? The Queen?' Jo Jums asked, struck by ineloquence as she rose from her well-organised desk and stretched her hands out like Julie Andrews on top of a mountain.

'The turnip is getting his George Medal on Friday and he forgot to tell me. I found the letter behind a cushion on the settee this morning, and when I confront him he will say, "Don't worry love, loads of time and the Queen will understand we've been busy".'

She turned and he stood there and she was pleased to see that he looked well and truly hung-over. She twisted her mouth, which gave her time to gather her thoughts and recover from the surprise of his presence. Where did he learn to creep around like that?

'How's your head?'

Jack beamed and looked back to Jimbo, half in and half out of the door; he was no fool that man. 'Did you enjoy my singing last night? I told Jimbo, works every time, women love it – Ouch!'

The sellotape roll Mandy had been holding hit him on the head. The subsequent roars of laughter meant Jack found it difficult to maintain the pretence that he didn't have a headache. The laughing changed to applause and he bowed like the eeejit he is as Mandy approached and he pretended to cower, leastways most people thought he was feigning. He kissed her, to calls of "Oooh er matron" and she was defused…again.

'Anything happening love cause I thought I might grab a nap in the deckchair before we go to the 'ospital?'

The effrontery of the man she loved knew no bounds and always amazed her. 'Well, not really anything that we would want you to worry about Jane. There are the demos; Jamie is getting uniforms to cover all of that for you. We were sort of hoping, if you didn't mind, if you felt like it that is…' Jack was beginning to suspect something was up, he had a sense for these things where women were concerned and he looked around for help, as Mandy continued, '…that you might, pretty please, brief us on what happened last night with the General.' She slapped her forehead, 'Oh Christ, I nearly forgot,' and she mock laughed, 'the Queen and the fucking medal. I have to get a dress and you have to get a morning suit. So no, not really,' and she mocked his cockney accent, 'you get yer 'ed down and 'ave a kip; you look a right two and eight sweetheart.'

'Thanks babes, I was hoping you would wear the emerald green dress, I love that on you and if you got a cream hat that would go lovely with the colour of the dress, yer skin and yer barnet. And I have a morning suit anyway. She looks really good in the green dress don't she Jimbo?'

Jimbo looked like he'd been caught in the headlights, but replied with creditable confidence, 'I thought you looked beautiful in that in Exeter. Del Boy and even Len thought so too, although Len preferred what Jack was wearing.'

The sellotape that had been retrieved by Mandy now hit Jimbo full on the forehead.

Jo interrupted the laughter as she fielded a call.

'Whoa, slow down Mike,' she listened. 'Okay, I'm with Mandy and Jack now. I'll come back to you.' She hung up, gestured with her head to follow her and went off to Mandy's office. Mandy followed and Jack tugged Frankie, thinking if he knew what he thought he knew they may need her.

'Mike received a call from someone who said he was a friend. Andrew?' Jo said, looking to Jack.

'Andrew Friend, ex SBS, steward at the club. Does he want to come in and brief us on what happened at the dinner last night?' Jack said.

'No Jack, he left a message that some Colonel has suggested that you may have pressed too many buttons last night, that certain people were going to react and it is likely to be quick and violent. We need to think what to do.'

Jack got up and called Jimbo.

'Jimbo, we may have stirred a nest of thingy's, ring Wilf and tell him to keep his 'ed down and let Del know, if Mike hasn't already; I think it's happening now.'

'What is happening now?' Jo said, looking to Jack.

'Well, the thing about putting your toe in the water is that sometimes you can't see what's below the surface and a crab may bite your bleedin' foot off.' Jack looked at Mandy and gave her his naughty boy look that he knew, secretly, she liked. 'I think we just pushed them a tad too far,' and he pinched his forefinger and thumb, to indicate that it was only a tiny tad.

Jimbo got Wilf on the phone just as Mandy took a call from Hissing Sid; she listened and put the phone down. 'Sid has just taken a call from Central, your house was just strafed Jack; Wilf is wounded, superficial, but two civilians that happened to be passing have been badly wounded. The serious incident team are on their way, so what the fuck do we do?'

Jack flicked his fingers, 'Frankie, my phone darlin'.' She tossed it to him and they looked on in wonder as he flicked the icons, pressed for a call and waited; an agitated foot tapping. He began issuing orders, 'Mandy, get Alice an armed guard up at the 'ospital; Jimbo call Bombalini, tell him to get Michael and Winders in Europe and get onto Bristol as well to ensure Alana and Josh are safe. You have a guy with Liz and Curly?'

'Yes Jack, we have and it's being reinforced as we speak. They're in the flat, the girls are safe,' Jimbo replied.

'How will you find Michael and Winders, Jack?' Mandy asked.

Jimbo answered, 'We have someone with them,' he took a call.

'They're safe Jack.'

Jack could hear a distant voice, like an ant calling from the floor, 'Jack I think you have someone on your phone.'

'Oh, fanks Frankie.' He took the call. 'Andrew thanks for the tip, bit late though, so watch out. You have your lads?' he listened, 'let's call them team B,' and Jack chuckled, 'close the club for the time being there's a good chap.' He hung up. 'Jimbo tell Del he's to meet Andrew with team B at the fun fair and to not go on the bumper cars, it's a rip-off.'

'Jack, can we skip the levity and the juvenile behaviour please, some people have just been seriously hurt,' Mandy said looking at him and she could see he was mortified. He'd put that to the back of his mind. She stood and went to him, 'It's okay love,' she said quietly, rubbing his back.

'No its not, I thought only of our children. Jimbo, Alana and Josh, are they safe?' he flicked his fingers again.

'Can't raise the cover team,' Jimbo called back, calm but with a nervy look.

Jack jumped up and narrowly avoided a collision with Mandy's nose. 'Fucking Ada, what're they up to? We expected this and they're not ready?'

'Give us time Jack,' Jimbo said back, equally agitated.

'You expected this?' Mandy shouted. Jack ignored Mandy, he paced. Mandy had not really seen him this panicky before, she assumed he would be okay when he heard that all of the kids were safe.

Jimbo took a call, nodded and closed his phone. 'They're safe Jack; Del says to focus.'

'Well fuck Del,' He continued pacing and rubbing his unshaven chin, began clicking his fingers again, disconcerted, nervous energy spilling out from his every fibre. He looked at his phone. 'Come on Len. Fucking 'ell, where are you?'

Frankie reacted, pushing herself off the wall again, 'Len? You made contact with Len?'

'Course I feckin' did, he'll know what's happening top down,

Andrew and his team will give us bottom up and then we'll have the turnips in the middle, obeying orders from their martinet, wanker senior officers.'

Mandy and Frankie made to challenge Jack when his phone went. They curtailed their comments as he pressed to receive and listened, 'Me too Len, must 'ave ate something off. Okay, okay. I said fucking okay!' He closed the call and looked to Mandy, 'Len,' he said.

'No kidding Tonto, got a headache has he? Poor sod,' Mandy said, trying to appear understanding.

Chapter 32

'Well?' Mandy said.

'Well what?' Jack said.

'Well what the feck did Len have to say?' Mandy said, and Jack sensed she was running out of patience; don't ask how he knew, it's just where women were concerned he had a seventh sense.

'He's got an 'eadache and said, as we're in London on Friday, he'd book a Promenade concert for me - well us - and the kids. And I suppose Len as well. It's one of my favourites, Tchaikovsky Violin Concerto, and guess who's playing? Only bleedin' Alexander Pantsoff!' Jack shook his head and flicked his eyebrow, unable to believe his luck.

Jack looked like he was thinking things through, Mandy was impatient, 'And?'

'And what?' Jack said.

'And what else did he say, and what are you thinking about?' Mandy said, a tad impatient Jack noticed - his uncanny ability to detect the moods of women had just proved itself again. Now all he had to do was try to develop a skill to avoid them.

'Yes that would be very helpful,' Mandy said, 'now what did Len say, and what are you thinking about, please?'

'I was wondering if Alice will be well enough to come to the Palace and we'll need to get a hotel booked for all of us, Mike could probably help there.' He looked up at Jimbo.

Jimbo reacted, 'I'll see if Mike can get a hotel then?'

'If you wouldn't mind Jimbo, how's Wilf?'

'He's okay, just a nick,' Jimbo was dialling. 'Mike...' he

disappeared out to the corridor, not because it was confidential, more in response to Mandy's look.

'Jack, focus please,' Mandy said.

'Make your feckin' mind up will you. This morning it's why haven't I told you about all that medal stuff and now I'm sorting it, you get all uppity.'

'Uppity?'

'Yeah, I think that's it...' but he did look nervous, not fully confident with "uppity". She was about to respond when his phone went again. 'Del, good, okay, no, the bumper cars are a rip off and you have to go round and around in one direction and they don't like you bumping into people case they get hurt - feck calling them dodgems, it's only good if you can bump people. Hang on Del, I've a call waiting.' Again they all marvelled as he piloted himself around the phone. 'Andrew, hold on old son,' he switched back, 'Del, Andrew's there now and says the 'Erbert's are in the clubhouse opposite the hotel and fun fair. It's all very open there.'

Jack thought for a minute. Del's squeaky voice could be heard summoning Jack back to the real world. 'Del, that's where the helicopters land for the dignitaries, Royalty and the like going to the dock yard. You don't think they're going to helicopter off from there do you?' He flicked the icons again, 'Andrew, we think they may be waiting for a helicopter to take 'em off; you have firepower? I won't ask. Hold your cover; the spooks'll be there soon, police tactical are on the way as well and so are Jimbo and me. '

'No you're not.'

He held his hand up to Mandy, it quietened her but she fumed as he returned to his phone. 'Okay Del; Andrew and his team B are there and holding station, they said they have this one but I think we should be there to make sure they are there, so to speak. Tactical is on its way and so are Jimbo and me.'

He flicked the close icon and tossed the phone to Frankie. 'Give that a bit of a tickle will you sweetheart, battery looks low and we'll be off in half an hour. I want tactical and Del's boys to set up first, and Frankie, tip tactical to keep an eye on Andrew's mob eh, just in case; I'm not sure about anyone in the feckin' military these days.'

'Jack, please?' He looked distant and Mandy tried to call him back, 'What the hell are you thinking now, where we will have dinner on Friday and what is team B?'

Jack responded, shaking his head and flapping his hands as if this was the least of his concerns at the moment. 'Len will fix up dinner and team B sounds more impressive than just Team. And I'm wondering where I can get a bazooka or whatever they use to shoot helicopters down these days.'

'I know where to get one of them Jack.'

'Brilliant Jimbo! Mind you, do we have dinner before the concert or after? I think after, what d'yer fink love? I hate the sense of rushing and we can have a bag of crisps before we go in. I'll 'ave cheese and onion; I wonder if they do the big bags at the Albert Hall? I bet they only have the pansy-arsed little bags. Tell yer what, we could have a pie at a cabbie place beforehand, there's one in Knightsbridge I fink?'

Mandy sat back in her chair and relaxed, you have to take the relaxation where you can with Jack, and this seemed like a good time. She spoke calmly to Jo Jums, 'Jo, can you sort our guys please, no front line, just support. When we get through to his nibs here...' she flicked her head, '...perhaps we will find out what's happening and we will likely be needed to mop up the aftermath, as I have no doubt there will some significant mopping to do. What is it Jack?'

'You got my shoulder tablets sweetheart, and d'you fink they'd work on 'eadaches?'

Mandy dug around in her bag, found the carton of pills, pressed two out from the foil sheet and handed them to him, pulled a bottle of water from her drawer and gave him that too, loosening the top for him.

'Thanks love, you prolong active.' She nodded and sat back in her chair, to recommence the relaxing bit. Jack stretched out on the orange PVC chair which he had pushed back to the wall and he was now looking out of the window at their tree, humming If you were the only girl in the world. He didn't even look up when there was a

187

knock at the door and Jackie appeared.

'Hi Mands, got a call from Jo, you wanted me?'

'I did Jackie,' and she gestured with her head. 'It's turnip, I think he may have lost it again.' Jack remained unmoved, just sat there as Jackie crouched in front of him, she had a skirt on and even that didn't elicit an unsubtle penetrating eye movement.

Jackie rose up from her haunches. 'He's asleep,' and they both giggled.

'Jackie do you have a cream hat?'

* * *

Andrew and some of his former SBS buddies had placed themselves in the hotel opposite the Garrison Sports Ground clubhouse. There had been a little tussle with the hotel manager but someone called Tony, who looked a bit like Charles Hawtry, had sorted it. Andrew was not sure who was more relieved, him or the manager. The manager looked like he did not know what to do, faced as he was with five muscular and seriously-testosteroned men in his foyer who were responding to commands from someone who looked like Charles Hawtry from the *Carry On* films. He did wonder if this was candid camera, or if they were making a new *Carry On* film, but that illusion was soon extinguished when some police arrived and told him to quietly evacuate his hotel, via the seafront side. He then watched a small arsenal of machine guns being delivered, and the manager appeared to want to relieve himself.

* * *

'Jackie none of this is funny and yes you will be invited to London, and with Gill if you insist. In fact I insist. I am not sure I could deal with Jack on my own. Should I be worried about him Jacks? '

'Not sure Mands. I want to see how he is when he wakes up, but whether he should go to the Garrison Sports Ground? I don't know. All my senses say no, but he does have an innate sense of command

and ability to read situations, and then control them. Maybe he should be there?'

'How do you know that?' Mandy asked.

'I am in with your spooky gang now and I've read all of Jack's files.'

'You have?'

'I have, and yours too. They like you Mandy and were watching you even before you and Jack got together.'

'They were?'

Jackie nodded, 'You know Jack asked me to take on Alice did you?'

Mandy sighed, 'No.'

'It's very perceptive of him, he even offered to pay me, but I am told the spooks are covering that and the surgery she will need afterwards.'

'Can you talk her into coming to the Palace on Friday? She's apparently physically fit enough, it's just she's embarrassed about the boatrace and the pain of course.' Jack was awake.

'You will have to leave that to me to decide Jack. Welcome back, nice sleep?'

'Yes thank you Jackie and I would be honoured if you and Gill would join us at the Palace; they have plenty of room there. And the concert as well. I'll get onto Len to arrange the tickets.'

They all looked to the door responding to the knock, Frankie stepped in with Jack's phone, 'Charged up as much as I can and it's Del.' She waved the phone, tossed it and he missed the catch but fortunately it landed in his lap. It looked like an exchange was about to ensue between Frankie and Jack, but Mandy stepped in.

'Jack, take the call please.'

'Del,' he listened, humphed a couple of times and then closed the call. Jimbo stepped inside; he knew what Del boy had said.

'We have a safe spot on the roof Jack. Mandy if you would like to come along? Del is there as well. Jackie, I think you should maybe stay back a bit.'

'No fear there Jimbo, I want no part in any of this, I just pick up the pieces.'

Jimbo carried on, 'Jo has the con and she's managing this with Nobby.' Mandy thought this must be where Jack got the term "con" from. Frankie confirmed the sat-cams were up and running. 'Good, well, Tony has secured the scene, the hotel is empty so shall we go?' Jackie responded, 'Give me a minute Jimbo; I'll meet you and Mandy outside. Just a moment alone with you Jack please.' They left and Jackie got up and pushed the door shut and heard Mandy go ouch. She sat herself down on her haunches and this time he did notice the skirt.

'Jack, focus please.'

'I am Jackie!' She playfully slapped his thigh.

'Tell me how you feel? Be honest, I am not going to stop you going.'

'I feel a bit light headed, I've had the shits and a headache, all of which I put down to the beer, except maybe the shits. I wanted to go in the harbour you know.'

'I know, Jimbo told me. You're scared, that's all. Its natural and you should allow yourself to feel that, it will protect you.'

'I am scared Jackie, in fact I'm not sure I can do this. They want us on the roof, did you know that?'

'Do you feel this is bringing back the Dr Mead episode on the roof of the tower block?' Jack nodded; she saw his hands shaking and held them. 'So long as you know and understand the feelings and what they can do to you, you will be okay. Would you like me with you?'

'It could be dangerous but if you feel you can, then yes please.'

'Good Jack, we are making progress and you are not alone, you have all of us around you. I will be there for you as well, so come on.'

She helped him up and he hugged her and whispered, 'Thank you Jackie.'

He was aware he wasn't a lesbian, although he often thought he wouldn't mind a crack at that.

'You'd make a shit dyke Jack, now shift your arse.'

'Did I...?'.

Chapter 33

The hotel guests had been herded into the amusement arcade building. The funfair continued to operate for the holiday makers and hub-bub of people, the shouts and screams of artificially created fear, all of this hit Jack's senses and contributed to his nausea. He was experiencing real fear. He tried not to show it but Jackie saw and Mandy sensed. They pulled him aside in the hotel foyer, gently pushed him against the wall; they both studied him.

'Okay, which one of you is having me first?' he said, and they burst out giggling.

'Helicopter in-bound Jack.'

'Okay Tony, we set up on the roof?'

'Yes Jack.'

They went to the lift and as the doors closed Jackie looked out at Tony. 'He looks just like *Charles Hawtry*,' Jackie said, and Jack gave his *Sid James* laugh and they were all laughing as the doors opened as Mandy told him to "stop mucking about" in her *Kenneth Williams* voice.

'Del, good of you to meet us. To the roof?'

'Yes Mandy, to the roof.'

They followed Del into a second stairway and as they exited onto the roof they were hit by a blast of off-shore wind, effused with brine and seaweed. Jack's mind went immediately back to Southsea Castle, then the tower block where he was eventually rescued from a life-threatening situation by a paedophile doctor. He heard Jackie whisper in his ear, 'It's okay to remember Jack, the feelings are normal.'

Mandy stopped and looked back at them and Jackie passed on a reassuring glance.

'Into the tank room.' It was Jimbo, in control. Beside the parapet Jack saw a rocket launcher, inanimate but capable of deadly fire power when brought to life.

There were five other men in the tank room with them, all armed with sniper rifles. Mandy never knew guns; she was as bad as Jack in that respect. She shivered just being in the proximity of these powerful looking weapons, but they had a hypnotic effect, she could not take her eyes off them. Jimbo took a call then spoke to them all, 'It's landed, Andrew get your guys to their stations. The ground team will caution the men as they try to make their escape to the helicopter. We are here only if needed.'

They went out onto the roof and watched as Andrew's men fanned out, professional and clearly well trained. Jack leaned over the parapet and looked down toward the playing field. The doors to the pavilion were on the far side and they could see nothing other than the spinning rotors of the Navy helicopter, side door open. He looked over and felt Mandy tug on the belt to his trousers. 'Don't lean out too far,' she shouted over the noise of the helicopter. He was about to respond with a brilliantly amusing quip when it all happened. Men appeared, running for the open door of the helicopter and stopped, shocked, as they were challenged by the ground team. A brief delay, then they opened fire on the challenging officer. They saw the officer go down but later crawl to a safe area; a vest hit. The men running for the helicopter were professional, they didn't want to kill the policeman, but that hadn't stopped them seriously wounding innocent civilians outside his house. God knows what else they had done, and would do if he didn't stop them.

The men sprayed shots in the direction of the tactical support team who were safely behind cover. Andrew took aim and dropped a man with a leg shot. The reaction was a fusillade of bullets to the parapet and Jimbo was hit and fell back. Mandy reacted, dropped to the deck and when Jack ventured a peek, the men were in the helicopter and it was ready to take off with a man firing from the open door, directing his fire to the ground team, now cautiously advancing and shielded by parked cars.

Jack picked up the rocket launcher and looked for the instruction book. He heard Jimbo say, 'It's ready to go Jack, just point and press the trigger.'

Jack shouldered the weapon, winced, 'Jack no!' Mandy called.

'Get back Mandy,' Jimbo called from the roof surface.

Jack was up and pointing the weapon, he had the helicopter in his sights, thought for a moment about the deaths he was about to cause, then thought again of the civilians who had been hurt. He sighted again, now with more determination, the door of the helicopter was in the cross hairs, he squeezed the trigger and fell immediately back and saw the beautiful blue sky; he only heard the explosion.

'My feckin' other shoulder Mandy,' he shouted in pain.

'Shut up bozo, you've blown up the sports pavilion,' she said, hardly able to contain her laughter.

Although Jack had been hopelessly off target, flying pavilion debris became caught up in the helicopter rotors and smashed them. The craft was on fire and completely disabled, and the men bailed out and made for the fence with their hands up, dragging the man with his injured leg. The men were being rounded up as the helicopter exploded. It made Jack jump and everyone else on the roof looked at the feckin' "shite shot" eeejit.

'What?' he said, a portrait of innocence.

'Shut up and come here,' and Jack went to Mandy and she hugged him. He winced, both shoulders. 'Please stop being a girl's blouse Jack, it's embarrassing.'

'Yeah, but your girl's blouse Amanda, eh?' he said, saving the day.

'Yes,' she sighed, an exasperated acknowledgment of her fate - not worse than death, but very close.

Jack was reenergised, 'Good, let's see Alice and ask if she'll come to London on Friday?' Mandy and Jackie's eyes went way, way, up to the open sky, where they were joined by Del Boy's and then Jimbo, who had very little choice as he was flat on a stretcher being carried off the roof.

'What did Jimbo say Del?' Jack asked, not really interested.

'He asked could he have the Queen or Prime Minister protection duty, it was a lot safer than looking after you Jack.'

'Oh. Has Mike got a hotel sorted for us all yet?'

'Jack, I want to bring Len in,' Del said.

'Lenin, when did you become a socialist Del? Not yet Del, give me the weekend; we're nearly there, what does Samuels say?'

'He unfortunately agrees with you,' Del sighed.

* * *

'Jo Jums, I'm going to the hospital...' Jo interrupted Jack's phone call with enquiries as to his health. '...I'm fine, we're all fine, well Jimbo took a shot to the shoulder but I told him that's nothing, I didn't even cry when I got mine.' He waited while she finished laughing, 'Okay, now can we get on with some serious police work?' Mandy could hear more energetic laughing from the phone as she sat next to Jack in the squad car, heading for the hospital. She took the phone from him and he looked hurt. 'You said I could do this.'

'Yes, but we need it done now,' and Mandy spoke to Jo. 'Jo its Mandy, we are going to the hospital and afterwards we would like to meet with you and Frankie, we need to talk through what you release to the press.' She listened, then turned to Jack, 'She says the press are all over the Commander wanting information, suppose that is to be expected, more shootings in peaceful Southsea and a blown up sports pavilion, what should we say Jack?'

'Hmmm, Hmmm.'

'Jack please?'

'Hmmm, Hmmm.'

'Okay, I'm sorry Jack, you can have your phone back, but please tell Jo what to do.'

He looked at her. 'Pretty please?'

'Yes Jack pretty please.' He took the phone. 'Feckin' Turnip,' Mandy managed to say so Jo could hear.

Jack waited for the laughter to die down. 'Hi Jo, Captain Sensible here! Len will be in touch with some names and some diatribe to put out from his side. For us it's more of the same, focus on cutbacks and just managing to cope but report that this is the military taking action themselves; say we are still trying to get to the bottom of it but it seems that some former front line people have had enough and acted alone. Leave a lot of room for the press to add conjecture. We can expect some financial revelations close on the heels of this stuff as well, so 'ang on to yer drawers Gertie.' He laughed to himself, but the phone was silent and so was Mandy, just the sniggering from Del Boy in the front seat and the driver.

Del Boy turned to face the stern face of Mandy and the boyish grin from Jack. 'Financial Jack, I thought we'd had that already?'

'Del Boy, stick to yer guns you feckin' turnip, can you not see anything?'

'No Jack,' Mandy said, 'neither of us can, please explain.'

Jack was about to explain when their car was rammed by an old land rover. The squad car rolled and was carried on by its own speeding momentum, eventually righting itself. Jack kicked the door open, unsnapped Mandy's seat belt and pulled her roughly towards him. He rolled out of the car, dragging her with him as a burst of machine gun fire hit the car's side panelling. Jack opened Del's door and pulled him out too. The driver was bloodied and clearly dead; Del had also taken a couple of shots.

Jack snatched Del's gun, looked up and fired off several rounds towards the departing land rover, hitting the bonnet of a parked car and shattering a fish and chip shop window, scattering customers. He aimed again at the departing driver and hit a kebab sign. Not one of the bullets hit the speeding land rover but another car, trying to avoid the chaos, did. Jack ran to the crashed land rover, pulling open the driver's door; the driver had hit the windscreen but was coming around as Jack stumbled from wrenching the door open and accidentally put a shot in the man's knee. He said sorry and tittered. The passenger lined up his pistol and Jack blasted again, a skimming bullet to the head knocking the man back. Jack went around the car and held the gun to the passenger's now grazed forehead. The man looked amazed that he was still alive. Clearly he had not heard about Jack's legendary skills on the shooting range.

'Put the gun down now and step away from the car, keep your hands in the air or we will shoot.' Bullhorn words from a tactical police officer; the squad had been instructed to follow them.

'Oh shut up you feckin' planks, I'm looking for my warrant card; I'm a policeman!' Jack shouted back, waving his hands.

'Stay perfectly still...'

'He is a policeman, he is DCI Austin and I am Superintendent Bruce.' Mandy had her warrant card and then showed them his.

'You got my card darling?'

'Yes Jack, you forgot to put it in your sock the other day and I forgot to give it back to you.'

'You know I don't need you looking after me all the time, I am perfectly capable.'

'Hold still sir while I check the cards.' The tactical police officer still had his weapon trained on Jack.

'You do need me Jack and frankly I need you, and right now I need you to fucking grow up and stand still.'

'I am standing still...' he remonstrated, waving his arms about. The officers clicked their weapons; Jack was oblivious, had he heard? '...and I tried growing up and didn't like it, d'you remember, I told yer?'

'Jack.'

'Yes.'

'Shut the feck up, please.'

'You do know your language is getting worse don't you Amanda?'

'Yes Jack, I fucking do.'

'Oi officer, how come you don't know me, you not from round 'ere, and I will need a poo in a minute, just sayin'...' and Jack tramped his feet up and down to demonstrate the imminence of the call of nature.

The officer was confused at the dialogue taking place in a highly stressed and far from normal situation. 'We've been called in from Guildford. You do not have enough resources down here to deal with all that's been happening.'

'Oh, I'm from Guildford originally, do you know Winker Watson?' Mandy seemed animated and Jack was pleased, it meant the attention was off him and he needed to look around for a public toilet; some chance he thought, they'd all been closed due to council cutbacks.

'Winker? Yes he's Station Commander, do you know him?' the officer in charge replied.

'Yeah, is he still an old fart?' Mandy said, quite enjoying the exchange now.

The officer could not help himself and he laughed, 'Yes, you clearly do know Winker.'

'Look mate, my shoulder is aching holding me 'ands up, can you take this bloke on the ground for me please, I want to go and see Del Boy over there and the officer in the car. Also d'you know where the nearest bog is?'

Ambulances were arriving and Jack strolled with his hands in his pockets and went to the bullet riddled patrol car, ignoring the instructions to stand still from the tactical officers. The driver was dead as he suspected and the anger in him boiled at these people who were prepared to force their will on others, killing to achieve it. 'Collateral damage my arse!' Jack shouted, 'I will not stand for this, I will not!'

'Jack, calm down mate.'

'Sorry Del, how are you?'

'I'll survive.'

Jack knelt beside Del, he had a wound to his upper arm and thigh and a very close shave on his cheek. 'You were lucky Del, the uniform took the hit.' Jack stood and let a paramedic move in, 'I'll see you at the hospital Del.'

'Jack you were about to say what this is all about, the financials?' Jack stood, looked at Mandy chewing the fat with the guys from Guildford, looked back at the body of the uniform driver, farted then fainted.

Chapter 34

Blimey what happened there?' Jack said from the ground.

'You looked at the dead officer, farted and fainted.' Mandy answered.

'What was his name?'

'Jim Davis, married, one child and out of our Nick. Jack what is happening?'

'We are very close Mandy that is what is happening and it's not Len, it's worse than that. Give us a hand up luv.'

'No, the paramedic said to leave you there for a minute. Jack, you fainted when I was talking to those other men; were you jealous?'

'I didn't like the look of them sweetheart, I have to look after your interests. Did you know that bloke didn't even think I was a copper?'

She was on him like a shot. 'Are you a copper Jack? Because you actually don't look like one, and you certainly don't behave like one, and I have been thinking, have you ever solved anything yet without the help of Seb, Mike, Del Boy, Kipper or Maisie?' She didn't look angry so much as tired and frustrated. Definitely fed up though; he'd learned that look.

'I like you in the emerald dress, please wear that on Friday, pretty please, dearest lovely Amanda.' He was in trouble and so he brought out the big guns.

'Stop trying to change the subject and yes I will wear it, Jackie thinks it will be okay and she has a cream hat I can borrow. Mike's been on the phone and they have accommodation for us all. Len has several boxes at the Albert Hall and so I suppose this will all turn out all right in the end.'

'Give us an 'and up then girl.'

She stood from her crouch then realised he had made no comment about looking up her skirt, and eased him back to the ground. 'I want you checked out first.' She left him there to see Del boy off in an ambulance, only looking back when she heard him shouting again.

'Fuck off you bleedin' woodentop. Leave me the feck alone, you shithead pimply arsed ponce.'

She dashed back. 'Jack, be quiet, what's up?'

'This turnip wants to nick me for shooting the bastard in the car.'

'What?'

The constable addressed Mandy. 'Yes Ma'am, the driver says that DCI Austin shot him in the knee and he also shot at the passenger, grazing his head.'

'You do realise that these bastards just sprayed the patrol car with machine gun fire which killed an officer, and DCI Austin was in pursuit of these armed and extremely dangerous men, don't you?' Mandy hit back at the young constable.

'And I fell over love, tell him that, and tell him you will tell his mum on him,' Jack added.

'Ma'am, I would be failing in my duty if I didn't take the Inspector in for questioning.'

Jack thought, what it is to be young and unaware of the dangerous path you can tread when conversing with a woman.

Mandy shouted now, and Jack thought here it comes and battened down his own hatches in case of collateral damage.

'Listen you little fucking tosspot, get your head screwed on right or I'll kick your arse from here to Kingdom Come. Who's your sergeant? Get him to ring me. Jack Austin is going to hospital now, so bugger off sonny or you'll miss the *Magic Roundabout* on telly.'

The young constable trailed off with his tail between his legs, still not sure what to do, should he ring his sergeant or just leave it, and what was the *Magic Roundabout*?

'Diplomatically handled that love and if I am right the *Magic*

Roundabout finished some time ago, though it was later than *Captain Pugwash*, I do admit. You do know I can see up your skirt don't you?' and he flicked his one eyebrow and grinned salaciously.

'Righto Austin you're alright, up you get...we need to brief Jo Jums and you need to tell me just what the hell is happening.'

She stuck her hand out and tugged and he winced his way up; she was immune, so he stopped, there was no need to waste good wincing.

* * *

'Jack, I seriously can't keep up with this lot.'

'Jo Jums, you don't have to, it will all pan out and all you will have to do is tidy up the bits and pieces.' That sorted, he returned to looking out of the window at their tree. Jo and Mandy looked at each other, then a cursory look out of Mandy's office window to see what the tree was doing.

'That's it is it, that's all the explanation we are going to get?' Jo said, thoroughly irritated. She was immune to tree calming; no chance of her becoming a Buddhist, Jack thought.

'A Buddhist?' Jo said, but the tree had calmed Jack and he turned to face them, rubbed his cheek and they sat in anticipation.

'I wonder where they'll put the kids?'

'Pardon?'

'The kids Amanda, I wonder where they will put them?' Jo looked at Mandy, they both looked back to Jack; he was away with the fairies again. 'I hope it will be nice for Buckingham Palace.'

Jo got off her seat and beckoned to Mandy. They met in the corridor and Mandy closed the door, 'Is he okay do you think?'

'Christ knows, I sometimes wonder if he really does know what is happening but my guess is Samuels will be here soon and he will want to talk to Jackie as well. Maybe then we will know?'

'Who will want to talk to me?'

'Jackie, have you heard?'

She nodded, 'Where is he and who will want to talk to me?'

'Samuels. Jack is in my office, give him the once over will you please I'm worried, he keeps veering off track mid-conversation. He says he knows what is happening and why, then talks about Buckingham feckin' Palace. He's in there now, vacant brain, finger up his arse and looking at the tree, or it may be the sky; apparently the tree is boring today. He said something odd though; he said "It's only what they did themselves to get their wealth. Sort of natural justice I suppose". That's it, then he farted and fainted at the scene. Again.'

'Okay let me see him, where will you be?' Jackie asked.

'In the CP room helping Jo get ready to brief the press,' Mandy answered.

They went their separate ways. Jackie knocked on the door and went straight in to see an animated Jack on the phone pacing. He put his hand up to say hi to Jackie, indicated for her to take a seat. Jackie remained standing, she didn't like being pointed at or ordered around, especially by a loony.

Jack carried on talking, 'John we need to make the change of direction, you know what to do, you know the world of arsehole bankers, pension funds and finance, think of something that will give them all that they want for God's sake, we are haemorrhaging here, literally. Good, I look forward to your call.' He pressed the end button. 'Jackie did you speak with Alice?'

'No Jack. You need to do that, but I will be there with you if you want.'

'Okay, I'll do that in a minute, where are the gals?'

'I take it you mean Mandy and Jo?'

He looked stumped, 'Of course.'

'They're in the CP room; Jo is preparing for the press briefing, God help her.'

'Okeydokee' and he strode out and down the corridor, bashing through the door to the CP room, good arm straight out. 'Yo babes, I'm popping up the 'ospital, Jackie's coming wiv me and we're going to see if Alice will come to the Palace, and then I'm going on the missing list, a bit of dodgy business needed...and to be honest love, I'm bricking it. I can meet you all at the hotel on Friday morning, okay? Cushty.'

Mandy stood from leaning over Jo's desk. 'What? No! What? What? What?'

'Yeah babes, you've said that, but I have some things to do, I have a few doobreys, meetings and fings to sort, okay?'

'No, not okay, shall we go into my office?' Mandy said, morphing from confused to angry.

'Sure, but make it snappy, time is ticking and all that,' Jack said.

Mandy walked briskly to the door, clipped Jack around the back of his head as she passed. He followed with Jo, and Jackie traipsed after, Jo thinking this gets more like a children's school playground every day.

'Right, what on earth are you talking about?' Mandy said.

'D'you want to wait for Samuels? He should be here any minute is my guess, Father Mike will have picked him up from the station by now.'

Jack picked his phone out of his pocket, flicked the icons and put it to his ear. 'Jock, are they all there?' He listened. 'Call me when Michael and Winders arrive please, straight away.' He closed the call, hummed, then sung quietly to himself, *'Onward Christian soldiers marching as to.....der dee der.*

'You want to know something shite, my Nan was one hundred, never missed Songs of Praise, loved it, played the tambourine in the Salvation Army and all of that, I think that's where my musical talent must come from...' he stopped to think, as did Mandy, but she was thinking what musical talent? But Jack was back and explaining. '...She wanted to hear The *Old Rugged Cross* only she called it the "Rugged Crawlse". Anyway the bastards didn't play it, and blow me down only two years later she's feckin' brown bread. So what d'you think of that, eh?'

Mandy wasn't sure what she thought about that but Jackie did, 'Do you think of your Nan a lot?'

'Of course, doesn't everyone?' He was humming *The Old*

Rugged Crawlse, 'And that bleedin Cliff Richard, I ask you.' He was humming *Summer Holiday* now, then singing to himself, '*We're all going on a summer holiday, dooo dee doo dee doodey doo,*' recommenced humming, the words just wouldn't come to him. He stopped like he had just thought of something, turned, stopped again then went back to looking at the tree, hummed *Harry Potter*. Mandy knew he was thinking of the whomping willow and she started to cry. Jackie hugged her and indicated for Jo to take her out and she did. The door closed gently.

Jack instantly returned to an active sane state.

'Look after her Jacks, she's precious to me, I have to go somewhere dangerous and I have no choice. It can only be me and to be honest sweetheart, I'm crapping me pants.'

'So what's the idea then, you want me and Samuels to recommend that we "take you away" and then let you get on with what you have to do, while Mandy is oblivious?' Jackie said, angered.

'Feck me you're good Jackie, d'you think that will work? I was just going to tell her and ask her to try not to worry.'

'I'm sorry Jack...err, I think your way is best.' Jackie looked stumped.

'Did I ever tell you how I felt when I first saw Amanda?'

'No Jack, you didn't?'

'Can't remember what rank I was then, it used to fluctuate, always has I suppose, anyway she was new, in at DCI from Guildford and was in my Nick, not my team.' He sat looking out the window.

'What happened Jack?'

'What happened when?'

'When you first saw Mandy.'

'Oh, well I bumped into her in the lift. Christ she was beautiful, I couldn't take my eye off her and she returned the look, right into my eye, didn't even flinch. Want to know what she said?" he smiled warmly to himself.

'Yes Jack,' she sounded more than a little exasperated herself.

'She said,' and he tittered, '"I would ask if you have had an eyeful, but that would seem rude. I warn you however that I get out on the next floor so make the most of it". That's it, word for word; I will never forget it, that humour, I love it. I love it and I love her.' He cried and Jackie stood and came over to him.

'What is this all about Jack?'

She shook in reaction to his immediate angry response.

'Power for fuck's sake! Isn't it always about that? Power and greed, it will always trample on love, compassion and humanity. It knows no bounds, it recognises no moral scruples, it cares not a fucking jot if the rest of mankind suffers just so long as the few have the trappings that come with it.' He looked up at Jackie, looked into her frightened eyes and he calmed. 'So you see, I have to stop the most ruthless men in the world and I have no power to match them, only street cunning, only the wits of a jumped up barrow boy. My odds are not good, but I have to try.'

There was a gentle tapping on the door and Jo poked her head around, 'Samuels, Mike, Frankie and Mandy are in the conference room, shall we join them?'

Jack rose, turned to Jackie, 'Say whatever you want Jackie. I respect you and value your opinion. I think in my way I even love you, as I would a family member. You are a part of my life and I treasure that, but I must go. I have to go and will go; just hope I come back.'

She hugged him. 'Let's go then.'

And they did.

Chapter 35

Samuels took the side seat, Mandy the head of the table. None of this was conscious on her part, Samuels directed it. Jo sat on the other end, Mike opposite Samuels. 'Jack will sit next to me and Jackie will sit opposite him, I want the window light on his face so Jackie can better observe,' Samuels said. The stage was set, but what for Mandy thought? She was worried that Jack had lost it again, his mind was wandering; she trusted in Jackie though.

The door opened; no knock. Samuels stood and greeted Jack, the handshake, the hand on the wrist; they exchanged a look. He shuffled past Samuels, recognised where he would be sitting, went first to Mandy, she was standing and he hugged and kissed her, whispered, 'I love you, always have, since the lift.' She looked stunned. He sat and nodded to Mike who nodded back. Jackie sat down. Samuels opened up but passed the ball immediately to Jackie, 'I want to hear from you first Jackie.'

Jackie stood, walked to the window, paused in thought then turned.

'I believe in Jack.'

She stopped there, sat down and looked at Jack directly. 'He is suffering from PTSD but he is beginning to recognise the symptoms and maybe he is beginning the long road to recovery. I believe he has a sense for his own wellbeing, and in that I trust.'

'And?' It was Samuels, with his usual insightful but economic use of words.

'I know that Jack has to go off and do some things that are dangerous. I know he wants not to go. I know he is scared, but he knows only he can do this, and...' she paused, looked at Mandy. '... and he may not come back.' Mandy reacted with a very slow intake of breath. Jackie put her hand up and Mandy released the air equally slowly. 'I don't know what it is he is going to do, where or why, and I will probably never know as you will likely ask me to leave right after this, but I believe Jack has progressed enough to have a grip on self-preservation, that he wants to return and he wants his life with Mandy. That's it.'

She folded her arms but her eyes never left Jack's face. 'In my way I love you too John Austin, I have gotten to know you and I will worry with Amanda while you are away. I will stay with her.'

'What do you mean while he is away?'

Samuels stopped Mandy. 'Tell us now Jack, what is this all about? I know what you intend to do, and everything you have asked for is in place, but please set it out for us all. Jackie you can stay.'

Jack looked up from the table surface and he hardly drew breath. 'This is all about the world of filthy lucre, debt and power. What we have is an attempted coup, pure and simple, with big corporate power players in league with disaffected military leaders. They have engineered a dire economic situation through the forced and widespread repayment of debt, and then used the media to enforce the right message, a message that tells the nation the time is right for change, that debt is killing our nation and destroying the lives of individuals not just now but for generations to come. Meanwhile they force through cuts in the public arena, but most particularly in defence and the military. Suppliers struggle and have to sell up because there is no more demand, and the nation (and the military themselves) are spun a message of a country that cannot defend its people. When the time is ripe the conspirators not only force through a change of government with military backing and the unwitting support of the people. They would then own it all – the power to strip the country bare while making billions from resupplying the military and privatising every industry that couldn't clear its debts. The money men get their profits and the military gets back its power. And the ordinary man on the street? Still saddled with a debt-ridden society and no promise of a future.

The banker who died in Southsea was going to go public and spill the beans. I was his contact and handler. He even had tacit support from some of the international financial institutions, the good ones that is. Len is also on our side, though I'm not sure he understands how. He is just trying to get us back to an age when we cared about each other and the common man had a support system around him. What motivates him? Christ only knows, but it may have something to do with never having anything to support him emotionally throughout his life, that and being buggered senseless at school; he's ripe for being used and so I'm afraid I've used him. I'm not proud of that but it was necessary. We have been divided so others can rule and I've been trying to make sure it doesn't come to pass.

'As Jim knows (a nod to Samuels), we know their plans and have had a strategy underway for a while now to stop them. I need to shield those on our side to give them time to not only stop the coup, but ensure the country is in a position to recover. The reason we have seen the violent action that we have in the past few days is because the game is up. They know we are on to them and that we are close. I'm sorry that this has been so cloak and dagger, but I have had to protect not just the future of our nation and its people, but you, the people I love.'

Jack sat back down and looked at Mandy, leaned across and took her hands, scooted his chair up to her. 'I promised you that I would tell you if I was going into danger, I would allow you your right to worry. Well now is that time and I am truly, truly sorry, but I can see no other way out...' he shook his head, '...I only wish I could.' The tear that had been held in his eye, rolled. Mandy's eyes in contrast showed resolve, determination, not tears. They stood and hugged and promised their love to each other. He held her out with straightened arms, locked the gaze, it was done and they sat back down.

Samuels took over. 'Okay, up until today we were unsure of the depth of the military involvement – we now know the severity of the situation. Your invite is done, Mike is your conduit, feedback anything you need and you will have every back up possible, you will have anything you want that is at our disposal to keep you safe Jack.' He swung his gaze to Mandy, 'And I promise you faithfully that this will be the case Mandy.'

'Thank you Jim and make sure you do, and in the meantime what do we do?' Mandy said.

Jack intervened, 'The family are now all at a safe house in Mayfair. I want you and Jackie, and Gill of course, to go there now, stay secure. God willing I will see you Friday morning and we will be ready for the Palace at eleven.' He paused, looked at nothing and gathered himself, 'Jim, Frankie and Seb have encrypted a contingency plan in the event this doesn't work, if I don't, you know...'

Mandy grabbed his hand, gripped it then let it go. He stood. 'Mike we need to move. Mandy, Jackie, I have no time to see Alice, please do all in your power to get her to the Palace. If she won't come, ensure she is well guarded and tell her I love her.'

Mandy stood. 'Jack can I have a moment with you in my office please?'

Mandy held the door for him and closed it as he passed, she turned the snib and held him. 'Jack would you like to make love?'

'Mandy darlin', it's all I can do to stop from shitting myself at the moment, and my winkle has shrunk to the size of raisin out of fear, but I'll take a rain check as the Yanks say, and I want it on a fairy to France, with seafood, a joint birthday celebration eh, Mr and Mrs Austin?'

'Yes Jack, I would like that very much and I will be worrying, but please now focus on what you have to do and come back to me, and for what it is worth, I have loved you since the lift as well.' They hugged and had a little cry. Jack opened the door in response to Father Mike's knock. Jack looked back to Mandy.

'What is it Jack?'

He walked back to her, held her. 'Martin, I want to see Martin; I miss him so much.' He was crying. 'Bring him to the Palace please, bring Meesh and I'll speak to the Queen; she likes dogs.'

Mike and Jack left together. Mandy ponderously climbed the stairs back to the conference room; they were all still seated, had not moved. Their eyes followed her as if there was nothing else to do. She walked to the large picture window, looked to the side, the weather had changed and she saw the tree top moving, picking up momentum, agitated, reacting to external pressure without any ability to stop itself, just going with it; relying on the structure of Mother Nature to resist the bending and swaying until the good times returned. This was not just Jack and Mandy's tree, it was them.

'Sit.' Mandy turned and faced Samuels.

'We must be able to do something Jim?'

'Yes, and we will work out what now.'

Chapter 36

'Tell us again Jackie.' it was Winders. Mandy noticed it was Winders, Josh and Nobby doing the talking.

Jackie explained again, 'I believe a short while ago Jack was not suicidal so much as *gung-ho*, couldn't care less what happened to him. If he died, was killed, then he thought he was prepared. He thought himself not worthy to live really, apart from a deep-seated care for his loved ones; he would never take his own life. He told me once that suicide was a selfish act that leaves so much pain behind, pain that the loved ones can never reconcile. Mourning the accidental death is easier; you stand a chance of recovery. He also said that suicide was a permanent solution to a temporary problem, although I think he has struggled to see his problems as anything but temporary. I also think that if this situation was not absolutely demanding his service then he would have retired, married Mandy and would be off somewhere with her, probably eating seafood.'

There was an all pervading eeriness in the large drawing room that had darkened as the night began to assert itself. The three glorious, full height, Georgian sash windows, that earlier were the source of blinding shafts of sunlight, were turning black like missing teeth. Jimbo entered and pressed a button, and thick curtains closed across the windows; a sense of cosiness was installed atmospherically, if not shared by the family. Can a safe house ever feel truly safe?

Jimbo spoke, 'We have dinner, if you would like to come this way.'

* * *

In nearby South Audley Street, John Sexton paced in front of his own Queen Anne windows. He could see the Mayfair street below him; not busy, just a few people on their own personal missions. Nobody seemed to be sauntering as he and Jack liked to do. He noticed the discreet and the not so discreet MI5 men and women. He had accepted this presence, mainly because the men and women that he could see seated at the table reflected in the window, demanded it. Personally, he thought it might alert people to their presence but knew also, if he was to be able to pull this off, he needed full and total support; no dissenters. He knew also that he had a meeting in Whitehall at midnight and he wanted to be able to report positive progress, albeit veiled, deceptive and temporarily and necessarily misleading. Dotting 'I's' crossing 'T's' this is what this was supposed to be about, but nothing is ever simple and these were the doves of the banking world, the peacemakers of the financial system, the people who wanted to facilitate for good not greed. They would do okay out of it of course, but wasn't that the way of the world? It was true that not all bankers were greedy bastards.

He turned to face the assembled money muscle, looked at the faces, benign even warm some of them, though he knew this masked a ruthlessness similar to his own. He knew also that he needed this ruthlessness to fight the malevolence that they faced, equally ruthless, and stronger because of the singular lack of care. A knock at the door provided the seven men and five women with refreshments. More sandwiches, wine and cold beer. They sighed collectively; they had been in this house since Thursday morning, coming from New York, Paris, Bonn, Zurich and of course London. Each had their own personal worries, set aside for the greater good.

'Shall we start again, I want this all sorted before the Prime Minister and his Deputy get here,' John Sexton said, turning to face the table.

'Are they coming?' It was Jacqueline Parmentier, classically chic, classically handsome, a very strong woman.; powerful and probably the key to this meeting.

'I have great faith in the man inviting them.'

'Do you John? And does that faith extend to our own safety?'

John Sexton looked at the beautiful French powerhouse banker, 'Jacqueline you knew what you were getting into.'

John Sexton looked at Jacqueline, then panned his eyes around the table, they all nodded, one by one, and then so did Jacqueline, with a sensuous smile directed at John that said she was up for the danger.

* * *

'Jack you feckin' turnip, you can't just walk up to Downing Street and meet the Prime Minister.'

'I've an appointment. Well, an invite for drinks.'

'Even so, you aren't exactly dressed for it. Look at all those toffs in suits, done up to the nines...' Mike realised he was talking to himself; Jack was already at the gates and had shown his invitation and ID, all care of Frankie. John Austin of Cedric James Bank, an obscure department, International Resources; sufficiently intriguing and sufficiently anonymous, but the copper at the gate appeared not so intrigued, and shaped to reject him.

A suit tapped the constable on the shoulder. 'One of mine.' They exchanged a look and Jack was through, followed rapidly by Mike.

'Well I thought you could have managed a suit Jack. Still, Samuels did say you might be in your Morecombe and Wise shorts as it was so warm, we must be thankful for small mercies at least I suppose.'

There was no response from Jack. He was determinedly striding to Number Ten. He'd been to Downing Street before, in many guises and for many different reasons and currently this was not friendly territory, or indeed prospectively, not a pleasant or friendly meeting. He did not like the occupants but he had to allow for democracy he supposed. Samuels had arranged for a briefing paper, so Jack saw himself as just the final lever. Having said that, he was prepared to take the extra step if needed and he had said as much to Mike. When Mike pushed, Jack had said he wasn't sure what that step might be, but he was sure something would come to him, levers usually did, he was good at steps and levers wasn't he? Mike had not been particularly reassured.

The press contingent flashed and clicked and shouted as other suited and booted guests arrived. Jack sidled along with them, trying to remain as anonymous as possible, if that was achievable, sticking out as he did like a sore thumb. He was in his dirty cream chinos, black tarmac on the seat where he had fallen back on the roof earlier. A nice shirt he thought though, short sleeves, powder blue. A little tear in the sleeve but that was hardly noticeable and Mandy had always liked this shirt on him, the colour matched his eye she always said. He would mention this to the Prime Minister if he asked. And of course the tan brogues with juice, everyone liked them.

* * *

Behind Shepherd's Market the Austin family and friends sat down at a large formal table, even Martin the dog had a seat and was on his best behaviour. Jimbo sat with them, two other men alert and ready on the large landing outside the dining room.

Nobby fed Alice and this endeared him even more to the family. They had talked through all that needed to be said earlier in the afternoon. Some pleasantries were exchanged but mainly silence reined, except for the clank of cutlery, the chink of china.

'There's a TV behind the unit over there, if anyone is interested?' Jimbo said, 'We may get Jo's press briefing?' A screen dropped from the ceiling and he fiddled and summoned up BBC News 24. There was news of the troubled Euro, the debt crisis hitting Greece and Portugal.

'Fucking hell, that's Jack going into Downing Street!' It was Winders, but the sentiment was repeated by many, including Jimbo who pointed, winced and looked to his shoulder.

'Oh no, Jack, please...' was all Mandy could say, but Martin was able to reassure her with just a gentle paw; she'd missed his reassurances and knew how Jack felt, and Martin looked back to the telly to watch his former master about to make a tart of himself without his dog to save him; only an equally inept tart, in a dog collar at least, traipsing behind.

The reporter was talking of a select few invited for an evening garden party, drinks and canapés.

'Jack and canapés?' Winders said and Mandy reacted defensively.

'Why not, he does have some refinements you know.'

'He does?' It was Alice, but she was obviously not alone as they all laughed.

* * *

Jack shuffled in the line of stuffed shirts in the hall of number ten. He was singled out and ushered to the side. Ah he thought, probably going direct to the PM's private office. He was patted down and the giggles started when the officer got to Jack's socks and produced his warrant card. The officer, still crouched, waved it around laughing and telling anyone who would listen, what he had found and where.

The security man handed it back. Jack bent down and returned the card to his sock, looked up to find a uniformed officer discussing Jack's attire. But Jack wasn't listening, he was distracted by another guest.

'Bonzo you old dog!' The line concertinaed to a halt, as Jack left the officer talking to himself and went up to a former Home Secretary.

'Jane? What are you doing here?'

'Little bit of biz with the boss. What about you, fraternising with the enemy?'

'We do talk to each other you know.'

'Could've fooled me,' Jack said, shrugging off the uniformed arm that was starting to get forceful. He looked back at the young officer trying to get his attention, but only half listened.

'I need you to leave sir, you have an invite but it is lounge suit only.'

'Well that's alright then, I'm not going in the lounge, I just want to have a word in the shell like of the PM.'

The security guard was unsure what to do, especially as the former Home Secretary took Jack by the arm and steered him through the hallway and eventually out into the floodlit garden and some welcome fresh air. The hub-bub that greeted them slowly subsided as the gathering of Knobs and Big-wigs saw Jack step into the garden, unsuitably attired, arm draped over the former Home Secretary and talking loudly about a very serious shoulder wound, but for the life of him, he couldn't remember which shoulder it was now.

'Drink Jack?'

'No thanks Bonzo, I'm working.'

'Working?' His eyebrows went up. 'Can I ask?'

'You can, and one time I might have told you!' They were still laughing as the current Home Secretary came up to them.

'Jane Austin, I was warned to expect an unsubtle entrance but at least you are not covered in mango.' Jack related to Bonzo that she had visited him in hospital after he had been blown up in an Asian supermarket and ended up covered in squashed magno.

Jack whispered in Theresa's ear, gesturing with his head, 'Tell the goons to feck off will you?' She chuckled, flicked her hand and the men disappeared, just as the Prime Minister walked up.

'Okeydokee Bonzo, Trees'a babes, s'laters,' and he turned to the PM and noticed the Deputy PM there as well now. 'Right, shall we go and parley then?' Jack strode off in the direction of the PM's private study. He knew where the office was, he'd been several times before, sometime ago admittedly but you never forget.

'Mr Austin my office is this way.'

'Ah, moved it have you Dave, good, never liked the old one.' The PM and Deputy PM looked confused. Had nobody warned them? So much for PM briefings Jack thought. An officer opened the door for them and they passed through, the PM taking up an erect posture behind his desk, Deputy standing to the side.

Jack paced but eventually turned to face the two politicians. 'Okay, I have very little time and I presume you have read the briefing papers, so you know what is happening. I take it you've been briefed - yes? Want it chapter and verse?' They both nodded. 'Okay, sitting comfortably, then I will begin...' Jack laughed at his *Watch with Mother* reference and noticed it was lost on the two politicians and put that down to having been at boarding school and likely never having watched anything with mum, so he saw no point in doing his imitation of Spotty dog.

'There is a meeting of very senior financiers going on right now, and they are arranging to reschedule the GB debt, and possibly other countries debt, over I think sixty or seventy years, maybe more. This will allow the country to both recover, and stop those who are seeking to bring it down from fulfilling their plans.'

'What?'

'You 'eard,' Jack said, fed up with dealing with hippopotamuses.

'Do you mean ignoramuses Inspector?'

'I've not got time to pansy arse around with you two....'

'Now listen hear, you can't just stroll in here and dictate...'

Jack showed the PM his famed stopping the traffic hand, an open palm.

'Here is what will happen if you carry on blindly and ignore what's happening. First, the military have already started reacting. You will have read that in your security briefing papers, if not, watch the telly. A truly ugly sports pavilion, which I'm sure nobody really wanted, was blown up, and whoever did that did the world of architecture a big favour. I'd like you to remember that. Anyway, I digress. Their co-conspirators will continue calling in debt, the stock markets will collapse and the tosspots who are pulling your strings at the moment will collect all of the goodies, and we are not just talking about buying up all the blue chip companies that will be on the floor, savvy?'

'We have read the reports from MI5 and frankly we find it quite fanciful. This is Britain not Africa or the Middle East.'

Jack sighed, he looked tired and felt it. 'Suit yourself, I am acting anyway but it will become known that you resisted, preferring to save your own poncey arses and be right royally fucked by your best public school buddies. ' With that choice appraisal of the situation Jack turned and headed for the door, he was pretty sure he could remember where it was.

'Stop.'

Jack did stop, looked back and said nothing; this was fill the ether time and he used the pregnant pause to see where the door was, he'd been heading in the wrong direction. There was silence for a short while, but the PM could not resist a void, he was a politician after all.

'There has been a small but significant mutiny in Helmand province. Have you heard of this?'

Jack waited and thought, then said, 'Well what would you do, fight knowing that when you get back to your bunk, you will open an envelope that says you will be redundant when you get home, if you get home? This is just the start. I want you to speak to nobody else. We cannot trust all of your colleagues, especially your Cabinet Secretary and your Chief Whip.'

'What?'

'You 'erd; are they here now?'

'Well err...no, we were wondering where they were?'

'I know exactly where they will be later tonight, along with the proposed next Head of the Military. We intend to arrest them tonight. This gentlemen, is your very narrow window to save your own arses.'

'What should we do?'

'There is an MI5 Jaguar outside and it will take you to a safe house where you will be briefed by the caring side of the financial world. They will give you the plan that you should announce at a news briefing already arranged outside the door of number ten, at nine am tomorrow. Speak to nobody in the meantime; word is out and these people are ruthless. And what can I do for you Jack? I hear you say.' They each looked mystified. 'What, did you think I would save your arse, and not look for something in return? I have learned some things from your world you know.'

'What is it that you want?'

'Your financial institutions will be relieved of the pressure of immediate debt. You will announce an alliance between Coalition and Labour. The joint task, to resurrect the country. You will then restore the NHS, the teaching systems, forgive student debt and begin to countermand all of the huge cuts that you have made. You will announce a tripartite programme of restoring the caring society, not the Big Society, not small, just fucking Human. Kick the Big feckin' Society into touch please, you have no idea what is happening out there.'

'But…'

'No buts. Your speech is being drafted now and Ted Milliband will be informed later…'

'Ed, not Ted.'

'That's what I said. Anyway, Ted will join you here at about one, you will have the rest of the night to prepare together…' he paused '…you will likely have news of other events…try to not see them in too much of a negative light.'

They looked tired and overwhelmed. 'Like what?'

'What? What do you like?'

'No, I mean like what events?' the PM looked like he was a smidge annoyed, Jack could tell because he'd met Tories before and they smidgened things.

'You do not need to know.' Jack answered.

Is this all the explanation we are to get, Mr Austin?'

'Yes and no. One other thing, you will instruct an arrest warrant for one Lionel Thackeray. He will have his day in court which will be embarrassing for a lot of people, and then you will issue a pardon after one year in a psychiatric institution; the paperwork agreeing to all of this is drawn up and will be presented for signing by you two and Ted, at two am.' There was silence as the enormity of it all sunk in.

The PM spoke first. 'I don't know what to say?'

'Look mate, I always says it's rare to find a person that's not redeemable in some way. Well, you might just turn out to be no worse than your average self-serving politician, so do what I've asked and think country before self. It used to be a pre-requisite of your job, start a trend eh? Oh and don't worry, I still won't be voting for either of you.'

They left and Jack looked out the window. Scratched his growing stubble and allowed his adrenaline to ebb, controlled his shaking hands and wondered if he could remember where the toilet was.

Chapter 37

Jack hooked-up with Mike outside Downing Street and they made their way up Whitehall and across the bottom end of Trafalgar Square, Jack briefing Mike as they went. They had agreed to meet the Colonel and Andrew Friend in the Two Chairman's pub.

The Two Chairman's was discreetly placed just off Trafalgar Square, you would hardly notice it if you didn't know it was there; narrow inside, sawdust, and Jack loved it. They were on a mission, and he could think of no better pub for counter conspiracy; it had a nice bar counter as well, Jack thought to himself, acknowledging that someone had to do the counting.

The Chairman's was sparsely populated. It was a drinking hole through the day more than late at night. The location of the pub suited Jack as it was just along from Pall Mall, hopefully his last port of call, and a call where he might need a bit of leverage in the form of the SBS, and the odd Marine Colonel.

'Andrew, Colonel.' The military men stood to greet Jack and a puffed-out Mike as they entered the pub.

'Call me Brian,' the Colonel said, and Jack couldn't think of anything funny except the snail out of the *Magic Roundabout*.

'I suppose they call you Snail do they?'

'What, like out of the *Magic Roundabout*?'

'Yeah.'

'No.'

'Oh.'

Mike stepped in and saved the stultifying conversation. 'Jack will you brief, while I get us some drinks.'

Jack briefed the two soldiers.

'How do we stop what is already in motion?' the Colonel asked.

Jack stroked his chin bristles. 'Well I imagine, after the PM's address from Downing Street tomorrow morning, anybody running an op would be able to see that the gig is up. And we have asked for a root and branch investigation into the military, to dig out the dead wood, the self-interested martinets; how does that sound?'

The Colonel smiled, 'That sounds about right, and I wish you luck.'

'Don't wish me luck Colonel, I've recommended you and the General to run the commission.'

'You did what?'

'You 'erd,' Jack said, insensible to the signals batted back from the military men. 'Now, are you aware of any Ops planned for tonight?'

'Yes, and the main one is to seek and find you actually, and that is accomplished now. So if you wouldn't mind telling me where the financiers are meeting, then we will be getting along.'

Jack became aware the Colonel and Andrew had silenced pistols resting on their laps. He thought he should have noticed them before, but they were silenced and so he didn't even hear them, although he conceded he was a deaf twat. Mandy may have mentioned it a few times, not that he had heard her. He chuckled to himself, which confused them, and then Jack shouted out to Mike at the bar, 'Don't get these tosspots a drink Mike, save your money.' Jack shook his head slowly. 'See what you've done, you've spoiled a good friendship and done yerself out of a beer in the process; will you never learn?'

Mike was back with just two halves of London Pride. 'What is it, you guys leaving?'

'We are Mike, unfortunately you two will be staying, permanently, just as soon as Jack has told us where the Prime Minister is meeting the financiers this evening.'

'Oh yeah, like I would tell you even if I knew! What is it you have planned? Wipe out the coalition, which had you asked I could have helped you with, and then do the same to the good guy bankers?'

'Don't bullshit us Jack, just tell us where the meeting is.' The Colonel looked rattled.

Jack thought he could rattle him a bit more. 'That's the trouble with you military types you just don't think the whole fing frew or even laterally, by the side of the box in the sky...' Jack thought, '... is that right Mike?' Mike ignored him, knew he meant outside the box, or blue sky thinking, but frankly he was more concerned about being held at gunpoint.

Jack was continuing, 'Did you not stop to think that I might expect something like this? And, even if I didn't have back up outside and you were able to get me out for some delightful interrogation, I would not want to know, because frankly I'm not very good at pain and cry easily. You may have heard?'

Mike nodded and added that Jack was a wimp, which Jack thought was maybe a bit too severe for role play. The Colonel thought on; Andrew watched and waited for his orders.

'Bet you wished you'd 'ad that drink now, eh?' Jack raised his one eyebrow and went to stand.

'Where do you think you are going?' the Colonel barked.

'Lads, please bear with me, I need the bog. It's this PTSD you see.'

Jack stood and Andrew levelled a gun. The barmen saw and went for the telephone. The Colonel released a round that shattered the back bar mirror. He now had the attention of everyone in the sparsely populated bar.

'Well I have to say this is not doing my Thomas Crapper dilemma any good at all. Andrew d'you want to come with me?'

Andrew looked at the Colonel, who flicked his head to indicate go with Jack. Jack, closely followed by Andrew, made the tricky descent down a tight flight of stairs to the cellar toilets. 'I don't mind telling you Andrew I've had a few beers in this pub mate, used to work a lot just off Half Moon Street, down the way in Piccadilly, d'you know it?' Andrew ignored Jack, just kept his distance and the gun levelled. 'D'you know what one of the main symptoms of PTSD is Andrew, do you even know what PTSD is?'

'Of course I fucking know what PTSD is,' Andrew replied.

'Well then, your starter for ten, what is one of the key symptoms?'

'I don't know.'

'You said you knew.'

'Yeah, I know what PTSD is, just not what the key symptoms are.'

'Well then, shut up and I'll tell yer, if I don't shit meself here and now, trying to educate a bleeding sailor boy. '

'What are you doing, keep your hands away from your pockets,' Andrew reacting to some disgusting trouser department rummaging by Jack.

'Oh don't be a bleedin' tart Andrew, I have some supersonic paracetamol for my seriously wounded shoulder.' He sighed as he reached the door to the toilets. He went in and as Andrew followed Jack shut the door hard on Andrew's extended hand. The gun dropped and Jack picked it up, and it spat bullets as he accidentally touched the trigger. Unfortunately for Andrew, Jack had not been aiming at him because if he had, then obviously he would have missed. Jack tried to mention this to Andrew as his life ebbed away on the tiled floor , but Jack couldn't think about that right then as he definitely needed toilet.

* * *

The PM and Deputy PM had finished their meeting with the financiers and were headed back to Downing Street. The garden party had been wound up shortly after they had left, with the explanation being there was urgent state business to attend to. The car whistled through the emptying late night streets of London, a short trip from Mayfair, through Whitehall and into Downing Street.

As the two men climbed from the back of the car, the driver handed them two envelopes.

'Sirs, your draft speeches, I'm off to get Mr Milliband and we'll be back here by one. I was asked to remind you not to talk to anyone, not that you need reminding, but Jack said to say we hear all the conversations in and out. But I suppose you already knew that?'

The car took off with Wilf, the driver, smiling and thinking that should give them something to think about. The Jaguar left Downing Street, turning into Whitehall and speeding up to Trafalgar Square. Just a short distance to the Two Chairman's to pick up Jack and Mike, and then on to collect the Labour Party leader. Jack and Mike needed to be back in Pall Mall for around one am.

* * *

Jack appeared at the top of the stairs and the Colonel and Mike could see him walking like he had not made it to the loo in time and had crapped on his feet, all highly possible of course. Gingerly Jack made his way to the table, making no secret of the fact that he carried a gun. He appeared to be more pre-occupied however with the blood soaked soles of his tan brogues. As he approached the table, he offered an explanation of sorts. 'Your mate's a bit of a hothead, still I'm more worried if I can get his blood off me boots.'

The Colonel looked confused. 'Where is Andrew?'

'I told you we had back up, so don't act surprised you feckin' turnip.' While Jack had been in the bathroom the Colonel had ushered all the patrons and barman into one spot. Jack got the Colonel's attention.

'Oh, they want to know if you will give yourself up or die like Andrew?' The Colonel looked distressed and depressed. 'Do you suffer from depression Brian?'

'PTSD Jack, Afghanistan.'

'Oh...' Jack said as he sat and leaned back into his chair, the two front legs raised as it tilted and strained against his not inconsiderable weight, '... tell me about it, it can be a nightmare eh?' The Colonel nodded, as Jack returned the chair to its upright position and the chair and Father Mike were relieved. Jack leaned across the table, took a sip of London Pride, leaned back again. 'Give us your gun old son, I 'ave to go and get the Leader of the Labour Party now.' The Colonel looked so confused and very sad.

'The meeting you wanted the address for?'

'Yes?' the Colonel managed to say.

'Well it's finished and there will be a statement at nine tomorrow morning. Sorry old son, I win, you lose, and was it ever so.' Jack considered beating his chest like a silverback but thought better of it, and the gun, which up until now had proved a tad temperamental, might go off, and so Jack tried to inject a bit of maturity. Sadly however the chair collapsed and Jack shot the ceiling.

'You ready Jack?' It was Wilf talking from behind a fruit machine, his head covered in plaster dust. 'We're all getting a bit fed up, and its murder out there with the traffic around Trafalgar Square.'

The Colonel looked up at Wilf.

'Take the Colonel's gun will you Wilf,' Jack said, 'and give Vine Street Nick a call and see if they can accommodate him.' Wilf relieved the Colonel of the gun, lifted Jack to a semblance of vertical, and then pulled the Colonel's arms behind his back and snapped on a plastic cable tie. Jack turned to the bar, wrinkled up his mouth while he thought what to say and rubbed his chin 'Oh feck it,' he said, 'we're spooks and this bloke and the dead one downstairs are the baddies, don't ask me where their black 'ats are or my ID is. Wilf, have you got some?'

'It's in the car Jack, don't worry, Vine Street police will be here soon,' Wilf said putting his phone back into his pocket.

'Oh shite, we'd better make a run for it, Andrew's dead downstairs and you know how antsy the filf can get about dead blokes,' Jack responded.

'Tell me about it,' Wilf said, gesturing with his head.

Jack turned to the barman, 'Listen mate, Vine Street are on their way and I really 'ave to go, so can you hold this bloke for a while, pretty please?' Jack had no time for brass knobs. 'Tell the filf there's a dead bloke downstairs and be careful how you go, because if you get blood on your shoes it can be murder to get out...' And then he rolled up, looked at Mike and Wilf giggling. 'Murder to get out... oh

feck me I must remember to tell Amanda that one. Come on then.'
And they followed Jack out of the pub.

They got outside and stood back and looked at the wheel clamp
on the MI5 Jaguar and they were preoccupied cussing as the Vine
Street old bill arrived, flashing lights and discordant music, and they
swooped and sealed off the road and pavement.

'Wilf, I take it you know where Ted Milliband lives?'

'Yeah of course, well I think so, I thought I might give HQ a
tinkle on the way, they'd be bound to know wouldn't they?'

'Yeah I'm sure they would.' Jack was then interrupted by a rather
forceful police officer who was asking them to move on. 'Alright,
alright, we're going, just that someone has clamped our bleedin' car
mate.'

The copper was young and clearly intimidated, but recovered
some poise. 'This is a crime scene now sir.'

'Well it might be a crime scene to you mate, but that was our
wheels and we need to pick up Ted, the Leader of the Opposition.'
The uniform screwed up his face and looked even more confused
when Jack asked if they could borrow their squad car, and showed
him his library membership card that appeared from somewhere.
Jack promised to have his car back by tomorrow, the weekend at
the latest.

Clearly believing he was speaking to some drunks the policeman
replied, 'Oh of course sir, now bugger off will you, we have a job to
do.' And he disappeared, following his colleagues into the pub.

'Well I have to say that was really nice of him. You drive Wilf I'm
not so good with the old one eye you know.'

'Mike, phone in and get Ted Milliband's address will you?' Jack
ordered.

Mike phoned and they got the address, it wasn't far and
they stopped outside the townhouse, sirens and flashing lights
announcing their presence and Jack thought it was lovely how all the
neighbours greeted their arrival.

The door opened. 'We need to get you to Downing Street sir.'

'You do?'

'Yes,' Jack said.

'Look, I'm not sure who you are, but you might need my brother Ed?'

'You not Ted then?'

'No, and its Ed.'

'You're not Ted then?'

'No,' slightly irritated now, which Jack expected from politicians, no patience you see, or was that doctors. David Milliband looked definitely irritated in his stripy schoolboy pyjamas.

'Oh, so where does your brother live?' David Milliband wrote down the address and handed it to Jack. 'Well, where the fuck's that?'

Wilf leaned out of the car window and called out, 'Got the address from HQ, let's go,' and Jack jumped back in the car and they tore away.

'Wilf, we need to get to Whitehall, we will have to go back for Ted. Look, tell you what, go back to his brother's gaff and he can tell Ted to get around to his house and we'll pick him up later. We know where he lives now you see.'

'Yes, I can see, but it's a bit arse about face.' Wilf said, irritated like a politician.

'Keep it simple stupid,' Jack said, and Wilf thought what was simple about any of that, except for Jack? But he knew resistance was futile and turned the car around and Ted's neighbours looked really pleased to see them again.

Jack got out the car and waved as he approached David, who was already at his door. 'We have a situation we have to attend to in Pall Mall, any chance you could get Ted over here and we'll pick him up, around one thirty, two o'clock...depending on if we get into any more trouble.'

The other Milliband gave the impression of not following the logic, but reluctantly agreed, and Jack jumped back in the squad car and they drove off to Whitehall, Jack arguing that there must be a filf radio that they could use to find out how to switch the blues and twos off.

Chapter 38

The Cabinet Secretary, Chief Whip and Admiral Chit Wesley sat patiently around the table, blissfully unaware of what was going on no more than a few hundred metres away. John Sexton was late, but this was not unlike him and they were not worried, he had a little bit of a reputation for maverick behaviour and in the rarefied circles of high finance, being a tad late for meetings often got you tagged as eccentric; transgress more than once and you were a maverick. Still, even by John's standards, this was late.

They sipped and savoured the Pomerol.

* * *

The meeting of Bankers in Mayfair broke up. He had promised Jack he would attend what he hoped would be the last meeting of the Pall Mall Star Chamber. Some bankers stayed over in the safe house, others, who lived locally, made their way home or to residences retained by their companies.

It was a lovely balmy night and John Sexton thought he would walk the short distance through St James's and up Pall Mall towards Whitehall. He had a spook for company, who had argued forcefully that it might be more prudent to drive, but John liked to walk in London. He loved the town, and he loved the West End especially. They used to say the money is made in the City and the gentlemen live in the West End. That must have been a long time ago he thought, because many of the businesses he dealt with had a presence in the

West End and not many of them were gentle folk.

He walked and enjoyed the pleasant, warm night air, through Shepherd's Market, buzzing with people as usual, along Piccadilly, past the Ritz and down St James's wide open boulevard. He was looking at the blackness of St James's Palace in the distance when a car screeched, window down and a gun levelled - a shot was fired that hit the spook as he dived to push John Sexton to the ground. The spook spun and although wounded, fired several rounds into the car which careered into a nearby lamp post. The spook called it in whilst covering the car; there was no movement. John Sexton was beside him, looking around, bewildered. This had been a close call. He had known the plan they had instigated this evening would rattle some cages, Jack had said as much, but how would anyone know where he was?

Beryl knew, and she watched as the ambulance took the spook away and the police held onto John. Vine Street she imagined, and she would pick him up later. She walked in the direction her husband had intended to take.

* * *

Len was getting a bit fed up waiting, and then became disconcerted as a police car pulled up with its siren and lights going. It was at that moment Len knew he didn't want to be arrested just yet, and felt a sense of relief as Jack called out, "Get in plank". They drove past Trafalgar Square and saw the coppers pointing to their own car as it went by. 'They'll probably tow that,' Jack said.

'Yeah and someone will be in for it tomorrow, and that someone's name begins with Wilf.'

'What's the time?' Jack asked.

'Ten past one, we're late and we still don't have Ted,' Wilf answered.

'Wilf will you stop worrying?' Jack answered.

'Well, can I worry a little bit, because we have a cop car following us and he seems to want to catch up?' Wilf replied, irritated.

Jack thought he needed to calm things down a bit. 'Well that's a good thing isn't it; they can tell us how to switch the siren off because frankly, I'm getting a bit of a headache, what about you Mike?' Mike was getting one too but they were there now. Wilf parked up and they got out as the pursuing police car also arrived, slewing to an angular halt. They switched their siren off.

Jack called out to the uniforms as they approached, rather rapidly; probably pleased to see him he thought. 'How'd you do that mate, turn the siren off, we've been trying for ages?' The two police officers rushed all four of them; Wilf flipped one and had the other with his hand behind his back and a gun at his temple, telling the recovering first officer to cool it and to switch the feckin' siren off. In the confusion they missed Beryl disappearing off towards the steps, down to the Mall and into a hailed cab.

The officer switched the siren off and Wilf identified himself as MI5, flicked his head to suggest the others were too. Wilf released the officer and showed his I.D, Mike sketched a blessing and this seemed to do the trick.

'Righto Len, let's be 'aving you; show us where we're going.' Jack ordered and then turning to the filth, he told the uniforms to look after the cars and if they could arrange for the Jaguar to be returned, they would all be most exceedingly obliged.

Len lead them to the back of the classical villa, fiddled with a gate lock and they popped through a postern gate into the rear walled garden. The back garden was immediately illuminated by security lights that blinded Jack, and as a consequence he stepped into an ornamental pond, 'Shite...'

'Shush,' Len said.

'Shush yer feckin' self,' Jack said to Len, and then to Wilf and Mike, who were convulsing with laughter.

They entered a hallway, through another door and into the main entrance foyer of a very substantial classical house. It was impressive, hallowed halls indeed.

Jack looked down as they ascended a staircase, puffed out some unneeded air as he looked at his pond soaked trousers, edged in blood, and the brown tinge to the leather uppers of his tan brogues. Len called from the landing a flight up.

'What is it Jack?' Mike asked.

'Mike, how can I see the Queen like this tomorrow?'

'You weren't going to see her dressed like that anyway were you?'

'Yeah, I forgot my morning suit was an afternoon one, so I phoned and left a message to tell them, to tell the Queen, I might not have time to get a morning suit, or I could come along in the afternoon, of course. I said to come back to me if there was a problem with some slightly soiled cream chinos. I said the shirt was nice, just a little tear in the sleeve and to tell the Queen that Mandy liked the colour on me, and the shoes of course would be perfectly acceptable as they have juice; but look at them now.' He flicked his hands in despair. 'Anyway, nobody's come back, so...' He shrugged his shoulders in an ipso facto way.

The uniformed officers had entered the building and Jack told them to follow. The group passed through a key pad controlled lobby and into an ante room. Len tapped in another code and opened the far door, revealing a brilliant light over a highly polished table. They could see distant walls, as the light from the door violently intruded into the gloomy environment. The table was splintered, and then they saw three men slumped on the floor, riddled with bullets. Jack asked for the room lights to be switched on. He'd already recognised the Cabinet secretary and the Chief Whip, and then became aware of the bullet perforated form of Admiral Chit Wesley, his hair still perfectly coiffed.

The room lights flooded the space as the uniforms reached the doors; they saw the carnage and moaned. 'Seal the scene guys,' Jack said, 'have you got the Jaguar back, only we've got to go and get Ted Milliband.'

The uniforms looked to Jack and then at each other, thought this could not be happening. 'Look, who are you guys?' the uniform took his notebook out.

'Put that away son, you won't need it. Ring this number, quote this code and hold the scene until you are relieved, and watch the news tomorrow.'

Jack looked at the police officers and turned and walked out, leaving the uniforms to call the scene in.

'Saved you a job Len,' Jack said as he squelched down the stairs. Mike, Wilf and a very quiet Len trudged after him, all with hands in their pockets and little black clouds over their heads.

Jack decided to walk out of the front doors, he could see the Jaguar and police cars just outside.

'No Jack...' Len called, but too late, Jack had opened it and all hell broke loose, bells, whistles and alarms and they all just slid out as a portcullis gate closed off the hall.

'Christ, I've got a headache; when we get in the Jag I want the radio off okay, and did any of you see if there was a bog around, I need the loo.' Jack said.

Chapter 39

'Can you remember the way back to Dave Milliband's gaff ?' Wilf said.

'It was up and off the Edgware Road wasn't it?' Jack said, 'And 'urry up I need his bog.'

'We didn't go anywhere near the Edgware Road,' Mike replied from the back, leaning over the driver's seat.

'You sure? Ring in Mike and find out.'

Len wondered if he would ever get caught if this was the way the authorities behaved, and then realised he was actually caught right now. 'Are you arresting me now Jack?'

'D'you want to do that now Len, or a bit later? Because, to be honest wiv yer, I could do without the 'assle right now and I need a bog but Wilf's driving so bloody slow.' Wilf sighed.

Len answered, 'A bit later if you don't mind, I want to be at the Palace with you, then a really nice lunch and of course the concert.'

'Yeah well, hold your horses there Len, Jack forgot his afternoon suit and we'll have no time to get one in the morning, if you pardon the pun,' Mike said.

'Don't worry about that, I have one Jack could borrow,' Len said.

'Brilliant Len, sorted. Okay Mike, Ted Milliband, then a bog.'

'Alright, alright,' and Mike phoned, listened to it ring out, with a nagging thought about the size difference between Len and Jack. 'Okay, understood we'll go to Downing Street now.'

'What's that Mike?' Jack asked casually.

'David took his brother in the end; both are in with the PM and Deputy now. We'd better get along and join them; we don't want the two brothers fighting.'

'Right Mike, good idea, phone that in will you.'

Wilf turned the Jaguar into Pall Mall and headed back up to Piccadilly and then swept down Haymarket. They waved to the coppers outside the Two Chairman's, as they circled mischievously around Trafalgar Square and then zipped down Whitehall to Downing Street. They could see Downing Street floodlit, the gates surrounded by crowds of press and TV reporters; they more than sensed something was up, they knew. They had been told to expect a big news item at nine.

Wilf slowed the car as the cameras swung and focused on them. Not surprising really, there were very few cars on Whitehall at this time of night and a Jag, indicating to turn into Downing Street, was a dead giveaway. A Policeman stood out and Jack thought he did a passable stop the traffic hand, but thought also he could maybe give him a few tips, so he got out and walked to the officer and Mike followed to get Jack out of the anticipated trouble. There was a whooshing sound and the Jaguar exploded.

The blast threw Jack and Mike into the air and they had little time to recover, as automatic gunfire began strafing Whitehall and the entrance to Downing Street. Jack and Mike rolled away and threw themselves into the panicky press melee, picked themselves up and ran for cover into Downing Street, past the flattened security guards. Jack had interpreted the situation correctly. It was him being targeted. But that hadn't helped Len and Wilf who surely couldn't have survived the explosion.

Special Branch opened fire into the parapet of a nearby building. The firing stopped. Special Forces flooded out onto the street and across to the other buildings. Jack left them to it and told Mike he was going into number ten. The policeman on post and from his crouching position, arranged for the glossy black door to be opened.

Mike bundled in, pushing Jack over the threshold, having made a dash from across the street accompanied by machine gun fire.

The PM was in the hall, surrounded by secret service, and made to say something but Jack stopped him, talking directly to the secret service. 'Call it in; Wilf and Len caught in a rocket attack, I couldn't see but I'd be surprised if they got out.' He turned and pointed to Mike, 'Get him some attention please I think he's hurt, and I need the loo.' Jack went in the direction of the garden and opened a door, stopped and looked back to the PM. 'Len just died and he was lending me his morning suit to meet the Queen tomorrow, well today, well in a few hours really. Can I borrow yours Dave, seeing as we're about the same size?'

* * *

Mandy was up, having had a restless night; she'd been worried for Jack and she also had the fidgety Meesh and Martin in with her. She shuffled to the dining room where everyone had gathered for breakfast in their fluffy white dressing gowns that came with the house. She could see Alice's eyes focused on the TV in the dining room and went to go in, but was she was steered by Jimbo into a study. He called for Jackie to join them.

'How are you Jimbo?'

He shushed her. 'Mandy, it has been one hell of a night and before you watch the TV you have to know that Jack and Mike are safe. Wilf and Len, I am sorry to say, are dead, as are a number of other people. We are still sorting it out and overall Jack has been successful and there will be a press briefing at Number ten in a minute, nine a.m. If you watch the TV, the Downing Street cameras pick up a car exploding and Jack and Mike being thrown in the blast.'

Mandy was stoical, it was a feeling she recognised from the hospital. She felt Jackie's arm around her shoulders, hugging, and despite her inner strength, Mandy felt she needed this hug and leaned into the comfort.

'Jack and Mike are okay but they have a number of blast wounds that have been patched up in the Downing Street Operating Room. I hear that he and Mike won't be able to sit down for a few weeks, but Jack can at least kneel to receive his medal I suppose. Okay, so when you see the news you will see basic carnage around the city and it has followed in Jack's footsteps. We are gathering all of the information and it sounds like he had no choice in any of it. We have a man debriefing Mike and Jack in Downing Street now. I understand Jack has borrowed a morning suit from the PM; they seem to be getting on like a house on fire, can you believe that? It's just the shoes wouldn't fit, but he said to tell you not to worry about that, and here I quote, he said, "He's left a message for the Queen and she's fine with his tan brogues even with the blood on them, the suit is a perfect fit and he will get to you as soon as he can".'

Mandy was speechless, Jackie wasn't. 'I'm sorry about Wilf, Jimbo, did he have family?'

Jimbo nodded. 'A wife and two kids, 16 and 18.'

Mandy hugged Jimbo then walked out of the study to the now full dining room, the TV up loud.

Samuels was also there. 'I've explained the situation to everyone, I suggest we sit back and watch the Prime Minister's press briefing, and then get ourselves sorted for the Palace.'

'Jim,' it was Mandy and the room quieted, 'is this it now?'

Jim Samuels looked exhausted and Mandy presumed he'd been up all night. 'Well you can never say never, but I think the renegade military will see that they have nothing to fight against, and the rogue bankers are sensible enough to know when they are beaten. They will rally, lick their wounds and all of their money, and then think about how to do it all over again. It's the nature of the beast, so I think we can say it is likely over.'

Mandy didn't like the way he put his crossed fingers into the air, but for now she relaxed. The sigh around the room was palpable; relief most likely, but also thoughts about Wilf and even Len. But all that ended as the Prime Minister, Deputy Prime Minister and the Leader of the Opposition, stepped out through the shiny black door and took the few steps to the bank of microphones and the gathered press, greeted by the whirring and clicking of cameras but no shouts. It was eerie – a lot had happened and this looked serious, not least the nearby rocket damage and strafed buildings.

The PM started. 'My government has been working tirelessly behind the scenes to resolve the debt crisis that this country of ours is mired in. There have been many investigations, some of which have now borne fruit and reports will be issued by the various government departments in the next few days. This is neither the time nor the place to expand on these issues save to say, the debt crisis we believe, was a result of an engineered plot. I have to say that although we have looked to blame the previous government, we now know they were powerless to deal with the wheels that had been put in motion. In the light of what we have learned, I can now say to you that our three main parties have worked together to thrash out a solution, and last night a plan was approved and is now in the process of being implemented. I say first of all, we focused only on the debt crisis facing Britain, but we believe the solution offered could be repeated across Europe and the world. It is simple and it will mean here in Britain at least, that we will completely review all government fiscal policies. My government will work with Labour and our partners the Liberal Democrats and we will rebuild the damaged economy together. I think that this tripartite working agreement is unique in our history, and I want for us to be proud of the maturity shown by all of the party leaders and supporting Civil Service.'

The press threw questions which all amounted to "What is the policy?"

'We will give the detail in a press hand out later in the day after I have reported to Parliament, but simply put, we have agreed with a number of the more benevolent and substantial financial institutions that the nation's debt will be rescheduled, to be paid back over seventy years with an option for extension, and at a modest interest rate. I want to say that we are grateful to a number of our own City of London experts, who quite simply likened it to the repayment of the debt following the Second World War. This now becomes manageable and we can get our country back into positive growth without the yoke of saturating debt. The authorities will continue their work to bring to book the culprits responsible for our recent difficulties.

In our new working relationship we will be reinforcing the state support systems in health and education. Our armed services will still be reviewed, but with growth not cutbacks in mind. I will now ask the Deputy PM and then Ted, I mean Ed, Milliband, to talk to you, but then we need to get back to work.'

This did not receive the serious response the they were expecting. In fact it was received with roars of laughter.

The politicians stopped and looked behind them and there was Jack, poking his heavily bandaged head around the door of number ten, looking like an Indian Swami ready to make a run for it. He was of course recognised by some of the press, his eye being a dead giveaway and they had also seen him with his head bandaged before. "Inspector Austin can you tell us why you are at Downing Street?" calls from several of the journalists.

All three politicians looked back and laughed. The PM put his arm out and Jack tippy toed to the microphones, his face showing a full on harrumph and a serious grimace; he was hedging his bets.

'I just popped in to borrow Dave's morning suit, mine was blown up last night.' There were roars of laughter and Jack twirled and pranced like a top model, to show what a good fit it was, even though the waist was showing clearly three or four inches of an unbuttoned gap, the bottoms at half-mast and the jacket had no way of joining up, the shoulder seams being tested beyond design limits. Jack spoke again, 'A little snug in some places,' and he pointed to the waist. 'I can do the coat up nearly, and cover up where it has shrunk at the cleaners. I've phoned the Queen and left a message to say that my chinos have been blown to shreds and I understand she is happy to still meet me, otherwise I said, just post the bloody medal...' and he harrumphed again, '...sorry I'm cutting down on me feckin' swearing. So, must dash, can't keep Queenie waiting.'

And off he went, followed by Father Mike in his tattered priest attire, also to a huge roar. Mike stopped, sketched a blessing, then ran to catch Jack up but bumped into him as he was now returning to the microphones and rolling cameras.

'If you're listening Amanda love, I've left a message for the Queen so she knows she is also making Martin a Police Dog, you forgot, you daft moo,' and he slapped the bandage over his forehead and winced to the nation. 'Anyway, I'm going straight to the Palace, I've got no time to get back so I'll see you there, I'll have a wash later before the concert.' He waved again and then ran after Mike.

'Mum you had better get dressed, we don't have long.' Then she noticed that everyone was ready except for her and Martin. How long had they been in this trance? Martin looked at his fur and thought it would do, didn't even need a brush; but then again, if he was to make a good impression on the corgis...

Chapter 40

Samuels had arranged for cars to take them all, a Bentley for Mandy and Jack, except Jack wasn't there, so Jackie and Gill joined Mandy in the back. Martin sat next to the driver with his nose out of the window, he'd been to London before but it had been raining. Today was a glorious day marred only as he was a tad nervous at meeting the Queen's corgis; whether they would fancy him, and bark only in posh.

Jackie looked to soothe Mandy's nerves. 'At least he is on his way, you look stunning and nothing else can happen now, so let's get the feckin' medal and have lunch, somewhere... God knows where though, since Len upped and died on us. Then we have the concert presumably?' She looked at Mandy and grinned, her head to one side. 'Yes, I see, the only thing we know for sure is that Jack is on his way to the Palace, in a slightly ill-fitting suit and tan brogues, it could be worse...' she reflected some more, and then agreed with Mandy and settled back.

Mandy decided that it might be best to not give a toss, and of course Jackie was right, what else could go wrong. The Bentley pulled up at the Palace gates as Mike and Jack were crossing the busy wide road, to hoots from cars and calls from the normal tourist crowds gathered around the gates, now being rapidly supplemented by the growing world's press.

Jack arrived and Martin leapt from the car to greet him, 'Martin, old son,' and Jack cuddled and hugged his former dog. Amanda stepped from the car with a little more grace than Martin and Jack looked on.

'Amanda you look stunning, truly beautiful. I don't deserve you sweetheart.'

'No you don't!'

* * *

The ceremony was being covered by BBC. Jack and Martin were not the only recipients of awards, although they were the highest honour of the day and as such were last on the running order. Jack was like a cat on a hot tin roof. 'Stand still,' Mandy said, 'what is it, are you nervous?'

The Queen approached and Mandy curtseyed, Martin bowed and Jack laughed.

'What is it?' Mandy asked, offended.

'You, curtseying, whatta twonk!'

'Jack, jolly good to see you again, and Martin.' The Queen bent down and scratched Martin's scruffy ginger head. She came up, with the crown still on her head and Jack thought it must be superglued. 'I would say Jack that your companion's curtsey was a lot better than your bow. Superintendent Amanda Bruce is it not?'

'Err, yes your Majesty,' Mandy said, and buckled her legs again and Jack laughed some more.

'I am told that it should be you receiving a medal today, for putting up with Jane?' The Queen said, enjoying the use of Jack's epithet. 'I must see what I can do...' and she turned to Jack, '...in the meantime, I hear you are using all of the lavatories around London Jack, so please feel free to avail yourself of our facilities. In fact I must insist. The loo over there has a shower and Johnny...' she looked at her Equerry, '...will arrange for a razor, I think a rant and rave would be in order. Martin and you are last up and I would like you to be at least reasonably presentable. I hear also that your lunch arrangements are err...' and she looked again to her Equerry, '...up the swanee was it Johnny?'

'Yes Ma'am, and without a paddle,' Johnny replied.

'Then I think the very least we can do is provide some refreshments for you and your rather large family afterwards, I trust that will be in order?

'Lubbly jubbly Ma'am, cucumber sandwiches please, and if you wouldn't mind excusing me, I need the loo.' He headed for the "lavatory" and heard raucous laughter behind him; he always liked the Queen, a game old girl.

* * *

Mandy retired to the receiving room and was shown to her seat beside the family. Martin would sit next to Jack on the outside.

There was a fanfare to announce the Queen, very quickly followed by Jack making a clumsy and inelegant dash for his allocated seat. Martin at least padded in a stately manner. Jack looked as if he couldn't understand why people, including the Queen and Prince Philip, were laughing so much, but eventually the ceremony proceeded smoothly and finally Jack and Martin were called.

Jack rose from his seat, and with Martin, they walked slowly, reverently, heads bowed. The Queen seemed to be waving him on, probably wanted lunch and had a shepherd's pie in the oven, but Jack didn't see, his head was bowed almost to his knees. Mandy could see it happening before it did, and when it did, it was in a sort of slow motion film sequence; Jack tripping, the Queen being heard to Oomph, as Jack's head hit her stomach and they fell together, into what Mandy assumed was the throne. The stewards ran to assist but the Queen waved them away. Prince Philip sat down, he was in danger of falling, he was laughing so much, and Martin was embarrassed, not sure if he could see the funny side. Jack helped the Queen up, who was giggling like a school girl, she later confided to Mandy over a cucumber sandwich that she hadn't indeed had so much fun since her school days, and Jack's CBE of course.

The hub-bub eventually subsided and Jack did his kneeling and the Queen said that he only needed to kneel when being knighted, and when that happened, which she assumed wouldn't be too long, she would be tempted to take his head off with the sword. More guffaws and Jack ineptly, oomphed and aaahed from one knee to the other and then gradually he rose and without thinking, put his arm around the Queen and whispered into her ear. The Queen rolled back and said something to Philip who also rollicked in his slightly smaller throne.

After a while Jack was presented with his medal and Martin was given what looked like a Christmas tree decoration on a length of knotted string, *The George Bone swung* around his neck. There was polite applause, and blow me down if the Queen didn't peck Jack on the cheek. Looked like she was going for the second cheek and he stopped her, he whispered and she laughed again. The ceremony was over and people looked disappointed. The Queen and Prince Phillip retired and Jack and Martin followed. The Queen could be heard to say that there was no need to follow, that someone would show them where to go. More laughs, and Mandy thought that all of that had been on the telly and sensed a little of what Kate must have felt, but decided to roll with it.

* * *

The press waited a long time in the baking sunshine for Jack's party to come out after lunch with the Queen, which actually went off remarkably well, just a few embarrassing moments. The press corps became animated as Jack and his entourage approached the gates. The police cleared a gap and the cameras rolled, covering the impromptu press conference. Mandy stood next to Jack and she put two fingers up behind his bandaged turban and the crowd laughed as the press took photos. Then came the barrage of questions, they all wanted to know what he said to the Queen and what happened at the lunch?

'Inspector what are you doing now; how will you celebrate?'

Jack flicked his head and the crowd hushed, 'Not sure,' he said, 'we were going to tonight's promenade concert but a friend of ours who booked a box was unfortunately killed in the operation last night, so, who knows.'

'What was the concert Inspector?'

'A Prom, Tchaikovsky's violin concerto...' Jack said, '...and my favourite soloist, Alexander Pantsoff.'

The rollicking laughter was immediately silenced by a shocked retort from Mandy, 'Jack,' and she addressed the press, 'he means Alexander Petrov.'

'Yeah, that's what I said,' Jack said and then put his serious head on. 'Listen up please, last night and in the past few weeks some very brave people have put the good of the country before their own safety...' and he paused to reflect, '...and some have paid the ultimate price. I want, with my family here and with all of you, to show our respect for those who have died and those who risked everything to broker the deal that the Prime Minister announced this morning. I would like to ask for a minute's silence.'

His children, Alana, Michael, and Alice, with Mandy and the others, sidled beside and behind Jack. The press shuffled back to capture the wide angled shot, mainly to get all of Jack's bum in Mandy later said, and there was silence, just the hum of traffic behind the crowd. Mandy was blinded by the sun again as she looked to the sky and sniffed.

The silence was eventually broken. 'Was that a minute, only I haven't got a watch.' Jack then went on to say how he had a really good time with the Queen and Prince Philip, made a little show of how he ate his cucumber sandwiches and how he held his tea cup with his little finger sticking out. 'And they said I was a barrow boy!' Then he waved to the crowd and jumped into the Bentley with Mandy, Martin, and his four children, making sure that Mandy's leg was squashed against his.

Chapter 41

They gathered back at the Mayfair safe house, greeted at the door by a smiling Jimbo, though Jack could see the grief behind the welcome; Jimbo and Wilf had been long standing colleagues. Jack stepped aside and Mandy watched him disappear with Jimbo down a corridor, and she left them to it.

Jack eventually returned to join his family, gathering in the sitting room, the tall Georgian windows no longer black teeth but open eyes to the sunlight. Jack sat on a comfy, wide armed armchair, and Meesh and Martin joined him. Meesh had not really had time to recover from her perceived neglect by him over the past few weeks, Jack taking comfort that she was displaying normal childish reactions. He looked the waiflike girl deep into her emerald eyes, and could see her conflict, how to tell him off for not seeing her for so long versus how to vent the bubbly excitement of meeting the Queen. Jack kissed the cheek of the girl and whispered, 'Spesh darlin', I'm so sorry I've been away and not seen you; I've missed you so much.'

Job done, she was okay, and now she could talk to Jack about the Queen, what she had said to Meesh and of course all the silly stuff that he and Martin had done. He heard some raucous laughter from the dining room as one of the servants pushed a trolley in with tea and cakes. Mandy sashayed up and sat on the other arm of the chair. He looked up at her, raised the one eyebrow that worked, as she spoke gently to him, 'It's all on the telly, you falling over into the Queen, putting your arm around her and whispering. I hear from Jo Jums that the press are inundating the phones at the station, they all

246

want to know what you whispered that made the Queen laugh so much.' He looked at her, wary. 'Well, what did you say? I will not be angry, although I may be embarrassed.'

That was good enough for Jack. 'Okay, all I said was "are you using that throne, I might need the loo again soon".'

Mandy sighed, 'Well it's lucky you were not locked up in the Tower, and I have to say that none of this has turned out how I expected it.' She sighed again, 'The photos may be a bit disastrous though?'

'Pour me a girl grey please love and I'll have that piece of cake there,' he pointed.

'That cake is there to be cut up into slices.'

'What, you're kidding, there's just enough for me. I've only had cucumber sandwiches.'

'And a lot of ham ones, vol-au-vents, smoked salmon and not forgetting a big strawberry cake,' Mandy replied, hardly able to contain her giggles. 'I know this because apparently Prince Philip had his eye on that one and he mentioned it several times.'

Jack gave up and pretended he hadn't heard, sipped girl grey and watched as gradually everyone sauntered into the sitting room. He took in the panorama of eyes looking at him, lingered his sight on Alice, put his arm out and she came over to him. Meesh and Martin squashed in, so Alice could take the opposite wide arm to Mandy. He stretched out; put his arm around her slim waist.

'Alright Alice?'

'Yes dad.'

'You Spesh?'

'Yes dad.'

'You Martin?'

'Woof'

'Amanda?'

'Yes plank.'

Meesh and Martin giggled and Alice joined in. Meesh touched Jack's face, picked up a tear on the end of her finger and put it to her own lips.

They all heard the buzzer but nobody moved, there were people to answer doors but with all that had happened, Jack noticed a few were on edge; would be himself if he were not so tired. A stunningly beautiful Pakistani woman walked in, beamed a glossy smile at Jack and Mandy.

'Aisha, how nice,' Jack greeted the woman from his crowded throne.

'Hi Jack, Mandy,' she said, 'Samuels wanted me to deliver some clothes for you and Mike. I guessed Mike's measurements and Mandy told us your size Jack,' and she broke out into a radiant grin. 'I got Mike's at Simpson's in Piccadilly, but the traffic getting over to London Zoo was terrible, and then the Elephant House was closed.' They all shared a jolly good laugh at Jack's expense. 'Jim also said to say that he has been in touch with the Albert Hall and there are two, first tier boxes set up courtesy of Len. Jim will send cars for you all. So that's me, I just wanted to say a very good job; Jack, Mike, Mandy, just a brief word if I may?'

The comfy chair broke up, and Jimbo ushered them into the study to listen to Aisha. Settled, Aisha spoke, 'Jim thinks that the military is pretty much under control...' and she paused, looked to Jack, who finished the sentence for her.

'Pugwash is on the missing list eh?'

Aisha nodded. 'Seems your theory he was coordinating the military was right, his reason for the community policing role; everything falls into place. Well, Jim wanted you all to know that until Pugwash is picked up, he will keep the cover up on you and your family Jack.'

Jack thanked Aisha, gave her a hug and she left. He turned to Mandy, 'Amanda, will you tell the family I need a lie down, I haven't slept in a while.'

Chapter 42

The auditorium lights were dimmed, the focus was on the violinist and the conductor, the momentum was building in the final movement. Jack knew the piece well, loved how the soloist built his cadenzas. There was a faint buzzing in his head, the gunshot echoing around his largely ineffective ears and brain box and affecting his full appreciation of the music, but his soul was overwhelmed by the power of the performance and the measure of the piece.

He had been in a daze after Amanda had woken him from a deep sleep. He could picture her in the shower with him; she had dried and helped him dress. He could recall the look of concern on her face and Jackie's voice, like a slowed down echo, asking how he felt? He remembered brushing them all off with the pretence of all being well, kisses, embraces and arms around shoulders – he wasn't.

He remembered getting out of the Bentley at the Albert Hall as the shot zinged across the car, ricocheting; it missed because Mandy pushed him out of the way, she was hit as she protected him, spinning him and wrapping her arms around him, protection against the next shot. He remembered the growls and muffled barks as Martin launched a massive bite into Pugwash's bits and pieces, the scuffle, screams of excruciating pain from the sailor boy, or was he now a Wren? Pugwash was taken down by the protection detail. The paramedics on standby pushed Jack to one side, his shouts also in booming slow motion, deep and echoing in the hollowness of his head as he fell back to the ground in despair, crying to the heavens, trying to reach Amanda, the paramedics having to scurf him away.

The music climaxed and the audience rose to their feet. Jack sat, people were standing around him. He chanced a look to Amanda, at her bandaged upper arm and grazed forehead. The concert had been delayed but Amanda was able to be fixed up, and insisted the Prom take place and also that she wanted to be with her family and next to Jack.

Meesh and Martin cuddled into the both of them, as slowly the audience returned to their seats, then up again as the conductor and soloist returned, and slowly back down; hushed with an expectant silence. The soloist and conductor remained on the platform, and it caused Jack and Amanda to look up from their shared gaze. Jack's eye squinted as a spotlight trained upon them both. You could hear the footsteps of Alexander Petrov as he walked the few steps and mounted the recently vacated rostrum. The audience applauded, but this is not what he wanted and using his bow like a conductor's baton, he waved an expansive horizontal slice into the air; immediate silence ensued and the houselights dimmed, just two spotlights; soloist and Jack and Amanda. The violinist, who had so eloquently spoken with his instrument just now, opened up and addressed the audience but looked directly at Jack and Amanda.

'I wish to acknowledge two people today, and dedicate my performance to Detective Superintendent Amanda Bruce and Detective Chief Inspector Jack Austin.' There was applause and faces turned, but this was brought to an abrupt silence as the bow slashed again. 'I have been informed of the exploits of Jack Austin and Amanda Bruce and how the country owes them both a great debt, not of money but of honour and heartfelt gratitude. For me, I am grateful, as I understand if you do not have a nickname from Jack Austin, then you are just not a part of his High Society. And so it is with pride I accept and welcome my name Alexander Pantsoff.' There was polite laughter and applause, brought under control again with the swish of the bow. 'Actually, I have no choice, since everybody seems to be calling me this now anyway, even my wife. I have learned a lot in a short time about Jack Austin. I saw the selflessness of the man when he organised a children's arts festival in Portsmouth; I was invited with Fee de Prune and Milk'O and I saw the energy and enthusiasm for the arts that was generated for so many youngsters. And today, as many of you will know, Jane Austin...' he waited for the laughter to subside at Jack's own nickname, '... received the George Medal from the Queen, and we want to honour this man in our own way. We are going to play a piece of music for you Jane Austin. The piece is in E flat major. The E flat is a key often bold, sometimes heroic, grave and serious. The major introduces the humour, the upbeat contrast to the underlying mellow, and this best describes an extraordinary man, quintessentially English - and so we will play a quintessentially English piece of music for you. We will play Nimrod, from what I understand Jane Austin calls Elgar's Enema variations. Ladies and gentleman please show your appreciation for an extraordinary man; Jack Austin, in E Flat Major.'

The audience rose to their feet and applauded and cheered, the orchestra stamped their feet, the conductor exchanged places with the violinist at the rostrum and allowed the audience to settle. Slowly the music swelled, deep and sonorous, heartfelt, powerfully moving, built and dropped, built and dropped and eventually faded.

Amanda looked at Jack. He was crying of course, sobbing, a wringing grip on her hand, Meesh crushing his waist, Martin with his paw on a wrist. And she looked deep into his soul for this was her Barrow Boy.

* * *

"There are only three possible endings —aren't there? — to any story: revenge, tragedy or forgiveness. That's it. All stories end like that."

Jeanette Winterson

Jack Austin will return in Ghost and Ragman Roll,
book four in the Kind Hearts and Martinets series.

About the author

Pete Adams is an architect and designs and builds projects around the UK when he's not writing up a storm. Pete describes himself as an inveterate daydreamer, escaping into those dreams by writing funny stories that contain a thoughtful dash of social commentary. With a writing style inspired and shaped by his formative years on an estate that re-housed London families shortly after WWII, Pete's Kind Hearts and Martinets series of books have been likened to the writing of Tom Sharpe.

Pete says that the best feedback he's had on his work was that "it made me laugh, made me cry and made me think." People have said they laugh out loud reading his books, and if he can continue to get that reaction from his readers then he says he would be very content indeed. Pete lives in Southsea with his partner, the Irish nana, and Charlie the star-struck Border terrier, the children having now flown the coop.

Pete Adams

Urbane Publications is dedicated to
developing new author voices, and publishing
fiction and non-fiction that challenges, thrills and
fascinates. From page-turning novels to innovative
reference books, our goal is to publish what
YOU want to read.

Find out more at

urbanepublications.com